She had *trusted* him, had brought him home to her family

Kristin turned back to Malcolm. He had *kissed* her, too. And for the first time in a long time, Kristin had actually let herself imagine...*those* kinds of thoughts about someone.

"Kristin," Malcolm murmured. "Let me just explain."

But her ears were buzzing harder. She couldn't hear so well anymore. Malcolm was saying something to the receptionist, ushering her out, closing the door.

"Tell me the truth," Kristin managed to whisper. "Who are you?"

His Adam's apple moved up and down. "John Sage is my uncle," he said quietly.

She felt numb all over. Maybe she was in shock.

He had betrayed her. All along, he had lied to her about who he was and why he was in her plant, and at her home. He had made a fool of her in front of everybody who mattered to her.

She clutched her stomach. So many emotions rose in her, she was being overwhelmed by them all. She had wanted to believe in him so much....

Dear Reader,

Thanks for picking up *The Sweetest Hours,* my fourth book in the Harlequin Superromance line.

This story was inspired by my love for all things Scottish. In it, Kristin Hart, a young industrial engineer for a shampoo-and-body-products company, shows up in her Vermont factory one day to find a sexy, mysterious Scotsman in her office, sitting at her desk.

From there, it's off to Scotland for an adventure of her lifetime. Along the way, she traverses the countryside, stays at a castle, attends a Scottish wedding and falls in love with Malcolm, the Highlander of her heart.

I hope you enjoy!

All the best,

Cathryn Parry

CATHRYN PARRY

—

The Sweetest Hours

HARLEQUIN® SUPER ROMANCE®

Recycling programs
for this product may
not exist in your area.

ISBN-13: 978-0-373-71895-5

THE SWEETEST HOURS

Copyright © 2013 by Cathryn Parry

Printed in U.S.A.

ABOUT THE AUTHOR

Cathryn Parry is the author of four Harlequin Superromance books. A former engineer, she lives in New England with her husband and her neighbor's cat, Otis. In addition to writing, she enjoys conducting genealogy research, working on her figure-skating moves and traveling as often as possible. Please see her website at www.cathrynparry.com.

Books by Cathryn Parry

HARLEQUIN SUPERROMANCE

1756—SOMETHING TO PROVE
1820—THE LONG WAY HOME
1863—OUT OF HIS LEAGUE

Other titles by this author available in ebook format.

To Lou, for everything.

To Karen Reid, my editor, for all the hard work and encouragement.

To my late grandmother, for providing the sword, the Scottish genes and the support during my childhood Highland Dance recitals. I haven't forgotten.

CHAPTER ONE

KRISTIN HART HEARD the soft burr of a Scottish accent, and something inside her sang.

She crept closer to the edge of the open door and listened. A man spoke on the telephone. He was obviously not from around here. What was he doing in her small-town Vermont factory? And why was he in her boss's office?

"…I cannot…I'm sorry you did not…" The man pronounced "cannot" like "canna" and "you" like "ye."

Kristin missed most of the other words he said. But the man with the deep, rolling voice *was* Scottish—that was no mistake.

Her spirits brightened. For as long as she remembered, she'd wanted to travel and visit the country of her grandmother's birth, the land of castles and Highlanders.

Take me away, she thought.

Kristin rubbed her arms and stared down the corridor, lined with boxes and the remnants of their labeling-machine going haywire.

Outside, it was a gray, late-January morning, threatening snow, and inside, the cold factory was dimly lit and quiet.

Besides her, there was only a skeleton shift: three hourly workers and Kristin. As production engineer she was supervising an emergency crew while they manually affixed labels to shipments that were already several days late. Kristin had opened the doors early that morning and let everyone in with a key not usually entrusted to her, since her plant was rarely open on the weekend.

At least her makeshift team was assembled from volunteers who wanted the overtime. Kristin was a salaried employee, and she had lost her day off. Like living in the movie *The Breakfast Club,* stuck in detention, Kristin had been ordered into the building on a Saturday. But she was determined to make the best of it and find the silver lining somewhere. The factory floor smelled great: like the jars of the honey body cream they labeled. The people she worked with were kind, too. Unlike Andrew, the plant manager, none of them gave her trouble.

Everything had been sailing along just fine, until she'd headed to the break room to grab a hot chocolate for Mindy from the managerial staff's coffee machine, and she'd been sidetracked by the Scottish accent.

Now her feet seemed rooted to the wooden floor. She couldn't see the man with the deep, sexy Scottish burr, but she heard him from her spot in the corridor.

"Goodbye, love, I have to go now."

Kristin closed her eyes and sighed. Her imagination could very well conjure up a big, burly, kilted Highlander saying that to her.

Not forever, of course, just for…well, an afternoon would be great. With no worries or fears. Just enough fun to satisfy a sense of adventure that had felt squashed in Kristin lately—for far too long, actually.

Kristin sighed again. She wasn't delusional. Her kilted Scottish Highlander was a fantasy. A nice fantasy, but a fantasy was all he was.

Oh, but that accent…

Daydreaming will give you only trouble, she chided herself. *Move on. Go back to your crew in the factory…*.

She shook her head. No, she had to do something. The

Scotsman was inside *Andrew's* office. Her big boss. The manager in charge of the plant.

The guy who was very unhappy with her at the moment.

Kristin chewed on her thumbnail. Andrew's door had been locked when she'd walked past an hour earlier. He was hypervigilant about keeping everyone out of his space. And now it was silent on the other side of the open door.

If Andrew found out that she'd been aware of an intruder inside the building and had done nothing about it…

Kristin rubbed her arms over her coat sleeves. Her throat seemed to close with fear.

Drawing in her breath, she grabbed her heavy metal flashlight from inside her coat pocket and then shrugged the garment off so that her arms were free in case she needed to defend herself. For a moment she thought of calling to Jeff on the plant floor as a backup, but Jeff was seventy-two years old, and he had diabetes and a bad hip.

Be careful. Be smart.

She grabbed her cell phone from the other pocket of her winter-wool coat—at least she had 9-1-1 on speed-dial— and then crept to the edge of the door.

He sat right out in the open as if he belonged there, though at present, his back was to her.

He had short hair: dark brown, almost black. He wore a hunter-green collared dress shirt with the sleeves pushed to his elbows, as if settled in to work. He'd tossed a black coat over the desk chair, and by standing on tiptoe and adjusting the angle of her gaze, she could see that he wore a tie.

A tie!

Nobody wore a tie at Aura Botanicals. Even the CEO, Jay Astley, showed up in jeans, T-shirt and Birkenstocks, like the hippie he'd once been—at least until his passion for bees, coupled with his late wife's passion for making body products from the resulting organic honey, had resulted in Aura Botanicals. "Aura," derived from his wife's name, minus the *L*. God, Kristin missed her.

Now that she thought of it, Laura's death had marked the start of Andrew's campaign against her.

Andrew was the one person who made coming in to work upsetting for Kristin. Just last week, a friend of his from one of their suppliers had joined a group of them for lunch. The friend had returned from a cross-country trip, and Kristin had been interested in seeing his photos, imagining herself taking the same drive and living vicariously through him. But Andrew had sneered at her in front of everyone.

"I'm tired of you being distracted and lacking commitment," he'd said. She'd been mortified. But his lack of faith in her hadn't stopped there. From her own supervisor, Kristin had learned that Andrew often told his other managers she wasn't serious enough. "A liability," he called her.

Sometimes after a rough day of Andrew's opinions, Kristin went home and cried. She tried her best to prove herself in her job through hard work, but beyond that, what could she do? She stayed at Aura Botanicals because there were so many other reasons why this company was the best place for her, and she knew she shouldn't let the small "bads" outweigh the more important "goods."

If she did go inside and confront the stranger in Andrew's office, she'd need to be careful. Maybe the man was in the office with Andrew's permission. That was the most likely scenario. So she needed to be circumspect in how she dealt with him. And no curious questions about his accent.

She was standing there, still weighing her options, when the door swung open. The big, dark-haired Scotsman strode out, down the hall away from her to the end of the corridor and into the smallest office, shoved into the corner like an afterthought.

Her office. *Her* private space.

Shock flooded her. Without thinking, she walked quickly after him.

And then the Scot, who was trespassing in *her* office, reached over and turned on the portable electric heater. *Her* heater, that she'd brought from home.

"Hey!" She gasped in protest. "This is my space."

He swiveled in her desk chair, caught off guard. "Jaysus!" he said, when he saw her standing before him.

She froze, clutching the flashlight and her phone. His brows drew down, and his lips settled into a thin line of disapproval.

She stepped back. With the exception of Andrew, she wasn't used to anyone being so outwardly angry at her. Aura was peopled mainly by gentle types: laconic Vermonters. Like her goofy supervisor, Dirk, who really should be here at the plant with her instead of moonlighting at his weekend wedding DJ gig.

"Um, that is my desk you are sitting at," she said to the big Scot.

He gazed up at her. Blinked for a moment. Regarded the flashlight in her hand and made no expression at seeing her clutching it like a weapon. Instead, he remained seated, adopting a poker face. He looked cold and arrogant, which didn't jibe at all with the pleasant, romantic voice she'd heard him using on the telephone.

"I was directed to sit here." He said it in a way that let her know not only did he think there was nothing wrong with his barging into her office, but he was also irritated by her presence. His lovely, romantic Scottish accent was gone, replaced with a regular, nonexotic New England voice, much like she heard every day.

She was dying to ask where the Scots' accent had gone. But she behaved as a professional, only asking business-like and relevant questions that would not upset Andrew if he found out.

"*Who* directed you to use this office?" she asked, her palm sweaty on the metal in her fist.

"This is a company office, is it not?" That scowl was still on his face—he was not backing down from her. "And a *company* desk?"

"Well…yes," she said.

He stared back harder at her. She felt herself shriveling inside. Was she making yet another mistake? Maybe she'd missed a directive given to everyone in a staff meeting?

No, that was impossible. Placing the flashlight carefully on her bookshelf, she forced herself to smile at him. "For all I know, you could be a corporate spy, sneaking in here to steal trade secrets," she said in a light voice. "I'm sure many companies are dying for the secret formula for Aura's bestselling Organic Beeswax and Shea Butter Shampoo."

He stared at her for another moment longer. Then he leaned back. He didn't seem so arrogant anymore. "That's a reasonable concern, actually."

"I thought so."

He nodded. "It would alarm me, too, if I worked here." He made a half smile at her. Though it was creaky and awkward, the gesture did come off as charming. He seemed to be making a conscious effort not to be so personally offensive.

She felt herself relaxing. "Are you here with one of the managers?" She should have checked the cars in the parking lot before she'd strode in without thinking. That would've given her more of a clue as to what was going on.

"Yes, of course." He nodded again. "I was escorted by Andrew Harris."

She couldn't be positive, but those *r*'s in her boss's name sounded rolled, like a native Scottish speaker would pronounce it.

She peered at him.

His gaze narrowed back.

Maybe if she kept him talking, she could trip him up, and he'd slip into the Scots' accent again.

"I didn't know Andrew was here today," she remarked lightly, strolling over and standing in the blowing force of her electric heater. She pocketed her phone and held her hands palm up to the warm air. "Usually when Andrew works on the weekends, he stops by the plant floor to say hello to everyone."

"He left early."

Three carefully spoken words. She waited, but he had no further explanation.

"*Where* did Andrew go?" she asked patiently, hoping he would slip and roll another *r*.

Slowly and carefully again, he muttered, "Family emergency."

"Oh, my gosh!" she exclaimed, turning from the heater. "Did Robin go into labor?"

The stranger seemed to flinch. "Ah, if Robin is his wife, then, yes, it appears so."

Two rolled *r*'s! They were very, very slight—but those delicious burrs sent an unmistakable shiver up her spine.

The question was killing her. She couldn't help asking; she was dying inside.

"So, are you from Scotland, or not?" she blurted point-blank.

He gave her a murderous expression.

And then she realized she was doing it again. Too many questions. Too adventurous for her own good.

MALCOLM MACDOWALL HAD been assured that the only people present at the Aura Botanicals plant were located on the other side of the building, inside the factory proper, and that these workers would not be interfering with him—certainly not entering the managerial offices where he had only one day to gather the data he needed.

"No," he snapped at the woman, hoping she'd go away. The worst thing he could let slip was a Scottish accent. If she found out why he was here and who he was affiliated with, it would be disastrous. Letting his guard down and smiling at her had been a mistake.

But the blonde only blinked at him. She was just so damn different from what he was used to. Younger than him. Female. Short and curvy, bundled up in a turtleneck and woolen jumper—sweater, he corrected himself. The building was so cold inside, it made his fingers stiff on the keyboard.

That's why Andrew had suggested he set up shop in this cubbyhole of an office. For the heater.

"I'm sorry," she said, sounding honestly contrite. "I shouldn't have asked about that. But if you want, you can use a Scottish accent when you talk to me. I don't mind."

He crossed his arms. "That was a private conversation you heard. A joke between two people."

She tilted her head at him. Loose, butterscotch-colored curls brushed the top of her shoulder. "So, you've never lived in Scotland?"

"No," he lied. "What is this line of questioning about? *Who* are you?"

She crossed the room and reached behind some binders for a purse, hidden on the bookshelf. The sudden movement unnerved him. He had every right to be on guard. There were several very good reasons why she couldn't find out who he was, who he worked for, and where he came from.

She held forward her company badge. "I'm Kristin Hart. I'm an engineer for Aura."

He didn't take the plastic-laminated name tag she offered, but he looked at her photo, verifying her name and job classification.

He felt his brows rise. Interesting. She was the last person he would've pegged for an engineer. He supposed he had an image in his head of one who practiced the profession, and she was definitely not it.

Not that he was prejudiced against women as engineers. On the contrary. It was just that she seemed too young for the job, for one thing. She was pretty, with a Botticelli face and shoulder-length blond hair that curled, giving her a soft look that, on second thought, maybe made her appear younger than she was. A staff position at Aura required a four- or five-year college degree.

Still, she looked more like a cosmetic salesperson than an engineer in a manufacturing plant with noisy, automated equipment. How did she hold her own within the realities of factory life? The CEO of the company—*former* CEO, though Kristin didn't know it yet—was laid-back and kind. But Andrew, the man who'd deserted Malcolm to this young woman with the Botticelli face, was aggressive and foul-tempered. Not someone Malcolm would trust with his sister, but then again, there weren't many people he did trust.

"What kind of engineer are you?" he asked her.

"Industrial." A frown crossed her brow. "I'm with an overtime crew today. One of our labeling machines broke and we're here to finish packing an order by hand."

She was very free with her information. In a sense, it fascinated him.

"Does that happen often?" he couldn't help asking.

She laughed. She had a nice laugh. As she tucked her badge into her purse, her gaze kept sliding to his. "How did you learn to talk in a Scottish accent like that? Because it sounded real to me. Did you *ever* live there?"

He slid his tongue over his teeth, debating how much to tell her. One tooth was chipped and uneven. A reminder to remain careful. "I left when I was young. I don't remember much," he decided to admit.

Her face brightened and she smiled—it was a remarkable transformation. She had a way of looking at him as if he was the most fascinating person she'd ever seen. "I knew it," she said. "My grandmother was born in Scotland, too."

"Really," he murmured. He crossed his arms and leaned back. She was nattering on with him, unaware of the peril.

She nodded. "I've always wanted to go there."

"Maybe you should," he said mildly.

"Yeah, right. I don't even have a passport." She laughed.

"That's easily fixed."

"What's your name?" she asked, smiling.

Something stilled in him. He hadn't expected the conversation to go quite like this. But he needed to convince her that he wasn't a threat.

He looked her straight in the eyes. They were pale green and luminescent. The color reminded him of rolling fields in the springtime, but even more beautiful. "George Smith," he said.

It was another lie. A complete and utter fabrication, but he didn't feel a twinge of guilt, because it was his "security name."

A look must've crossed his face, because a crease formed on her forehead. "What are you here for today, George?"

He tensed slightly. The moment he'd been waiting for. If she had chatted around the bush much longer, he would have thought less of her. As it was, she was utterly charming about it.

He opened his briefcase and handed her the folded letter. He'd hoped not to have to show it to anyone other than Andrew. It only increased complications.

She glanced questioningly from the letter to him. He kept silent, steepled his hands and waited as she opened it and read.

The printed orders were on letterhead from the CEO of Aura Botanicals, her company. "To Whom it May Concern," it began, informing the reader to give "all and any assistance to Mr. George Smith, consultant."

She put down the letter. "You're a consultant? What kind?"

He frowned. "I specialize in brand expansion and cost savings."

"So you're a marketing guy?"

"Business strategy, actually."

"Why are you here alone on a Saturday? Is Jay selling the company?"

For a split second, Malcolm almost broke his mask. She was more perceptive than Andrew had been. "No," he said carefully. "Jay doesn't want to alarm anyone. He just wants suggestions to improve profitability so he can expand the label."

She digested his answer. "Are you talking about the 'Morning Botanicals' product line? Because I'll tell you, that's my favorite. People especially like the shampoo, but most can't find it in stores due to spotty distribution. Maybe you could tell Jay that."

"Kristin, there are one hundred twenty-five people in your company. Why don't *you* tell him?"

"Well, I would, but his wife died a few months ago, and Jay isn't as available as he used to be. He took her death hard. We all did." She shrugged, moving to stand in front of the heater again. "We don't see him as often as we used to around here."

Which explained the state of the company financials. But Malcolm would discuss nothing of the sort with anyone besides Jay, the CEO.

"May I get back to work, please?" He held his hand out for the letter. God help him if he had to use it again.

"What kind of work are you planning to do today?" she asked, holding back his letter.

He sighed. She just wouldn't let him off the hook. The irony was, it made him respect her more. "Fine, I'll tell you. Andrew gave me the computer password so I could retrieve the reports I need from the system. I also need to have a look at the factory equipment. Andrew gave me diagrams, but I'd rather observe for myself."

"Interesting," she said, perusing the set of schematics showing the layout of the machinery on the floor. "Did you know I made those drawings?"

"That's…perfect."

"Why?"

She was entirely guileless. And she seemingly knew everything about the operations and the company.

"Because I could use your help," he said.

"I don't know…." She shook her head, smiling, tapping the letter against her chin. "The directive to give you assistance is definitely from Jay, because I know his signature." She handed the letter back to him. "But, how do I know *you're* George Smith? You really should show me some identification."

He'd prepared for this, and he gave her his best sheepish look. "I'd like to, but my wallet is in the hotel safe."

"You came here without a wallet?"

"I was dropped off by a driver," he said honestly. The driver was supposed to stay with him for the day, but he hadn't felt well and had returned to the hotel to rest. A damned unlucky move. Malcolm took extraordinary measures to avoid unlucky moves, but what could he do? "I didn't realize I'd forgotten my wallet until it was too late."

"You must have *something* with your name on it," she said.

He had nothing on him that identified him as Malcolm MacDowall, and that was by design. Everything Malcolm did was by design. He was utterly careful, and he trusted no one.

But a piece of paper to identify him as George Smith?

He snapped open his briefcase again, reached into a folder and withdrew a printer copy of the reservation for his hotel stay. He passed the receipt to her.

She studied it. *George Smith*. The document did not list a company name for him.

She nodded and passed it back. "Thank you, George Smith. I hope you understand. We can't be too careful these days."

"I completely agree."

"To be sure, though, I need to make a phone call to my supervisor. Will you wait here until I come back?"

Malcolm tried not to wince. It wasn't his choice to prevaricate. Jay, the owner of Aura Botanicals, had made it a condition of his visit. Jay had seemed deeply sad, almost in a state of numbness the last time Malcolm had met with him. Personally, Malcolm didn't think it was wise to make business decisions so soon after the death of a loved one, but what Malcolm thought didn't matter.

And so, Malcolm was "George Smith" today. A generic "security name." Less messy for all concerned.

As long as Kristin's supervisor didn't raise any red flags.

CHAPTER TWO

KRISTIN STRETCHED HER arms, twisted at her waist and then bent down and retrieved her fallen coat. She'd been over-cautious in protecting herself from George Smith.

Clearly, he was not a physical threat, she thought, as she walked to the company break room. George seemed harmless enough beneath his rough exterior, once he'd lowered the gruff defenses he hid behind.

She hung her coat on a hook by the far wall, beside the vending machines and the coffee brewers. She couldn't help but still wonder about the phone conversation she'd overheard him engaged in, but it would've been unwise to push him too far. That call had been private...*intimate*.

In all likelihood he'd been speaking with a Scottish lady. A girlfriend from his homeland, perhaps? That would explain the accent he'd been using—and the reason he'd been covering it up. It could just be simple embarrassment.

Still, it was best she inform her supervisor what was going on in the offices. It was safest that way. She didn't want Andrew calling her "unprofessional" over her han-dling of the consultant, not if she could help it.

Carrying her purse under her arm, she slipped down the hall and into her hideaway in the factory. The best part about working at Aura Botanicals was the great smell of the organic body creams that they manufactured—a scent that was everywhere in the air, fresh and clean.

If she used her imagination and considered the silver

lining in every cloud, then working for Aura was like taking a spa day every time she came to work. The essential oils of juniper and birch cleared her head, and the milk-based lotions made her feel like Heidi on her own mountain in Switzerland.

But the scent of the beeswax—the honey—was her favorite, and it was most concentrated in the inventory storeroom she chose to make her phone call from. Lingering amid the racks and bottles to take deep, cleansing breaks was her secret escape during regular workdays.

Positioning herself near a small square window, high above her, she took out her phone and texted Dirk, her supervisor.

Immediately he rang her back. When she answered his call, she could hear the "Chicken Dance" playing in the background. Dirk was at one of his Saturday wedding-DJ jobs he loved so much. Who was she to stomp on someone's dreams?

"Yo, Kristin, I was just gonna call you. Did you hear that Andrew's wife went into labor?"

"I did." Kristin had forgotten about that in all the excitement with George Smith in her office. "Do you have any news?"

"No."

"What did Andrew say?" she prodded. "How is Robin doing?"

"Ah…he just said that there's a management consultant in the plant, and that you're in charge of him for the day."

"*I'm* in charge? Well, it was great of him to let me know about it." Too bad Andrew couldn't deign to talk to her himself instead of going through "channels." Mentally, she rolled her eyes. "What does he want me to do? The consultant asked to be let into the computer system, and he requested a tour of the factory, too."

"Hey, you know I would help you out, but I'm at work today," Dirk said.

Kristin gritted her teeth and took a breath from the smell of the honey around her, reminding herself to stay calm. "So am I, Dirk."

"That's great," he said. "Look, I'll see you Monday. You'll do fine, okay?"

"Wait!" She jumped down from the shelf she'd been sitting on. "Don't hang up on me yet." Her boss seemed only too happy to distance himself from the consultant's visit, and she wasn't getting a good feeling about this. "Do I have your permission to show him our operations?"

"Andrew said you're in charge. This is your decision."

"Well, what does that mean exactly?"

"Honestly? If anything goes wrong today, it's on you."

"Me?"

"Sure. You're the one who's *there*." Dirk made a laughing inflection of the word. "I can't cover you from *here*. If Andrew gets mad at you, then he gets mad at you. Shit happens, and it is what it is."

She hugged herself, pacing the small storeroom. More than anything, she needed to keep this job. Suddenly, there were more stakes involved than just being "distracted" from her work. Yes, she'd thought George Smith was interesting; she'd enjoyed questioning him. When he'd smiled, she'd been intrigued. His eyes were nice. Kind. Not threatening at all. And, of course, there was that accent…

She sighed, opening one of the lotion bottles and inhaling for fortitude. Dirk was, in effect, reminding her to be on her guard. Reminding her of her shaky standing at Aura of late. Ever since Laura had died, there'd been no one to protect her from Andrew.

"Kristin, I need to go. It's time to announce the cake-cutting."

There was nothing more to be done. Discussing the decision with Dirk wouldn't solve a thing. She needed to trust her gut.

"I'm just keeping you informed," she said. "Have a good wedding."

MALCOLM HAD WORKED with a lot of successful women in his professional life—CEOs, saleswomen, accountants—and what they all had in common were determination and strength of will. None of them were pushovers.

Kristin wasn't a pushover, either. She was just...surprising. She had a different style of operating, he supposed, that of a natural free spirit. When she smiled at him and tilted her head, he could see where he would have to be extra careful not to let himself be lulled off guard. Because at the end of the day, as the cliché went, everybody had their own interests at heart. As he well knew.

"Is everything all right?" he asked Kristin as she stood again in the doorway to the office—to *her* office.

She nodded grimly and set down two steaming mugs on his—her—desk. "It looks like I'll be taking care of you today," she said. "George."

He made sure not to flinch at the false name. His poker face in action, he nodded.

"Great. Er...I'm going to need some help with navigating this computer system. It's not an accounting program I'm familiar with."

"That's because we bought the rights to the source code, and it's evolved from an older software package." She slid one of the mugs toward him. "Here. I brought you some coffee. If you don't like coffee, there's tea and cocoa in the break room."

"This is...great. Thank you." He curled one hand around

the warm brew. Black, the way he liked it. "Could you, ah, show me the report screen?"

"Do you want financial reports or manufacturing reports?" she asked coolly.

"Ah…the shop floor reports with costs, projections and capacities would be most helpful for now." Damn, he was distracted. Good thing he already had everything else he needed, directly from Jay Astley himself.

Personally, he thought the man had made a mistake. Astley should have been here today. Instead Kristin Hart was bearing the brunt of it, though she was very good at what she did, judging from watching her as she leaned over him and tapped at her keyboard.

He closed his eyes. Malcolm got a whiff of that honey body lotion they sold, that the factory smelled of, actually. It was nice. It was driving him a little crazy, because it wasn't just the cream he was inhaling, but the scent of Kristin, mingled with the cream.

"This is the main screen. The printer is right there." She indicated a portable laser printer on a table behind them. "I need to go check on my crew now, but you can stay here and print whatever production reports you need. If you get lost in the system, just type 'MI10' here." She showed him a tab on the screen. "That's a back door to the main reports menu. You can go directly there instead of clicking through the hierarchy of screens."

"You know what you're doing," he said, impressed at the speed with which she paged through the system.

"I should. I installed a lot of it." Her voice was matter-of-fact. Not filled with the pride she should be taking in her work. "What else do you need today?" she asked, very cool and professional.

It threw him for a bit of a loop. There were dynamics in

play here that he wasn't aware of. Nothing had gone right about this day so far.

He forced himself to think for a minute, collect himself. "Why don't I print the reports later? As long as you're heading to the floor, I'll tag along with you now."

She nodded again, showing no emotion. "Fine." She glanced at her watch and winced slightly. "I've been gone too long, and I left Mindy in charge."

He followed Kristin as she strode down the hallway to a section of the old plant with ancient floorboards that creaked when he walked on them. A remainder from the original, nineteenth-century cotton mill it had once been, beside the great flowing river that cut through the classic, small New England factory town. He felt calmer. These were facilities he knew well, both from his university years and his work experience.

They rounded a corner and bumped into a woman who was headed in their direction, evidently searching for Kristin.

"I brought you your hot chocolate," Kristin said to the woman.

This was Mindy. And Malcolm knew, because she wore a "Hello, my name is Mindy" sticker affixed to her blue-flowered blouse.

Mindy was shorter than Kristin, and squatter, and when she suddenly sighed and wrapped both chubby arms around Kristin's waist, her head only reached the top of Kristin's breasts. For a moment, Malcolm froze. Such shows of affection in the workplace were so out of place, inappropriate…and yet, he couldn't tear his gaze away from them.

"I am sooo tired of snow and cold," Mindy moaned, her voice muffled between Kristin's breasts.

Malcolm swallowed, his heart feeling as if it had stopped. But Kristin wasn't fazed by the woman.

"I know, honey." Kristin hugged Mindy with one arm and patted her on the head while she juggled the mug of hot chocolate in her other hand. "It seems like it's been snowing for months and months, doesn't it? But it's only January."

"The new year," Mindy said. She pushed away from Kristin and faced him. Her eyes were spaced far apart, and she had a distinctive look to her features.

Ah. He understood. She was…what did they call it? Special Needs.

"Hello," Mindy said to him.

"Er…hello." He crossed his arms and nodded curtly. No hugs for him today, please, he thought.

"This is George," Kristin said to Mindy. "He's visiting us for the day."

Inside, Malcolm cringed. He did not want to bond with anyone here, did not want to risk getting to know them or, God forbid, *liking* them.

"What did you do for New Year's Eve?" Mindy asked him.

"Er…" He gazed to Kristin for help. She smiled and shook her head as if to say, "You're on your own."

Involuntarily, he swallowed.

"What did you do for New Year's Eve?" Mindy asked him again, louder this time.

He risked glancing at Kristin. She was watching him as if his response was of utmost importance.

"I…er…went home."

"Where is that?" Mindy demanded.

He felt a muscle in his jaw tick. He looked to Kristin, but she didn't say a word.

"I saw my family," he said quietly. And it killed him to think of it. His life was so out of sync with theirs. He'd stayed two weeks, for Christmas and for Hogmanay—what the Scots called New Year's Eve—but then after the "first-footing" tradition, he'd been right back on the road again.

He really was getting tired of the road.

"*Who* is in your family?" Mindy asked him.

"Come," Kristin interrupted, taking pity on him at last. "We need to get back to the packing room. How are Jeff and Arlene doing?"

"Good." Mindy stopped to take a drink of her hot chocolate. She downed half the mug in one long gulp, before Kristin gently took it from her.

"Let me carry that for you, Mindy," Kristin said. Mindy allowed Kristin to put her arm around her and lead her down the hallway.

And just like that, his interrogation was forgotten.

He paused, catching his breath. Even though it was cool enough to nearly see his breath in the below-room-temperature factory, he was sweating beneath his shirt. A cold perspiration, running in a thin trickle from his armpit down along his bare skin. He was in hell. Women and special needs workers. What was he doing?

Kristin poked her head around the corner. "Are you coming, George?"

It was like a dagger to his core. "I... Yes." But he gripped his notebook and made sure he had his phone in his pocket; he'd need the camera app to take photos of the factory floor.

He followed Kristin and Mindy. Slowly, he was turning himself numb inside again. Not fighting anymore. He would go with the flow, whatever the day brought. Let Kristin show him the way, but at the same time, stay safely wary.

But it turned out he didn't need to be; nobody challenged him. Kristin introduced him to Jeff and Arlene. Jeff was mellow and quiet. He had a thick white beard, wire-rimmed glasses and a habit of saying very little. Arlene was around the same age, but warm and nurturing. She babbled on about a trip to "the British Isles" she was planning to take, and it was only by the grace of God that Kristin didn't raise a brow at him or otherwise give him away as a possible inhabitant of the Commonwealth.

She was a blessing to him. And, as she'd promised, Kristin led him on a tour of the plant. It was a light, airy space with high ceilings and tall windows that overlooked a back parking lot and a pine forest that was picturesque—pure New England.

Malcolm knew the region well; he'd spent his childhood and teen years in two New Hampshire boarding schools, and then, his undergraduate terms in a college not too far from the location of this plant.

The snow falling on the pine trees outside made him feel sad. It was so quiet and peaceful. He and Kristin were the only two people on the factory floor, with all the empty, ghostlike machines. She led him from station to station, his footsteps echoing against the ancient wooden boards, warped and uneven with age. The space was small and cramped with devices—mixers, conveyor belts, bottlers and a label maker that Kristin said was broken, hence, the applying of labels by hand today. But no matter…all the other machines were dormant, too. On a Saturday.

Incredibly wasteful. His head had been buried in the levels of financials for this small, privately held company for weeks, and it was apparent to him that the business was mismanaged.

Malcolm took photos with his camera phone. He listened while Kristin explained each part of the production process, and how the layout was configured depending on the product to be manufactured that day.

"I thought you worked with the computer system," he remarked to her.

"I do. But I also schedule the machines. That's the benefit of a small company—I get to do lots of things." She smiled. "I like variety, so it's perfect for me. I don't think any other company would fit my personality. It's why I won't ever leave here."

He kept his careful poker face and just felt sadder. It was not good that he was getting to know his hostess. Not wise at all to let himself sympathize with these people at Aura. It was his job to stay emotionally aloof and separate from the actions he was required to take. He needed to remain neutral and businesslike. It was safer for everyone that way.

He went back to the computer in her office and studied the range of reports to choose from.

"George?" Mindy asked from the doorway.

It took Malcolm a moment to realize that Mindy was referring to him. *Damn it.* "Yes, Mindy?"

"Kristin says to ask you what you want for lunch. She's going to call in a sandwich order, and I get to pick it up by myself." Her chest expanded with pride.

Do not get too close to these people. "No, thank you," he said. "I'll take care of my own lunch."

"But, aren't you hungry?" Mindy demanded. "I'm always hungry."

His stomach was growling. He was thirsty, too, but for something cold. Andrew had shown him a Coke machine in the break room earlier, but Malcolm hadn't brought any pocket change with him. He was still hoping Andrew would call him, even though Malcolm knew it was highly unlikely—less than a one percent chance, he figured.

"I'll, er, walk someplace close by for lunch," Malcolm said to the girl. A lie, because he didn't have a wallet or credit cards, and his smallest bill was a hundred. He doubted a small-town diner would risk cashing it.

"*I'm* walking today," Mindy said. "To Cookie's Place. Kristin said I'm in charge." She scrunched her face at him, showing him that she was peeved. It occurred to him that maybe he was taking her job away from her.

"Ah…is there a bigger place nearby? A chain restaurant?" Maybe he could call his driver to phone in an order with a credit card. "How about a pizza place I can walk to?" Vermont didn't have fried pizza like in Scotland, but he would make do.

Mindy frowned harder. "If you are walking, there's only Cookie's Place."

Of course. It was a small town. And it had been a crucial, logistical mistake not to have access to a car. His fault, because how could the fictional "George Smith" rent a car without a driver's license?

Sighing wearily, he gave in. "Please order me whatever sandwich Kristin is ordering. And, er—" man, this was painful "—please ask her if I can pay her back later, once I have change. Okay?"

He would have to send an envelope with cash later, which gave him more logistical problems. The compounding of his torment today did not end….

"Kristin is paying for our lunches out of petty cash," Mindy informed him.

Well. That solved everything. "Fine. You win."

When the food came, he was grateful for it. Thick slices of deli turkey piled high on homemade white bread, also sliced thick, with crisp lettuce and Swiss cheese and a spread of fresh cranberry sauce as the main condiment. Absolutely delicious. He tried not to eat like a hungry wolf. They were all together sitting at a table by the big front windows, chewing happily, saying little. Malcolm downed his bottle of cool spring water, contented, no longer so dehydrated.

The snow outside was coming down in a thick blanket. At home, in Scotland, the roads would be at a standstill, he thought with amusement. When he'd been in Edinburgh over Hogmanay, the city had received just a few inches of snow, and the city government had literally called in the British Army to clear the streets. Scotland didn't have snow-clearing equipment like Vermont did. People just didn't drive in snow the way they did here.

But Malcolm was a great driver in snow. He'd had many years of long New England practice.

Then he realized that, without knowing it, Mindy had put a bug in his ear with all her questions. He suddenly felt homesick for his country. He unscrewed the cap on the bottle of Coke that Kristin had also ordered for him. If he were at home, he'd have asked for an Irn-Bru. Maybe Kristin would think it was nasty stuff—sweet, licorice-flavored, neon-orange-colored carbonated soda—but it was his *Scottish* nasty stuff, and that's why he'd always liked it.

He was just tired from too much traveling. Maybe he needed a rest....

The others went back to work, and he observed Kristin and her motley crew from a distance. It fascinated him how Kristin made a game out of finishing their labeling chore. She and Mindy sang all the choruses of "Walking in a Winter Wonderland." When they were through with that, they shared turns telling stories.

And then they lapsed into silence, quietly moving among the open boxes, filling them with jars, while Mindy closed her eyes and rested.

Outside, the snow covered the world in a peaceful white blanket. Malcolm got up by himself and wandered the facility, first completing his report-printing and diagram-photocopying, and then taking the last of his photos.

When he'd finished, he searched for Kristin. He found her sitting by herself at the table where they'd eaten lunch earlier. Her chin was in her hands and she was staring out the window, just watching the January snow come down. Hushed.

And it seemed to him that the delicious sandwich caught in his throat, because he'd known before he'd even started his day's work, known before he'd seen the first bleeding financial statement and the first silent, still piece of machinery that he was going to shut all this down on her.

He was the man responsible.

And there was nothing he could do to stop it.

NOT EVEN MINDY could melt this glacial man's heart, Kristin decided.

Thankfully, George had avoided them for most of the afternoon. Mindy had come back and reported to Kristin that George was "mean."

"He frowns at me," Mindy had said.

Yes, George was a frowner. Nothing cracked his reserve.

He was closed, disinterested, zipped-up tight. And she wouldn't complain about it, because he had treated her with nothing but professionalism so far. During their tour of the plant, not once had he said a single inappropriate thing or even cracked a smile again.

If anything, as he followed her about the factory floor, listening silently to her explanation of the processes, cutting in only now and then to ask pertinent questions, he was insightful.

Her anxiety since she'd spoken to Dirk had slowly slipped away. She had relaxed enough to leave George to his own devices while she'd helped her crew box orders and perform quality control with the invoices and packing lists. The shipping company was due soon, and Aura was behind with their schedule. They were always behind with their schedule lately, it seemed. Whenever things went wrong at work, Andrew would be quick to criticize her, but Kristin was determined this would not be one of those times.

She just needed to accept that George Smith was enigmatic. He was a "Mr. Rochester" type. Once upon a time, Kristin would've found a fun challenge in bringing him out of his shell. What made this guy tick? Why was he so closed off and brooding?

Jeff dropped a box he was carrying, and George jumped. Literally jumped.

So he was nervous, too. Behind that angry, serious facade.

But, she really didn't want to think too much about it or him. Things had changed with her since her younger more naive days. Now, she just wanted this handsome Scotsman bundled up and on his way so she could go back to her life as it was.

At the end of the afternoon, Kristin crossed the plant and found George standing in her office, sliding a folder into his briefcase. He glanced up when he saw her, and for a split second, his face brightened.

She hesitated. Maybe he was melting a bit.

"Did you find everything you needed today?" she asked cautiously.

He nodded, making a slight smile. "Yes, and I appreciate all your help."

Well. That was…good. "Do you think you could tell Andrew that for me?" She started to smile, too, but then stopped herself, remembering. "Please, just give me a good report. It really would help me with him."

"Yes, I'll tell him," George said warmly. "I'll tell Jay Astley, as well. Maybe he can do something for you."

Jay Astley? Her pulse elevated. "Thank you. That's…" She paused, thinking of their gentle CEO. "Did I mention that his wife recently died?"

He nodded, slowly drawing on his coat. "Yes."

"Laura…his wife…was the person who interviewed me for this job six years ago." Kristin couldn't help smiling at her memory. "We hit it off right away."

"She made a good decision hiring you," George said.

He thought so? She snapped her head up, but he had discreetly turned aside and was wrapping a winter scarf around his neck.

Kristin turned off the electric heater. Laura's sudden illness and then death had upset everyone. She had been the heart and soul of their little factory community. She had also been the most perceptive person Kristin had ever met.

Anybody else would've thrown Kristin out of her office once she'd seen Kristin's grades and college transcript. Kristin had not been top of her class, far from it. Back then, she'd been hopelessly disorganized. Even during her scheduled interview—so important to her—Kristin had accidentally dropped her purse, and to her mortification, two packaged tampons had rolled out onto the interview table.

But Laura had been gracious to her and had looked beyond the mistake. Maybe she had been able to tell that Kristin was bright and knew what she was talking about, despite the rough nerves. In any event, she'd simply smiled and put Kristin at ease. "It would be nice to have another woman besides me in the plant offices," Laura had said. "Tell me, what about Aura Botanicals drew you to us?"

And Kristin had relaxed enough to just be herself for the rest of the interview. Something all too rare back in those days.

Kristin blinked, coming back to the present. She bit the inside of her cheek and glanced at George. He had cocked his head and was quietly studying her.

She smiled at him. "When Laura interviewed me for this job, she asked me why she should hire me. And I actually said to her, 'Because I'm addicted to your Red Chestnut shampoo. It makes me happy every morning when I smell it.'"

Laughing, she shook her head. "What would you have said to such a candidate? You would have run away, wouldn't you?"

"Actually," George said slowly, "I like that answer. If said honestly, it shows that the employee understands the company's products. It shows a tendency to be loyal, and that's the most important thing to me." He swallowed, his Adam's apple bobbing up and down.

Something stirred in her heart. He looked so vulnerable and yet sexy at the same time. She pressed her palms to her sides and tried to stay calm.

"I definitely would've hired you," he said quietly. The soft lilt of Scotland rolled over her. Her heart picked up and seemed to float.

"Really?" she breathed.

"Absolutely." It was almost a whisper.

A spell hung in the air between them. Her knees weakened. She gazed at him, into his light, clear blue eyes, the color of the fading winter's day, and she could not stop that bond that had seemed to spring up and suddenly intensify.

With a sharp intake of breath, George stared down at his watch. "Four o'clock," he murmured. "My ride will be here soon."

"Yes." Flustered, she grabbed her coat. "I'll walk you to the front door."

He nodded to her. She wondered if he would reach

for her hand. But, no, as always, he was careful not to touch her.

"Well, I guess this is goodbye, then," he said. He kept his hands in his pockets.

"Yes. Of course," she answered.

His phone rang, and he seemed relieved to turn away from her. "Hello, I'll meet you out front," he said into the phone.

She went back out to the packing area, trying not to think of him. She had wanted him to leave, after all. By now, the shipping guy had shown up and was loading the stack of boxes into his truck. Kristin signed time cards for Mindy, Jeff and Arlene, and was saying goodbye to them when George approached her, looking worried.

"I wonder if I might ask for your help," he said.

So polite. But at least he hadn't reverted back to scowling at her. She nodded. "Certainly, George."

He seemed to flinch. "My, er, driver got into a small accident." With a rueful expression, he gazed out the tall factory windows. In the light that fell over the parking lot, the snow swirled. Two inches accumulation, she judged. The fresh snowfall had amounted to more than the dusting she'd expected.

"Is he all right?" she asked.

George shrugged. "He's not used to driving in snow. He skidded off the road and into an embankment. He called for assistance, and now he's awaiting a replacement vehicle. They estimate two hours before he's able to get here."

"Oh." She digested that information. What did it mean for them?

"Is there a taxi company nearby that I might call?" he asked, ever so polite. But she saw the worry lines on his face.

"Yes. Absolutely." She went to the bulletin board in the

break room and pulled the tack to release a worn business card, and then brought it back to George. "There's only one taxi service in town, but they're usually pretty reliable."

He held the card between his fingers while he pressed the buttons for the phone number. He had large hands, the nails bitten to the quick. No rings, wedding or otherwise. She glanced up at him to see his gaze dart away from hers.

She felt warm inside, from her face to her toes. Now, that was strange. She definitely didn't want that. A fantasy was one thing, but this…this physical attraction was reality. And it was still too dangerous—she didn't know this man. Yes, everything had gone well so far, but…

Even if their work arrangement didn't end tonight, she just wasn't interested in a relationship with him. She seldom dated, and never with anyone she'd met at Aura. It just wasn't who she was.

Frankly, these days, she'd pretty much resigned herself to the fact that she was meant to be single. The loyal employee, the quirky aunt, the want-to-be-adventurous sister. Maybe—on a good day—even the dutiful daughter. That was all that she was.

Thankfully, George Smith was leaving town. She turned away from him and marched from the packing area. She kept her hands balled in her pockets. She was far enough away that she couldn't hear him, which was good, because the sound of his deep, low voice speaking into the phone was doing a number on her, making her body feel things she didn't want to feel.

She busied herself by walking through the plant, checking that lights were off and doors were locked. Inside her office, she grabbed her flashlight from the shelf, along with a spare pair of mittens and a beret that she kept in one of her desk drawers. It would be a long walk home in the dark and the cold. She shut down her computer and closed up the room.

When she turned down the corridor, she saw George walking toward her. Her legs seemed to freeze. She stopped where she was, twisting the mittens in her hand.

"The taxi service isn't willing to drive me to my hotel. The snowfall is supposed to intensify, and they don't want to get stuck."

"Oh," she replied.

"Is there a diner where I can get something to eat and do some work until my ride arrives?"

"I… No." She laughed ruefully, not able to avoid gazing into his eyes. Sky-blue. So beautiful…

She shook her head, looking away. "We're a backwater town. All that's open on Saturday night is a convenience mart, a seedy bar I don't recommend, two gas stations and a twenty-four hour pharmacy."

His countenance fell. Kristin rubbed her arms and risked glancing at him again. He really was worried. Suddenly, this was not just his problem, but *their* problem. They were a team, and he needed her to help him solve this.

It made her feel sick and a little anxious.

"How about if I find someone to drive you to your hotel?" she suggested shakily. Maybe her brother was home. He had a four-wheel-drive vehicle.

But her brother was like her; he tended to talk too much and inappropriate things often popped out without him intending it. "On second thought, never mind," she said hurriedly, "I'll take you instead."

"No." George shook his head. "Absolutely not. I will not have you jeopardize your safety. It's out of the question."

"Then…what do you propose we do?"

He set his mouth in a line. "I'll wait in your office."

"No, we can't do that. Because of the alarm, you can't

stay in the factory without me being here with you." She rubbed her trembling palms against her sides—she had no choice, really. "How about if you wait with me at my sister-in-law's house?" Nothing could go wrong with that scenario. "My niece invited me for an early dinner tonight. We'll sit with their family while you wait for your ride."

"No, I don't want to impose," he said.

But she could tell he was being polite and cautious, refusing the invitation the same as she would have, in his place.

"Stephanie is a professional chef. To her, adding another seat at the table is a good thing. The more people who enjoy her meals, the better, as far as she's concerned."

He still looked dubious.

"I'll call her now and tell her." She had to—she couldn't leave George out in the cold.

Holding her mitten with her teeth, Kristin took out her phone from her pocket and dialed her sister-in-law's number. George gave her a pained expression, but he didn't argue.

Stephanie picked up on the first ring. "Where are you? You said you'd be here at five o'clock."

"I'm bringing a work colleague to dinner. That's okay, isn't it?"

George was now outright frowning at her and looking tremendously unhappy.

Kristin glanced away. "His name is George Smith, and he's snowed in for a couple of hours until his ride shows up. I told him that he could grab a bite with us, and that it wouldn't be a problem."

"You're bringing home a *man?*" Stephanie asked over the phone. "Our Kristin is actually bringing someone *home?* Are pigs flying?"

"Stop it," Kristin murmured. George winced. She smiled gamely at him, trying not to tremble.

"You used to be fun," Stephanie complained.

"I still am," she whispered into the phone.

"No, I mean, you used to date. You used to like guys, and want to have a family of your own someday. You were gonna have a set of twins, remember—so they would be best friends with my kids—and we were all going to vacation together, happily ever after. I even married your dumb brother for it."

Oh, no. Knowing Kristin's brother, some elaborately planned prank had backfired. She glanced nervously at George. "Um, what's he done now?"

"Nothing! That's the problem—he's refusing to eat my cooking. And me, a professional! You would think that after eight years of marriage, the dummy would learn."

"What's…going on, Steph?"

There was a pause, and when she spoke again, Stephanie's mouth sounded full. "Actually, it's a surprise. Ask George Smith if he likes haggis."

Haggis? For a moment, Kristin couldn't process the incongruity.

She glanced at George, confused. What was Stephanie talking about the Scottish dish for? Her family had never eaten or served it before, not once. From what Kristin had read, haggis was a pudding/meat kind of thing, made with sheep's heart, liver and lungs all ground up and stuffed, along with oatmeal and onion and spices, inside a big sausage casing and served on a platter.

At least, that was what she had discovered on the internet when she'd been explaining Scottish customs to her niece Lily for the girl's "What is Your Family Ancestry?" Girl Scout project.

And then it dawned on her. "Oh, my gosh!" Kristin

squealed. "Today is January twenty-fifth! You made haggis for Lily, didn't you?"

"Yes, I did," Stephanie said. "Though technically, I prepared it for you. Maybe it will spark some sense of adventure in you and bring you back to life. The whole family is invited and we're going to do it up—bagpipe music, toasts, songs—the works. Pretty good surprise, isn't it?"

With a smile so big it felt as if her cheeks were splitting, Kristin suddenly remembered George standing beside her.

She stopped giggling and turned to him, her hand over her mouth.

His face had turned paper-white.

Kristin covered the phone so Stephanie wouldn't hear her. "You know exactly what holiday tonight is, don't you, George?"

WORSE AND WORSE. That's how his day was going. He was in a section of Hades reserved for liars. Or at least, for imposters who were required to take security names as part of their jobs.

Malcolm bit his tongue, hard, not for the first time today, and probably not for the last time, either.

Kristin was right about one thing: he knew damn well what "Rabbie Burns" night was.

January twenty-fifth. Every year, a countrywide supper held in honor of the birthday of Scotland's national poet: Robert Burns. Malcolm had been out of the country and away from home for so long, he hadn't been to a Burns event since he was…

Ten years old. Exactly.

Damn it. He should've anticipated this. Kristin was obviously obsessed with his home country, romanticizing it like many women did.

The reality was, his home country just wasn't that damn romantic to him. Not in his experience.

"Have you ever eaten haggis?" he made sure to say in his best American accent. "Because I haven't. It sounds horrible. No offense to your sister-in-law."

"Seriously? You've never tried it?"

"Seriously. I've never tried it."

She smiled at him. "Then I guess you'll have to come along and try something new tonight," she teased.

Obviously, Kristin trusted him more than she had earlier. Her reticence had left her, and this was not good, for either of them.

What was she doing, believing in him?

Don't, he wanted to tell her. But if he confessed to her what he was really doing visiting her company, then he would violate the terms of his agreement.

You have to make the hard choices, Malcolm.

Really, he had *no* choice.

CHAPTER THREE

MALCOLM STRODE BESIDE Kristin in the early darkness, his mood matching the light. Snowbanks lined the sidewalk. It was so frigid cold outside that the hard-packed snow crunched underfoot, and his breath made puffs of air as he walked.

They'd left the mill building and were cutting through the middle of what passed for a downtown—a New England-style town green surrounded by shops, shuttered tight, and old homes, typical of the region. It reminded him of the remote village in New Hampshire where he'd first been sent to prep school as a boy, which only depressed him further. He hunched his shoulders in his coat as they passed through a section of street without lamplights. Malcolm pulled his torch from his pocket and turned it on.

"You carry a flashlight with you, too?" she asked, breaking the silence.

"Everyone should." If trouble warranted it, the heavy barrel could double as a weapon. He never went anywhere without considering the security implications.

She showed him her flashlight. Smiling sheepishly, she said, "Not everyone understands it, but a person has to protect themselves."

Something they agreed on. Still, he thought of his sister who was about Kristin's height, though slighter. He couldn't see her bashing anyone over the head with a piece of metal. *Too bad*.

"Did somebody teach you to carry that?" he asked her.

"Yep, my brothers."

He rubbed the back of his neck. "Ah…will they be present this evening?"

Passing beneath a streetlight, he noticed the dimple form in her cheek. "We may be blessed with their presence, yes."

Lovely. At least his luck was predictable.

Within another block, they were at her family's house, a multistory, clapboard Victorian. They climbed a set of stairs to a big wraparound porch. Stamping her feet to warm them, Kristin pulled a key from her coat pocket.

"You have a key to your sister-in-law's home?" he asked.

"I live in the apartment upstairs. My brother and sister-in-law own the house, and I rent space from them."

Interesting. Living here was safe, he supposed. "You have a short walk to work."

"I do." She smiled at him. Her hair was tucked inside her beret, and she looked…pretty. The fur from her collar framed her face, and her soft, green eyes gazed up at him. It made him ache.

He had too many secrets to keep from her. He only hoped he endured the night without incident. If he kept himself aloof from her and did not let himself care about her or her predicament once he left, then he would do fine.

"I have one thing to ask of you, George—please don't hold me responsible for what my family might say or do tonight," she pleaded, her hand on the doorknob.

He blinked. "Why? Are they likely to string me up because I'm with you?"

"Not *you.* They like strong, silent types."

Is that what he was? In any event, nobody would think well of him once his handiwork was made known. Kristin certainly wouldn't.

A gust of cold wind blew by, and he hunched his shoulders against the frigid temperature. "What are the risks tonight, then?" he asked.

"Me. I'm the risk. I'm bringing someone to a family event." She choked out a laugh, and then glanced at him helplessly. "Trust me, they would love to pair us up. And it turns out the whole clan is going to be here, not just Stephanie and Lily. So, could you please back me up—make it clear that we're work colleagues only?"

He stared at her. There were so many things ahead that could go wrong—so many potential traps she didn't even know about. But he could only fixate on one thing.

"Don't you have a boyfriend?"

"No." She shivered. "I am happily single."

For some reason he liked that response. He smiled at her. "Then we'll be happily single together."

She seemed relieved. Nodding, a look of grim determination on her face, she opened the door. "One more thing," she said, turning to him. "If you don't like the haggis, then you don't have to eat it."

"I'll be certain not to. You can count on that."

She smiled at him, and something in his chest pinged. This wasn't good. He was getting drawn to her despite himself.

There was a reason he'd done his best to keep his distance from her during the afternoon. But now here he was entering her private home, and it was too late to back out. "May I ask why your family is having a Burns Night? All these years I've lived in this country, and I don't think anyone has ever invited me to one. It's not well-known outside of Scotland."

"Meet my family, and I'm sure they'll tell you why it's important—well, important to me, at least."

The door was creaky, so she threw her hip into it. With

a rattle of glass and a squeak of hinges, they stood inside a warm kitchen. That distinctive odor of tatties and neeps—potatoes and turnips—hit him, and he wrinkled his nose. He also noted sheep—haggis—mixed in, and he grimaced.

He'd been following behind Kristin, but she was immediately whisked away by a female rug rat. She was a shrimp of a girl, a ginger, with the wildest red hair and a smattering of freckles that he'd not seen in ages. Such a combination usually only existed on his home island.

The ginger rug rat was wearing a kilt that clashed with her features. A bright red Royal Stuart tartan, displayed outside almost every tourist shop on Edinburgh's Royal Mile. He was having difficulty not chuckling aloud, so he squeezed his lips between thumb and forefinger.

"George Smith?" a woman asked him. He didn't answer right away; it wasn't registering that she was speaking to *him*. When it did occur to him, he turned abruptly.

And looked down. She was a shrimp of a woman, too, to match the shrimp of a daughter. Black hair, flashing eyes, and wearing a chef's white top, checkered loose pants and kitchen restaurant clogs.

That was a relief—she *was* a professional. Thus, it was unlikely he would be poisoned.

The lady chef grabbed his hand and pulled him into a small butler's pantry off to the side. And then she shut the door behind them.

Inside, with a bare lightbulb hanging from the ceiling, and rows of spices and jarred dry goods arranged on shelves, she grabbed a bottle of whisky—single malt—from a top ledge and unscrewed the cap. "A word with you, Mr. Smith," she said, pouring them each a wee dram.

Solemnly she handed him a glass. "I know you're an out-of-town guest, a work colleague to Kristin, but I am telling you, they are going to crucify her in there. And if you don't support her—or worse, if you join in on the laughter and the insults—then I will personally see you pushed into a snowbank. Do you understand?"

"I…"

"Of course you do." She smiled sweetly and raised her glass to him before slinging back the shot.

"Whoa!" she said. "That waters the eyes."

"Er," he said, still holding the glass of whisky, "I thought this was Kristin's family celebrating a Burns Dinner?"

"Sure, but they're not always an easy crowd, and definitely won't be tonight once they figure out what kind of food I'm feeding them." She shivered. "Trust me, I've known this bunch forever. Kristin was my nap partner in kindergarten. She kept me laughing so much, I never got my sleep. We were always in trouble."

"Kristin has how many brothers?" Were they big? How many stone did they weigh?

"It has taken me weeks to find a decent haggis recipe," she said, ignoring him, "and then, importing the ingredients and testing it in my kitchen." She poked him in the chest. "It's taken me a while to crack the code and make it palatable. The rest of them likely won't touch it, but you will. You will at least try to like it for Kristin's sake. Do you hear me?"

"I hear you." He slugged back the whisky shot. It burned his throat like comfortable fire. "That's good stuff," he muttered, smacking his lips.

"Damn straight it is. I'm bringing up a little girl who's fifty percent Scottish-American. My husband has three Scottish-American grandparents, and one Scottish grandmother, actually born in the old country. I figure that makes me Scottish by injection, and I plan to act accordingly."

He nearly choked.

"So, you'll play along with Kristin and me?"

Mutely, he nodded.

Thankfully, she pivoted on her clogs and stalked back to her instrument of his doom—a silver range with six gas burners, four of them currently going full throttle, shooting up vicious blue flames. He wiped his mouth and ventured out of her kitchen and into the lion's den.

With foreboding, he glanced into the dining room, where a crowd of men stood, drinking lager from brown longneck bottles. Unless they all ganged up on him, he figured he could handle each of them, alone, judging by height and weight. One of the men looked as though he might be bigger than Malcolm, but Malcolm couldn't be sure because the man, unfortunately, sat in a wheelchair and had a glum expression on his face.

Kristin was nowhere to be seen.

Malcolm raked a hand through his hair. She would be back soon, with the little girl in tow, he assumed, and introductions would commence. He could behave seriously and in a low-key manner, the same as he'd been doing all day.

Or…there was still time to confess to her. Pull Kristin aside and tell her his real name. His true purpose. Let her in on his thoughts about what her CEO had asked him to do. Maybe some steps she could take for herself to mitigate the fallout before anyone else knew…

It was insanity to consider it.

He'd planned to never see this woman again after tonight. She was not part of upper management at Aura Botanicals, nor was there any reason for her to learn of his past. If he came clean now…

Then that would break his agreement with Jay Astley to remain anonymous. Malcolm would be jeopardizing the new product branding plans. He would also be jeopardizing his own company and the people in it.

It was too risky.

He had to continue the charade. One last night of being George Smith before the security name was retired for good. Kristin would never find out who he really was.

The only difficult part would be the guilt.

No. Guilt he could handle. The worst part would be re-signing himself to remaining aloof for the next few hours. Like it or not, he saw all the ways that she was like him, with her heavy flashlight and her love and loyalty to her family and her employer. She had an innate capability for taking care of herself and others. And, she *was* fun. The lady was quietly compatible to him in a way that he hadn't known in years, in a way that pulled him in and attracted him.

It was downright dangerous, and he could be in trouble here unless he was careful.

Plus, he would eat no more than one bite of haggis—he didn't care what her dynamo of a sister-in-law threatened him with.

And, he would never let on to any of them that he knew what Burns Night was. He was simply an observer, killing time. His mouth shut. A ghost who would fade from memory once his driver arrived and he left this small Vermont town forever.

The brother in the wheelchair rolled over to him at the same time that Kristin came hurrying back into the room.

"I'm sorry," she said, her face flushed and her smile trembling in an "I apologize!" grimace. "My niece wanted help with her part in the festivities. I didn't mean to desert you."

She turned to the largest of the men, the one in the wheelchair. "George, this is my brother Stevie. Stevie, this is George. He's a work colleague, and he's stranded in town until his ride gets here."

"My sympathies," Stevie said, holding out his hand.

"Good to meet you," Malcolm answered, and shook the man's hand, nearly getting his fingers crushed in the process.

"This—" Kristin continued, with unmistakable worry in her voice "—is my mom. Mom, this is George."

"Er...hello," Malcolm said.

Mom speared him up and down with her sharp eyes that didn't appear to miss much. Clearly, an appraisal was in process.

Frowning, Mom asked him, "George? George what?"

"Smith," Kristin replied.

"And what does he do at Aura Botanicals?" Mom demanded.

"Marketing," Malcolm said without hesitation. The crowd was moving toward the dining table, so he followed along, praying the line of questioning would soon stop.

"And where did he go to school to prepare for the job?" Mom demanded of Kristin.

"Er, Dartmouth." Malcolm decided to answer her directly. "And later, Harvard Business School."

Mom whirled to stare at him. Her eyebrows shot up. In a heartbeat, her expression changed. "That's the Ivy League!"

He knew that. Kristin sighed and leaned over to murmur into his ear: "I went to a local college and my grades weren't stellar. No one around here lets me forget that."

"Engineering is difficult," Malcolm remarked. "I imagine that business studies are much easier."

"You're being nice to me. I appreciate it." She pulled out a chair and indicated that he sit.

He did so, and she joined him to his left. Her face seemed frozen in a mask of what appeared to be both trepidation and hopeful excitement. The dining table was large, and there were a variety of chairs jammed around it, due to the crowd the sister-in-law chef had invited. He wasn't sure who everyone was, and he was glad Kristin hadn't made the big deal of introducing him to everyone. He was just waiting for his ride. That was all.

He leaned back in his seat, cushioned and lined with fabric, while hers was an aluminum folding chair. Despite them each sitting on different kinds of chairs, he and Kristin were at the same height, so his thigh brushed against her thigh. His elbow rubbed her elbow.

She drew back, smiling sheepishly at him. "This is worse than airplane seating."

He stared, then realized she was talking about coach class in commercial airliners. He didn't know much about that.

The little rug rat climbed into the chair on the other side of him, his right side—his eating side—which was a relief because she was miniature size, and it was unlikely they would bash elbows during the course of the meal.

He smiled tentatively at the little girl. She grinned back, her freckles even more impressive at this close angle, and she cupped a hand, whispering into his ear, "Watch me, I'm going to dance later."

"You're…?"

"George," Kristin's mother said, simpering from across the table, "I apologize for our boardinghouse arrangement. We are not usually so uncivilized."

"Yes, we are," an older man contradicted her from the opposite side. He stood and leaned across the table to shake Malcolm's hand. "I'm Rich, Kristin's dad."

"Better than being poor," quipped the brother in the wheelchair as he maneuvered himself beside the dad.

"They're terrible," the mother said, fussing with the silverware that the sister-in-law had set out. "Pay no attention to them. We're usually not so disorganized, either."

"Sure we are," a tall man chimed in.

"I should probably explain who everybody is," Kristin murmured to Malcolm. Discreetly, she inclined her head. "That is my dad, Rich, and mom, Evelyn—both of whom you've already met. Dad works at the county Chamber of Commerce and Mom serves part-time in the town offices and the rest of the time in the café, helping Stephanie." She gestured across the table, still speaking in a low tone. "PJ, my oldest brother, is married to Stephanie. This is, of course, their house. Then there's Stevie." She tilted her chin toward the man in the wheelchair. "He's renting a basement room, for now, while he rehabs from his motorcycle accident." A cloud crossed her face.

"Will he be okay?" Malcolm asked softly. Throughout the entire conversation, he kept his gaze on the tableau of the room. Bustling, energetic, they weren't paying much attention to him—except for the mother. But at the moment, she was occupied with searching for napkins—giving him and Kristin a chance to talk safely.

"We hope so," Kristin answered in a lower voice. "Stevie was reckless, going too fast, and he lost control when a car coming in the opposite direction crossed over to his side. We're lucky he survived the accident." But she brightened and talked faster. "Over there is Neil, my second oldest brother. He lives across town."

"How many brothers do you have?" Malcolm asked, suddenly feeling nervous. So much for being aloof. The haggis hadn't been presented, and already he was betraying himself.

"Four. The last, Grant, just joined the marines. He's in boot camp. He's hoping to come home and join the police force after his tour of duty."

Brilliant. "Er, are you the youngest sibling?" God, Malcolm hoped not. That would bring out her brothers' protective instincts.

"No," she said, "I'm right in the middle. Two older than me and two younger."

Malcolm nodded. He didn't know why he was bothering to keep close track of everything. He would probably never see her again—he was counting on never seeing her again.

"Except for the marine, no one in your family tends to move very far from home, do they?" he observed.

"No, we do not."

Before he could ask why, the sister-in-law—Stephanie—strutted into the room. She'd changed from her chef clothes and was wearing a blouse with green and navy blue plaid in it—Black Watch, he automatically thought. She still looked formidable, the military tartan appropriate on her.

Clearing her throat, she said, "Attention, everyone!" She tapped a water glass with her spoon. "Thank you for coming to the Hart family's first annual Burns Dinner. This is a surprise orchestrated by—"

"Me!" the urchin to his right said, jumping in her chair. She squatted, her feet on the seat, and her kilt was in a most unladylike position. But, Malcolm had grown up with an urchin sister, and in his house, they hadn't stood on formality much, either.

He must've been grinning at the little girl, because to his left, Kristin turned in her seat and gaped at him.

"He smiles!" she said. "Hallelujah!"

The urchin giggled, her chubby hand splayed over her freckled face.

"Kristin," the girl's mother ordered. "Help Lily sit properly in her chair. Lily, use your company manners."

He couldn't help it, he turned to little Lily himself. Didn't say a word, just gave her his best comic glower.

Lily laughed harder. But she straightened her skirt and untangled her feet from beneath her, sitting solidly on her rump.

Meanwhile, the mother and father were arguing across the table. It was so much like his own family he was starting to believe there was something to the Scottish genes. Maybe he was homesick.

Stephanie clapped her hands, startling them all. "As I was saying, this is called a Burns Supper. Lily learned it from her aunt, who was teaching her about Scotland and her Scottish ancestry for Lily's Brownie badge."

"Oh, please," Evelyn said. "Here we go."

"Your mother was born in Scotland," Stephanie said, directing the comment at her mother-in-law. "I think we should be proud of that."

"Yes," Evelyn said, "but I know where this is going."

She shot a look at Kristin, who blushed furiously.

Malcolm wondered what was going on.

"My mother was *not* heiress to a castle in Scotland," Evelyn said to Kristin. "Get that fantasy out of your head. I don't want to hear a single word of it tonight."

"She was, too!" the urchin—Lily—cried beside him. He winced from the shriek in his right eardrum. But at the same time, it took all his self-control to restrain himself from bursting out laughing. In general, he didn't like to snuff out anyone's enthusiasm—he hated the look of sadness it gave Kristin—but Evelyn was right.

There were thousands of castles in Scotland. Malcolm had often met people who, just because of a last name indicating a few drops of Scottish blood, somehow felt they were related to Scottish royalty. It was part of the romance of the Scottish diaspora, he supposed.

"A long time ago, Nanny got a letter from a man in Scotland, and, and, and…" Lily threw up her hands. With a straight face, the little girl said to Malcolm, "My great-nanny owned a castle. In Scotland. Really."

"Is that so?" Malcolm murmured.

"It's a family story," Kristin explained, her face flushed. "Before I was born, my grandmother received word from Scotland, informing her that she was heiress to a castle."

"Probably a scam," her father—Rich—remarked.

"Certainly a scam," Evelyn agreed. "They were looking for money."

Kristin's countenance fell.

Malcolm wished he could make her feel better. "Do you have the letter?" Malcolm asked gently.

"My mother-in-law tore it up," Rich said. "She was a practical one."

Kristin shook her head. "My family tends to be…skeptical," she said to Malcolm.

Malcolm completely understood.

"Still," Kristin said, glancing across the table at them. "The story remains."

"It's like those spam emails the Nigerian princes send, looking for bank account numbers," her brother—PJ—remarked. He looked plaintively at his wife. "Honey, I thought I smelled hamburger in the kitchen. Aren't we going to eat?"

Malcolm had news for him—that smell was haggis. Not one person present was going to be pleased once they tasted it. If this crowd heaped scorn and poked fun on a "castle heiress," then the presentation of the haggis would really kick off a round of derision.

Kristin stared at her empty plate. There was a resigned sadness to her face. Malcolm suspected she had experience with the futility of arguing with skeptics. Why did she stick around in the same hometown she'd grown up in if she had to deal with this on a daily basis? She was an adult—why not move away like he had?

As far as her career was concerned, she'd told him she liked the products at Aura Botanicals and the variety of the work in a small company. He understood that. But why subject herself to such restriction when she obviously craved adventure? That was her true personality—he'd watched her in action all afternoon. He'd only known her this one day, and it was obvious to him.

He frowned. He shouldn't long to cheer Kristin up or to look out for her. He shouldn't be moved enough to care about anything she did.

Leaning back, he ran his tongue over his chipped tooth.

"I believe in the fairy castle," a small voice whispered in his right ear.

He turned his head slightly. The urchin was standing in her chair again. She was staring at him as if she expected an answer.

"Do you now?" he murmured.

"Don't you?" she whispered back.

But it was a loud whisper. He glanced at Kristin, who was gazing at him expectantly, as if she'd heard their entire conversation and was immensely interested in what he thought on the matter.

Malcolm didn't believe in fantasies of castles and lost letters. But he did believe in Kristin. The woman was eminently capable. So he smiled in encouragement at her.

"I do," he said.

She bit her lip and looked down at her hands in her lap. When she glanced up again, she was blushing.

"Mom, when are we going to play the music?" the urchin shouted to her mother in the kitchen.

Malcolm flinched again. Kristin covered her mouth,

laughing. She was beautiful when she laughed. Bewitching.

Damn.

"Hold your horses!" Stephanie clomped into the room holding a white note card. She passed it to Kristin, whose face brightened further upon receiving it.

Clapping, Stephanie said, "Attention! The Burns Supper is now commenced! Kristin Hart will please read the opening grace." Then Stephanie spoke behind her hand in a stage whisper to him. "I copied it from the internet. Let's see how Kristin does with the accent."

Oh, lord. It must be the Selkirk Grace. Would Kristin read it in English, or would she go for the vernacular?

Inside, he felt tense. If Kristin were going to give away his secret to her family, then now was her chance.

He waited, breath held...

Kristin cleared her throat, and with a flourish, she read:

"Some hae meat and canna eat,
And some wad eat that want it.
But we hae meat, and we can eat,
And sae let the Lord be thankit."

Yes, she gave the language a thorough butchering. And then she raised her head and smiled at all assembled, exquisitely pleased.

"I'd like some meat," her father said plaintively.

"Doesn't everything sound better with a Scottish accent?" Kristin sighed to no one in particular, ignoring her father. "God, I miss Nanny."

"What did that poem say, Aunty?" her niece asked her. "It sounded funny."

"I'm not exactly sure," Kristin answered. "But Robert

Burns was a witty poet in his day. I'll research it later and explain it to you once I figure it all out."

But Kristin didn't look at Malcolm. She hadn't given away her suspicions regarding him, either. She could have pointed out that he had admitted to her that he'd lived in the country and that he knew damned well who the national poet of Scotland was. She could have shared with the group that she'd overheard Malcolm speaking in a similar, heavily accented vernacular this morning. She could have offered him up to the laughter and the skepticism and the jocular infighting, all things he was so familiar with from his own large brood of cousins. But she had not.

She was keeping their secret.

He glanced down at his hands in his lap, feeling sick for what he had to do. At some point soon, he would have to betray her.

He felt thoroughly ashamed.

"Now?" the urchin shouted to her mom. "Can I dance *now?*"

"No!" her mother answered. "Not yet." Then she marched into the kitchen and returned carrying a platter filled with hamburgers, each containing lettuce, tomato, cucumbers and, instead of a commercial bun, assembled with that same bread that he had eaten at lunch.

He nudged Kristin. "This looks familiar," he murmured.

She nodded, smiling. "Our sandwiches today came from Stephanie's diner. She runs Cookie's Place."

"Who is Cookie?"

"The lady who owned the restaurant before Stephanie. When she passed away, Stephanie bought it. First thing she did was choose a new name, and everyone in town got mad and refused to patronize the diner, so Stephanie switched the sign back. The diner is, and shall remain for all time, Cookie's Place."

"People just do not like change," her father said. "It's a fact."

"Attention!" Stephanie announced. "I'm offering a substitution for those of you who are not adventurous with the new food that will be forthcoming."

She waggled her finger at Malcolm, indicating he restrain himself and wait for the joy of the pending haggis.

Everyone except for him, Stephanie and Kristin lunged for a hamburger.

Stephanie shook her head at them. "Your forebears would be shamed."

"Our forebears would be thankful we'd left the sheep behind in Scotland," her father-in-law answered.

Malcolm silently agreed, watching longingly as they ate. "How is business at your diner?" he politely asked Stephanie.

"Truthfully, there are two factions keeping my operation afloat. Aura Botanicals employees, and my in-laws."

"Yeah, and this is why we come to dinner at your house," one brother remarked to PJ as he sank his teeth into the bun. "Your wife knows how to cook."

Malcolm's mouth watered. A sane response. And it would also be a sane response to reach forward and grab a hamburger along with the other men at the table. He knew what awaited them.

Stephanie left the room and returned with her iPod stand. "Now," she said to her daughter. "Now it's time for your part."

Then she addressed the table: "Technically, I was also supposed to serve a Cock-a-leekie soup course, but since you people don't like soup in general, I didn't want to hear the bitching and moaning."

Only silence answered her. With the exception of him,

Kristin and the urchin seated beside him, the rest of them were munching and chewing happily.

"In any event, no matter, because it is time for the parade of the haggis. I'll start the music, and Lily will dance the Highland Fling. Everyone will show the traditional respect."

Malcolm had never heard of the Highland Fling being combined with the presentation of the haggis. He bit his tongue. *Do not laugh.*

The strains of a lone bagpiper playing a Scottish reel exploded over the small iPod speakers centered on the dining table. It was like nothing Malcolm had ever heard, and it struck him as uproariously funny. He wished his sister was here; she would appreciate the humor in this.

Don't laugh. Don't make a sound.

Stephanie planted her hands on her hips and scowled. Malcolm followed her gaze to Lily, cowering and doing her best to hide under the tablecloth.

"What?" Stephanie asked her daughter. "What is the problem now?"

"I need Aunty to dance with me!" Lily wailed. "I can't remember the steps without her!"

Malcolm glanced to Kristin on his left.

"Of course I'll help you, honey. Excuse me, George," Kristin said as she attempted to edge backward from the tight circle.

Malcolm stood and assisted, pulling back her chair for her.

"Oh, Kristin, really?" her mom admonished. "You have a guest." She glanced apologetically to Malcolm.

"It's all right," he said. "I'm greatly interested in seeing this."

"It's for Lily," Kristin mouthed to him, blushing further. But she held her niece's hand and smiled at her.

"Please start the music again," Kristin said to Stephanie, and took a position beside the girl. Kristin nodded at her, and they both turned out their toes like ballerinas, with hands on their hips.

Kristin looked down at Lily, nodding in encouragement. When they had eye contact, in a low voice, she said, "Step, bow, up on your toes... Go."

Malcolm couldn't keep his eyes off Kristin. Gracefully, like a dancer, she lifted her arms above her head and leaped in the stationary dance, said to have been traditionally performed on the face of a warrior's shield before battle. Her legs pointing and kicking, she looked like a true Highland dancer. "One-two-three-four, one-two-three-four, one-two-three-four, turn-two-three-four," she instructed her niece.

And, God love her, as his aunt would say, the little girl kicked and twirled right along with her aunt. It was thoroughly charming.

After they'd finished their short duet and he'd risen to help them both into their seats, he asked Kristin, "You took Highland dance lessons?"

"Not really." Her face still flushed, she smiled. "My grandmother thought she was paying for ballet classes, but unbeknownst to her, the dance instructor also taught us the Highland Fling and the Sword Dance so that we could compete at the Highland Games up in Quechee."

"Quechee?"

"Vermont. They host a Scottish Festival there every August."

"And did you compete?"

"No." She grimaced. "Nanny ran out of money to pay for the classes."

"Then what happened?" he asked.

"She passed away," her mother interrupted. "And that was that."

Blunt. Practical. Cautious. All words that could describe his own family, too. He sat back, watching as Stephanie strolled the perimeter of the room carrying her pride and joy on a platter: the perfectly composed haggis. It looked like a bloated rugby ball, exactly as it should. Stephanie set it on the table, to sniggers and wry jokes from the brothers and the brothers' friends.

There was a gap in the banter, a long, drawn-out, uncomfortable moment when it appeared that the night had failed. That the ceremony itself was patently ridiculous, and that other than Kristin and quite possibly her niece, no one else bought into the fun. Even Stephanie seemed peaked, tired of swimming against the current of everyone's bad opinion.

The platter just sat there. No one even bothered to cut into the haggis.

"I am not eating that," Lily said flatly.

"Me, neither," came a chorus of voices.

Kristin blinked silently. He couldn't be sure, but her eyes looked moist.

Malcolm edged the platter with the haggis on it toward his plate. His stomach was clenching and threatened to revolt. But he forced himself to do it. Maybe it was penance…but he said it.

"I'll be the first to taste the haggis."

All eyes were upon him. No one moved. He picked up the carving knife. He might have been the only one who even knew there was a ceremony to go along with the slicing, plus another poem to be read—"Address to a Haggis," by Rabbie Burns himself—but the verses were long, with many stanzas, and Stephanie was likely abandoning the readings due to lack of interest.

The more the tradition was being given up, the lower Kristin seemed to droop. Malcolm wanted that sadness in her to go away, even if just for tonight. He loved it when she smiled. He *needed* it. Worse, only he foresaw the sadness that he would soon bring to everyone around this table. It was the only way to explain what he was doing.

He sliced into the haggis, through the thin skin of intestine, releasing the mass of sheep's innards mixed with other assorted flotsam and jetsam—bits and pieces of spices and chopped vegetables—onto his plate. Somehow, he resisted the urge to plug his nose and instead, he picked up his fork....

Stephanie hurried to his side. "I'm told it needs a wee dram of whisky on the top." Without asking his permission, she opened a bottle and drizzled some whisky generously on, as if adding Vermont maple syrup to her pancakes.

Bless her. Diving in before it got cold or he lost his nerve, he shoveled some of the dark, steaming specks of sheep onto his fork. If Kristin could dance a Highland Fling before an unsupportive audience, then he could take one bite of Scotland's national dish.

Tentatively, he tasted it. Everyone stared at him. "It's... not bad." Actually, it wasn't. "It tastes like chicken," he pronounced. "Whisky-flavored chicken."

The father—Rich—held out his hamburger plate. "I'd like some whisky with mine, please."

"Is that haggis?" Stephanie demanded. "Because only the haggis gets the whisky."

Immediately, one of the other brothers pulled the haggis platter toward him.

The haggis got passed around—a teaspoon of ground meat plopped onto each plate, along with a drizzle from the bottle.

And afterward, Stephanie piled on some tatties and

neeps. The tatties were mixed with liberal amounts of butter, and the neeps had brown sugar and maple syrup added. Maybe she'd figured it couldn't hurt.

"All right." One of the brothers stood at last, wiping his mouth with a napkin. "That was great, Steph, thanks for inviting us. But Dad and I need to get going."

"Wait!" Stephanie said. "We haven't sung 'Auld Lang Syne' or read a Burns poem yet."

"Sorry, sis. We just don't have time."

Just then, Malcolm's phone buzzed. He glanced at the incoming text message. It was his driver, waiting for him. Malcolm looked at Kristin. She knew what the text was for.

"Actually, Steph, it's okay," Kristin said brightly. "It was a great dinner. Thank you for organizing it and for inviting us."

And with a light smile on her face that he knew was fake, she pushed her chair back. "Besides, George has to leave, too. His ride is here."

She turned to him. "Thank you for coming. We appreciate it. I hope you liked the dinner."

He felt even worse now. Pocketing the phone, he stood. "I, er, would like to read a Burns poem as my thanks to you all, and I'd like to have everyone's indulgence while I do so."

Kristin stared at him.

He smiled at her mother. She was the one person besides Kristin who seemed predisposed to like him, so he played that for all he could. "I don't know if I told you, Evelyn, but I went to prep school with a fearsome English professor, one who drilled poetry into our heads, and he made us stand and recite verses until we knew them by rote."

Evelyn nodded. "I had teachers like that, as well. They don't exist anymore."

"No," Malcolm agreed, "they probably don't."

A brother was putting on his coat, and Malcolm turned to shoot a look at him. "Please, sit down. This will only take twenty seconds."

The brother sat.

"Thank you, George," Kristin said softly. "What will the poem be?"

If he were alone with her, he knew exactly what line he would recite to her: *The sweetest hours, that ever I spend.* Because his short time with her had been sweet, and he was sorry it had to end.

But, they were not alone; he was sitting with her family. And, their hours together could not continue into the future.

So, he turned to her niece and smiled at the wee one. "This verse is called 'To a Mouse.' It's by Scotland's national poet, Robert Burns, and I will recite it in your honor." He took a breath:

"The best laid schemes of mice and men
Go often awry,
And leave us nothing but grief and pain,
For promised joy."

And then he looked directly into Kristin's eyes:

"Still you are blessed, compared with me,
The present only touches you.
But oh! I backward cast my eye,
On prospects dreary.
And forward, though I cannot see,
I guess and fear."

She stared at him. He swallowed, and knew he had to repeat it once more. This time, as it should be read.

"That was the English version," Malcolm explained.
"And *this* is the proper recitation:

"But Mousie, thou art no thy lane,
In proving foresight may be vain:
The best-laid schemes o' mice an' men
Gang aft agley,
An' lea'e us nought but grief an' pain,
For promis'd joy!

"Still thou are blest, compared wi' me!
The present only toucheth thee:
But Och! I backward cast my e'e,
On prospects drear!
An' forward, tho' I canna see,
I guess an' fear."

The table erupted in applause.

"That was my best Sir Sean Connery imitation," he
said lamely.

Kristin beamed at him, a quiet, shared look.

"Will you be back?" her mother asked him. "You're certainly invited to our home, anytime you'd like."

He shook his head. "Unfortunately, I'm here for just
the day."

"A one-day contract?" Kristin inquired.

He nodded, finding himself unable to speak. A heavy
sadness had descended over him. The night had been
sweet. The sweetest hours. He was immensely sorry he
could never see her again.

SHE'D KNOWN ALL along that George was leaving.

Kristin put on her snow boots and followed him outside to the porch. A black car was waiting for him, idling at the end of the driveway.

He stood still, staring at the car with his hands in his pockets and his coat open, seemingly unconcerned about the wintry weather that enveloped them.

She sensed sadness coming from him, but it wasn't her problem, not any of her business. He was off to some other faraway place, the black car on the corner set to whisk him away.

She felt relieved that nothing had happened with George to risk her already shaky standing at Aura. But still, part of her wished she didn't have to lose his companionship just yet.

He'd been good to her at dinner tonight, standing up for her. He'd even played along, though she knew he hadn't wanted to—encouraging the others into tasting the haggis and reciting the Burns poem.

She'd seen what he'd done for her, and she'd appreciated him for it. With each secret glance he'd given her during the dinner, each reactive dimple in his cheek toward her, she'd felt herself drawing closer to him.

She blew into her hands, so cold in the dark night. She couldn't see George's face clearly in the dim light from the porch bulb, only the outline of his tall, broad form, the flat plane of his sexy, razor-stubbled cheek—a cheek that she could too easily get used to gazing upon.

How could she say goodbye to him? Instead, she fumbled for something to say. Something trivial—anything to prolong the moment.

"I hope that everything went okay today," she said, "and that you got all you need from us."

He turned, his expression illuminated, and smiled at her, descending two steps lower than her on the stairs. He was at exactly her height now, his eyes level to hers.

"I did," he said, staring at her, his gaze not breaking. "Thanks to you, of course."

Biting her lip, she looked down. "I'm sorry about some of the comments in there."

"There's no need to apologize." His voice was gentle. "I understand families."

"Yes, you do." He'd been so good with them, even Lily. She lifted her head, her eyes searching his again.

His hand touched hers, warm from the dinner table inside. His fingers brushed her knuckles, just once. Kristin was glad she hadn't put on mittens. She liked the feel of his skin against hers.

"Kristin," he said in a low voice.

She waited, barely daring to breathe, his wool coat rough against her knuckles. She inhaled his unique smell, mixed with the earthiness of the whisky he'd consumed. Involuntarily, she shivered.

He opened his coat, enveloping her in his warmth. It was a tender, protective response. A stolen moment in an evening that was turning out to be magical.

Maybe she was a sheltered person…she supposed so. She'd only been away from Vermont for a short time, until life in the city had crushed and overwhelmed her. She'd been back home for years now, in this small town she knew and trusted, with people who—though they may sometimes tease or criticize her—on the whole loved her and cared for her, no matter what.

Yes, they gave her trouble. Yes, she longed to break free. But in the end, she needed this safety. And by his actions tonight, it was clear to her that George understood that.

She stepped closer to him, inside the shield of his heavy woolen coat. Tentatively she touched the solid wall of his broad chest, feeling his cotton shirt and the silk of his necktie beneath her fingertips.

"Is it bad that I don't want this day to end?" she whispered.

"No, lass." His voice was throaty. The gruff...Scottishness of it seeped into her, as if spilled from one of Laura's potion bottles. "I won't forget you, Kristin."

His eyes held hers. And as she swallowed, he angled his head and leaned toward her.

And then he kissed her.

At the first brush of his lips on hers, the heated whisper of his breath against her cheek, she sighed and tilted her head back, wanting to feel all of it—everything about him—so she could remember him.

He was tender, his lips molded gently over hers, moving with sweetness, as if to remember her fully, too.

Her heart fluttered in her chest, and she made a little moan.

He gave her the joy of a long, passionate kiss. Mouth to mouth, honest and solid, because that's who George was. He was just so damn sexy.

The car at the end of the drive flashed its lights at them. Once. Twice.

George cursed softly. He straightened and drew back. The warmth of his coat dropped away from Kristin.

"I will put in a good word for you at Aura." Back to formality, his tone sounded tortured. "You can count on that."

"I believe you," she said.

"I'm sorry I have to go." He looked toward the car. "Maybe someday I can tempt you away. To Scotland." His tone was teasing, and the accent was there.

She smiled at him. Maybe if she were a different person, in a braver place, she would dare to follow him and kiss him again. Prolong their interlude that had felt so sweetly romantic and special.

But she wasn't that fearless.

"Goodbye, George," she whispered, touching his hand one last time.

"Kristin?" His voice caught.

"Yes?"

"I hope you find your castle."

And then he was off, into the winter night, the snow swirling quietly in the lamplight.

CHAPTER FOUR

DURING THE NEXT six weeks, Kristin heard nothing from George Smith.

She returned to work the Monday after he left, expecting questions about her time spent with him, but most of the office was busy celebrating the news of Andrew's firstborn daughter. In the excitement, no one remembered to ask Kristin anything about what had happened on Saturday.

She sat at her computer and checked her company email, but found no messages from George—not even about Aura Botanicals. She thought he might at least have some lingering questions about the company and its products.

Kristin felt...well, sad. Not at all relieved. Maybe even a little bit hurt.

Of course he was busy—he spent his life traveling, he'd said. And he had thanked Stephanie for dinner; he didn't owe them anything more than that.

But, the night *had* affected her—how could it not? Even not knowing that he and Kristin had *kissed,* her family still talked about him.

George had sat congenially around their dining table, and he'd read the Robert Burns poem in the accent of his country. Even without the kiss, that alone made him more memorable than any other man she'd known.

I hope you find your castle. He'd meant it figuratively,

of course. But how did she go about doing that? She had no idea what her mythical castle even was.

Kristin signed off her email and chewed her lip. Maybe George would contact her when his report to Jay Astley was finished. That was what she hoped for.

Or maybe she would never hear from George again.

She didn't know.... She felt so confused.

She leaned back in her chair and stared at the water-stained ceiling tiles. The night had certainly been an adventure. And to think that before George had shown up, she'd been feeling depressed with her life, traveling along in her rut of routine, longing for something to change, but every time she'd tried, getting into trouble.

Unlike George, she couldn't just pick up and leave her hometown. She'd trapped herself here. Her rut was just something she had to figure out how to live with.

WEEKS LATER, TOWARD the end of her shift on a bleak, drizzly Monday, Kristin's supervisor, Dirk, poked his pony-tailed head into her office. "Jay Astley has called a meeting with management. You'd better step in here, Kristin."

The owner of her company considered her management? That was something new. Kristin perked up.

She pushed away from her desk and hurried after Dirk. Her gangly supervisor diverted his path to the coffee machine, but she followed the other managers into the conference room, the place where Laura Astley had interviewed Kristin for her job six years earlier. Kristin hadn't been to many meetings inside the gleaming, modern plant manager's lair since then. This was Andrew's turf, and Andrew didn't hold her in confidence.

Inside the sunlit space, most of the office staff were already present. The top managers had staked their places around the polished board table; the lesser supervisors lined the walls behind them. Kristin found a spot at the back of the room and squeezed in.

Dirk wedged beside her, a coffee mug in hand. "Man, Astley looks like hell," he said to her in a low voice. "I just saw him come inside the plant with two bodyguards flanking him."

"Bodyguards?" Kristin asked. "Why would he need that?"

"Why do you think?"

Everyone hushed as Jay Astley entered the room and took a seat. He'd seemed to have aged ten years since Kristin had last seen him. One glance at Astley's face—pale and broken, thoroughly lacking in sleep—and she felt sorry for him. Even at Laura's funeral he hadn't been so stooped and withdrawn, shoulders slumped as if he carried a heavy, sad burden.

A burly man wearing a suit and security-guard expression lingered in the doorway, staring them up and down. "He looks like he's packing heat, doesn't he?" Dirk whispered.

She did notice a bulge on the man's hip beneath his jacket. Kristin swallowed.

Dirk sipped his coffee.

"I don't think this is a good thing," she whispered back.

"Probably not." Dirk grinned. "At least I have my DJ business to fall back on." Behind his hand, he said to her, "I hope our severance check is sweet—I'd love to get some new amplifiers. I'm looking forward to the unemployment checks, too."

She stared at him. "We are not getting laid off."

"Sure we are."

How could Dirk even *think* that? She'd never been through a layoff before, but she'd seen a movie about it with George Clooney once, and this was not the way it happened.

In the movies, George Clooney met with people one-on-one.

This…this…was a mass announcement. Something different was going on.

Jay Astley, their CEO, turned slowly, gazing from face to face, regarding even the people standing behind him, including herself. A single tear ran down his cheek.

Kristin's jaw slackened. This was really bad.

"You're probably wondering why I called you all here, so I'll just get to it," Jay said in a raspy voice that didn't sound like his own.

It seemed to Kristin that everyone hushed and leaned forward.

"I've had to sell our company," Jay said.

A collective gasp rang out. Kristin put her hand to her mouth.

"Yep," Dirk muttered. "I was right."

Kristin elbowed him. "Shh!"

"Without Laura, I just…can't do it anymore." Jay's voice faltered and then stopped.

Kristin's heart went out to him. This was horrible. Laura had been the heart and soul of Aura Botanicals, and it seemed she'd been her husband's heart and soul, as well. As awful as things were for him now, Kristin couldn't help thinking how wonderful it must've been to have a love as great as that.

"An outfit overseas bought the rights to Laura's products." Jay gripped the edge of the table, unable to look up. "In your next paycheck, there will be a bonus." He took an audible breath. "I'm hopeful you'll all see fit to stay with me through the end of the month. We'll need help disassembling the machinery and moving the inventory to the new location."

New location?

"But what about *our jobs?*" Andrew asked, putting voice to the question on everyone's minds, judging from the nodding and murmurs. "Will the new company keep us on?"

"Andrew…" Jay began.

"Will they keep this factory open, Jay?" Andrew demanded.

Jay didn't answer.

"You *owe* us better than this," Andrew hissed.

Kristin clutched at her throat. If she had a knife, she could cut the tension between the two men. No one else spoke. Their plant manager had challenged their CEO, and the CEO was on the hot seat. And yet, she desperately wanted his answer, too. What *about* their jobs?

Tears rolled down Jay's cheeks, one after another. It was excruciating to watch. Their boss was falling apart in front of everyone. This was not how it happened in the movies, either. In the movies, company owners hid in the back room or at an off-site location and let the consultants deliver the bad news. Here, their CEO faced them himself.

Kristin thought she might be sick to her stomach. Everybody present had something on the line here. This factory was the lifeblood of their community. It was the center of Kristin's life.

"I thought…I could save the company…for Laura's sake, I *tried*." Jay's loss of control was outright now. "You have to understand," he pleaded, "this was Laura's baby… her only baby…but now it's losing money, and despite the recommendations, I had no choice but to sell. It's the only chance her formulations stand of surviving…."

Oh, Laura. Kristin blinked her eyes against the stinging she felt. She knew what it was like not to have kids or a family of your own. She'd watched Laura pour all her considerable love into her work—her balms and her lotions, her healing aromatherapies. To Kristin's mind, the world was a better place with Laura's potions in it; and Jay was right, it was good that somebody wanted to rescue them so they would live on.

"*Whose* recommendations did this?" Andrew challenged Jay, standing to face his boss and the bodyguard—now hovering beside Jay—from across the length of polished wood. "Was it that consultant you sent here?"

He's talking about *George,* Kristin realized.

"What did the consultant tell you?" Andrew pressed. "I thought he was supposed to be advising us in good faith, helping us find ways to improve our financials. Not giving you recommendations to sell the company out from under us."

George would not have recommended the sale. Kristin was convinced of this. George had broken bread with her family, and he understood what Aura meant to their community.

"The consultant *did* try to save us, Andrew," Jay said. "We all tried. No decisions were made lightly. In the end, I didn't have a choice."

Jay placed his hands on the table and stood. He seemed shaky, like an old man, and even the stone-faced security guard beside him broke form and wavered, as if considering helping Jay up by his elbow.

Jay turned and deliberately looked to each of them again. "You are all my management team," he said quietly. "It's been a privilege to work with you. Thank you for your service all these years. And now, I'm asking for your assistance as I inform the rest of our workers. Today is Monday—we have one week before the new owners arrive to begin the process of packing the equipment. I gave them my word that all would transition smoothly. Today, we will speak to the employees and inform them about the situation. You all—the management team—will stay with me for the week, and then, in an agreement I made with the new owners, you're welcome to stay for another month at double your salaries. I was able to negotiate this point for you in writing, if you choose to accept it. The hourly workers will be paid one month's work, though the presence of most of them won't be required."

"What then?" Andrew asked. "The factory closes? Is that it?"

Astley solemnly nodded. "I negotiated the best I could," he said quietly again.

And then everything was a blur to Kristin. The security guard hustled Astley out. The meeting broke up. As quickly as it had started, it was over. She felt confused. Adrift. As if she didn't have anything to hold on to anymore.

Somehow she staggered back to her office. As she stood in the doorway, wondering what to do next, Andrew corralled her. With one hand on the door jamb, making her feel trapped, he glared at her. "What *happened,* Kristin?"

She didn't understand. "I…"

He stepped forward, and by instinct, she backed up, into her office. Her heart pounding, he shut the door behind them.

"What happened with the consultant?" he demanded. "You were here that Saturday with him. Alone." His voice was accusing.

"He…downloaded some reports and took a tour of the plant."

"*What* did you tell him?"

"Nothing!"

"Did anything untoward happen?"

"No!" What did that even mean? She felt herself shaking.

He pointed at her. "I'm not going to forget this. Nobody here is going to forget this."

With a last, warning look, he opened the door and left her.

He thought it was *her* fault?

For a long time, she sat at her desk, running through all the moments of that Saturday—everything that had happened—over and over in her mind. Wondering what had gone wrong?

Nothing had gone wrong. George had even thanked her. He'd said he would commend her to Jay Astley.

George had not recommended that their plant close down. She knew this in her heart. George would not have accompanied her to her brother's house, and he would not have recited poetry for Lily, and he would not have kissed Kristin otherwise, not if he was going to recommend this happen.

She needed to talk with Jay Astley—now. Grabbing her purse, she hurried to the plant entrance, hoping she hadn't missed him. On the way, she passed Mindy, holding her hands on either side of her head, wailing, as Arlene tried to calm her.

This was horrible. Mindy loved her job. What would she do now? So many people were affected by this heartbreaking decision.

Another worker walked by, also looking shell-shocked. Kristin wished there was something she could do to stop this tragedy of the plant closing. Even though a rational part of her knew Andrew was wrong for blaming her for it, she couldn't help feeling somewhat responsible for finding a solution. He was right about one thing: Kristin was the only person on the management team who'd been present in the plant that Saturday.

But where was Jay Astley? Kristin gazed out the front windows. Across the street, a steady stream of Aura employees seemed to be heading toward the cheery glass storefront to Cookie's Place, surely to congregate and talk.

Stephanie, Kristin thought. Oh, no. Her sister-in-law likely would be a basket case. She was already worried about her business's cash flow as it was.

Without returning to her office to grab her coat, Kristin ran into the cool spring afternoon, dodging the rain puddles that pooled on the asphalt. Pulling open the heavy glass door, she wove her way through the small crowd inside the diner.

A line had formed at the counter, and Kristin's mom grimly poured coffee and manned the cash register as best she could. Inwardly, Kristin groaned. Even her little niece Lily sat on a red vinyl stool beside the cake and muffin display case, observing the somber proceedings with big, scared eyes. Jeff, Kristin's normally quiet and calm production worker, was stomping his feet and hissing under his breath to the woman in line behind him.

"Have you seen Jay Astley?" she asked Jeff.

His lips pressed thin, he jerked his head toward the window.

Outside, a black SUV had pulled to the curb. Jay Astley was getting inside.

Kristin bolted. Without thinking, she sprinted out of the diner and across the street, waving her arms like a madwoman. "Mr. Astley! Please! Wait!"

One of the security guards blocked her path.

"I want to know about Laura's Born in Vermont line," Kristin called. "I have Laura's plans. Please, sir, talk to me."

"Let her through," Jay said quietly.

He indicated she come into the SUV beside him. She stepped up and slid over the cool cushions, the leather creaking beneath her slacks. The bodyguard shut the door behind her and then climbed into the passenger seat. The driver accelerated away from the curb. A line of people watched them roar off.

"Once we're out of sight, pull over farther down the street," Jay instructed the driver. He turned to Kristin. "You have Laura's plans?"

"She gave them to me, sir. I keep them in my filing cabinet, and until now, I'd forgotten about them, to tell the truth." She smiled at Jay, hoping to convince him. She *had* to convince him. "Please—if you tell the new company about the Laura's line, then they'll have to keep our Vermont plant open, right? I mean, Laura had great hopes for the line. It's a high-end body care collection with all-organic ingredients and green packaging, and the point of it is that everything, from raw ingredients to the labor used to produce it, is all born in Vermont. She commissioned the marketing studies, the sales projections, the pricing strategy, the sourcing of all the formulations…."

Slowly, Jay nodded. "I remember those plans."

"She left them with me because she wanted me to help her work out the production aspect. But then she got sick. I just…sort of forgot about it until now."

Jay looked down at his hands. Then he gazed at her sadly.

"I don't own the company any longer, Kristin. I can't do anything for the line."

"But…what if you told the new owners about it?"

"It's too late. It's Sage's decision."

"Who is Sage?"

"Sage Family Products. They're European—they distribute soaps and shampoos all over Europe, mostly. They were looking to acquire organic and green brands to integrate into their portfolio."

"But…this line would *have* to be made here. It's not Born in Vermont if it's produced in Europe. Maybe we could save a few jobs."

"As I said, you'll have talk to John Sage. He's the CEO."

"Me? You want me to tell him?"

"I'm not part of it anymore, Kristin," he said gently.

"Is this John Sage coming here next week?"

Jay laughed dryly. "I'm sure he'll send a team of underlings. John Sage is one of the wealthiest men in Scotland."

"Scotland! Mr. Astley, what did George Smith have to do with this sale?"

He shook his head. "Oh, no, no. Not a thing. George Smith is a, um, New York management consultant, that's all. He doesn't know these people."

"Oh." What a relief. She would never be able to bear it if George had betrayed her and if she'd been the person responsible for inadvertently selling out her own town.

"In fact," Jay said, smiling, "Mr. Smith put in a good word for you. I instructed payroll to add a bit extra to your bonus check. I wish there was more I could do for you, Kristin, but there isn't."

FIFTEEN MINUTES LATER, feeling determined, Kristin sat on the stool beside Lily in her sister-in-law's diner, typing the name "Sage Family Products" into the search engine on her smartphone.

Stephanie leaned over, a pot of coffee in one hand. "What does it say about them?"

Kristin scrolled through the company website. "They're family-owned, not a public corporation. I can't find an email address for anyone specific, but that's not surprising."

"Maybe you should call them?"

"So they can laugh at me? Steph, I'm just doing research as I think this thing through."

"Where are they located?"

"Edinburgh. The capital of Scotland, ironically."

Stephanie snorted. "I should send them my haggis recipe."

"I doubt they would appreciate it, hon."

Stephanie took the phone from Kristin and swiped her thumb across the screen, scrolling through text and photos of the products. "You should go over there, you know. In person. Show them Laura's Born in Vermont plans and force them to reconsider before it's too late."

"Right," Kristin said breezily. "I'll just hop on my private jet and use that passport I have tucked away at home. No problem."

Stephanie walked off, taking her coffeepot with her. She came back a moment later and slapped a piece of paper on the counter before Kristin.

"What's this?" Kristin asked.

"Arlene Ross posted it a few weeks ago. She's looking for a roommate on her British Isles trip."

Arlene was a worker in the Aura factory. She'd been one of Kristin's overtime crew that fateful Saturday. Kristin saw her sitting across the diner at one of the tables in the corner near Jeff and Mindy, who was still crying. Kristin turned back to Stephanie. "And?"

"And," Stephanie said, poking at the paper, "look where the trip starts and ends."

Kristin glanced at the itinerary. "Edinburgh."

"Yup." Stephanie grinned at her. "You've always wanted to go to Scotland. Why not now? This is perfect. You'll be with a group, and you'll be safe. And once there, you can do *good* for us, Kristin. If anybody can convince them, you can."

"But I don't have a—"

"Passport. I know." Stephanie nodded. "But since the flight leaves on Thursday night, we can get you an expedited one at the passport office in Boston. By the end of the week, you'll be on the plane." She leaned over, peering at Kristin. "Don't you see? This is it—your chance. You've always wanted to go to Scotland. Do it, Kristin."

"You can find our castle," Lily piped up.

"Oh, come on," Kristin protested. "You two can't possibly be serious."

Both Lily and Stephanie stared at her. It appeared that they were.

CHAPTER FIVE

KRISTIN STOOD AT the intersection of a busy, bustling street corner in the city center of Edinburgh, noise from traffic overwhelming her and the roar of passing buses and taxis fraying her nerves. She pressed her hand to her chest, struggling to gain control of her worry and fear.

Was this a day terror, or was she having a real, live panic attack?

Breathe.

Rhythmically, she forced herself to inhale and exhale, bringing much-needed oxygen to her bloodstream.

Gradually, the clamminess in her skin subsided, though the grit of exhaustion remained in her eyes.

She fluffed her plane-matted hair. Last night, on the red-eye flight from Boston via Dublin, she had spent hours in a cramped coach seat, wide-awake while Arlene snored beside her, oblivious to everything. Kristin's thoughts had bounced between fear of the huge task she'd set for herself and, truthfully, an excitement over finally seeing Scotland.

And now, on this late-morning, cold-and-breezy spring day, here she was. A gust of wind roared through her, shaking her to her core.

But Kristin straightened. Pulled her wet-weather coat, lined with warm wool, closer to her body. She had packed sensibly, with sturdy, waterproof boots—she was in the British Isles in March, after all. The weather was similar to Vermont in the mud season, she supposed, though Edinburgh had surprised her with a pale blue sky, rather than the rain she'd been told to expect.

Edinburgh was certainly busier and more beautiful than she'd counted on, too. Though this section was quaint, with hilly boulevards and cobblestone sidewalks, it was still much larger, with more people strolling the Victorian-themed streets, than she was used to at home.

Clenching her teeth, she patted her jacket pocket, wishing she'd brought her flashlight. She also felt unsafe without her cell phone. But the inner circuitry didn't work in Europe, and she hadn't found enough time to arrange for an alternate. All she carried with her was her purse—containing her Born in Vermont reports, a new passport and her wallet lined with Scottish pound notes—strapped bandolier-style over one shoulder.

There was just something about actually being there that shook her anew. Yes, the buildings looked familiar—she'd seen the bird's-eye version from the internet website cameras, after all—and yet, being here in person was completely different.

The air felt dissimilar from home; it was heavier and damper. She didn't see the familiar signs of spring, either. In Stephanie's front garden, the purple and yellow crocuses were just barely pushing up from the earth, the first of the spring bulbs, but Edinburgh was farther north than Vermont. Closer to the Arctic Circle. It felt colder to Kristin. More foreign.

What am I doing?

Now that she was here and realized how frightened and anxious the whole scenario made her feel, she briefly wondered if she should give up this crazy errand. She still could. The rest of her family—her parents and her brothers—didn't know her true reason for signing on for this trip. Listening to their skepticism and criticism had been hard enough. If they knew she was single-handedly trying to save the Aura plant, the ridicule and the reasons against attempting it would have been deafening.

At home, only Stephanie had her back. Kristin had left her travel plans with her sister-in-law. If Kristin backed out, she could continue on the tour with Arlene, with no one the wiser.

Keep going. If she could find the headquarters of Sage, get inside and convince John Sage to listen to her, then she might be able to help save her factory. She could help Mindy. Arlene. Jeff. Stephanie.

She could help her town.

Kristin took out her city map. Righted herself. Crossed the busy boulevard many blocks away from her hotel near the Royal Mile, and checked the numbers on the buildings against the number on the slip of paper in her hand. She was on course, and she would stay on course.

The architecture surrounding her was beautiful. Edinburgh was beautiful. If she didn't have this task, she would have enjoyed exploring the neighborhoods.

She passed food shops—so many food shops, with cheeky, silly names. This was just her type of city—interesting, independent and vibrant! She couldn't help stopping to stare at every window—the cheeses, the chocolates, the whimsical pastries. Stephanie would love it here. And there was a bagpiper—oh, a bagpiper, in his kilt and sporran! She shivered, letting the drone of the haunting Highland songs seep into her bones, soothing a part of her she so rarely let out in her day-to-day life.

Yes, the pomp was for the tourists, true, but she was a tourist. And there were ancient-looking pubs and cheery tearooms along her path. And those accents. The rolling Scottish brogues that drifted along the streets and alleys like music. She could drink in that accent, lie in it all day long. Maybe she should just embrace this temporary insanity.

So much to explore. Even if she were to just stay in Scotland for the duration of her two-week tour it would be a dream come true.

Arlene had gone off with her friends to tour Edinburgh Castle and the Royal Mile down the hill between the castle and Holyrood Palace. Later, they planned to shop in a woolen-mill store and taste some whisky before dinner. Kristin had been sorely tempted to join them. Oh, how she wished that—

There. Kristin stopped. The company headquarters for Sage Family Products loomed ahead.

She speed-walked toward the building until she was at the pavement before a great, revolving door. Tilting her head back, she gazed up at the stately stone facade with tall windows. Ornate. Gilded. European.

From her research on the internet, she'd learned that John Sage was a wealthy man—nearly a billionaire, or at the very least, worth hundreds of millions of dollars. And this rich man had decided to buy her tiny, local factory—strip it of all its wealth and then put it out of business? The factory that made healthy, honest, *healing* earth-based products, for body, mind and soul?

That had been Laura's dream. Laura, the only person who'd ever truly believed in Kristin. She had given Kristin a chance and taken her under her wing when no one else would.

Now that Laura was gone, who else but Kristin could stop her company from being stripped and destroyed?

Armed with hot anger, feeling freshly indignant, Laura's spirit fueled her. She strode through the rotating door and marched inside the vast, white lobby. Nearing the lunch hour, it was busy inside the cavernous space. Suit-jacketed business people, many of the women wearing high heels that *click-click-click*ed across the marble tile. The men sported short haircuts and carried nice leather briefcases slung over their shoulders. They were attractive office workers, sophisticated and confident, especially in comparison to her small-town factory folk. Her coworkers at Aura dressed more informally, acted more casually. She couldn't imagine Mindy here. Or Dirk. Or even Jay Astley, with his slumped shoulders and defeated expression.

She could, however, imagine Laura. Laura accepted guff from nobody. If she were here, she'd tell Kristin not to let anyone make her feel inferior. Besides, Kristin had nothing to feel self-conscious about. She'd changed her clothing in the lobby restroom of her hotel. She'd repaired her hair and makeup as best she could and had dressed in a knee-length black skirt and a business-formal silk blouse that brought out her most striking feature: the green in her eyes.

Usually, Kristin dressed like a country cousin, but today she looked as if she belonged here in the city. And she did belong: technically, she worked for Sage Family Products now. As far as she knew, she was drawing a paycheck signed by John Sage.

Focus, as Laura used to say. In Kristin's bag, she carried the plans for Born in Vermont. She took them out and clasped them to her.

Concentrate. Do not let the lack of sleep get to you. As Laura so often had done, Kristin fixed a smile on her face, lifted her chin, and forged ahead, plowing toward the elevator.

Amazing how no one stopped her. A security guard nodded at her, mistaking, perhaps, the white Aura employee badge that Kristin wore clipped to the hem of her coat for the same employee identification card that Sage used. The elevator—or lift, as it was labeled—was open, so Kristin stepped inside. She searched the directory posted on the wall, and found a listing for Visitor's Reception.

That would do. She took a breath, kissed her finger for luck, and pressed the button for the floor she wanted. She was officially jumping without a safety net....

The elevator door opened to the waiting area for a wealthy, modern company. A woman dressed and made up like a trendy young fashion model handled a telephone call, smiling at Kristin as she did so.

Finally the receptionist hung up. "May I help you?" she asked Kristin in a pleasant voice that, while definitely British, Kristin clearly understood.

"Yes." Kristin placed her shaking fingertips on the desk and did her best to solidly plant her feet on the carpet. *Breathe.* "My name is Kristin Hart. I'm an engineer and a new Sage employee. I need to speak with the person affiliated with the Aura Botanicals acquisition."

The receptionist paused. She didn't seem to know what to do.

Kristin smiled at her and held her ground.

"You're...American?" the receptionist asked.

"Yes. I'm from Vermont."

"I don't know..."

Please, Kristin silently pleaded.

And then a smile spread across the receptionist's face. Kristin smiled, too, until she realized that the receptionist was gazing at someone behind her.

"Hello, Mr. Sage," the receptionist said.

Kristin turned and saw a group of four men exiting the elevator, traveling together like an entourage. In the center was the short, balding man she distinctively recognized from his company photo on the internet. John Sage.

Kristin smiled directly at him, saw the twinkle in his eye, and felt hope.

Before she could talk herself out of it, she stretched out her hand to him. When he took it, she felt relief.

"Mr. Sage, I'm so pleased to meet you. My name is Kristin Hart. I'm a new employee of yours, from America. The Vermont Aura plant."

"Ah." He shook her hand and nodded. His grip felt firm, but cool.

Swallowing, she held out her report to him. She had his attention, and she needed to keep it, so she forged ahead. "One of the formulations was overlooked in the transition between our companies. I've come here today because I believe it could be very valuable to you. This business plan should show you why the proposal for the Born in Vermont line should be implemented *in* the Vermont factory."

Two short lines formed on his brow. "You'll have to work with Malcolm MacDowall on that."

"Malcolm?"

"Yes. Jean here—" Mr. Sage nodded to the receptionist "—will set up some time with Mr. MacDowall for you."

"Who is Mr. MacDowall?"

"He is our vice president in charge of acquisitions."

Jean picked up the phone. Kristin understood she was being handed off. Mr. Sage passed the report to the man beside him and looked beyond her, seemingly ready to move on.

Kristin had just a split second. She knew how corporations worked.

"When?" she asked Mr. Sage.

"When?" he repeated blandly.

"When may I give a presentation to you?"

Mr. Sage smiled indulgently at her. "You may speak

with Malcolm on Monday. I'll make sure I discuss it with him today."

Monday? That meant she would have to stay in Scotland through the weekend. She would have to leave the tour and Arlene, and stay on her own in Edinburgh.

She swallowed. Did she dare? She would be alone. Then she'd have to catch up with the tour later. But this offer…wasn't this why she had traveled all the way to Edinburgh—to keep her town's factory from being closed?

Mr. Sage was walking away and through an intimidating set of doors. She needed to make her decision quickly.

She *had* to stay. She could not lose the Aura factory.

"I'll see you on Monday," she called.

Mr. Sage turned. "You'll see Malcolm."

"Yes." She nodded. "Absolutely."

She glanced to Jean, the receptionist, who was busy looking up phone numbers on a printed list of names.

Kristin needed to prepare herself for this Malcolm person. She wouldn't leave until Jean had called him and set up an appointment.

MALCOLM CLOSED DOWN his spreadsheet and leaned back in his chair. He keenly felt the frustration from weeks of massaging numbers, and the numbers still refusing to give him what he'd wanted them to.

Numbers are always right. They do not lie.

That fact was a solid rock to hold on to in a hostile and dangerous world.

He stood up and stretched his arms, his attention drawn, as always, to the large but delicately painted oil landscape mounted over his desk. His sister's work. She had an amazing talent. The rolling green hills and glens and the deep, sparkling loch where he'd been raised were faithfully reproduced in such a way that the place looked mythical.

He'd hung the painting there because it was his touch-stone. The reason for everything he did—whether good or bad.

He'd been gazing at it for six weeks now. It had aided his conscience—necessary, because he was a man in a business where a conscience wasn't of much use.

Yet again, he touched the edge of the envelope he needed to mail. The note inside, on official letterhead, had taken him a while to compose so that the message was delivered just right.

He couldn't save Kristin Hart's factory for her. There was no possible way to keep that facility open without continuing the financial bloodbath that Jay Astley had started. The only sensible decision on Jay's part had been to sell the brand. Malcolm didn't feel guilty for his acquisition; he never would.

But Kristin…she'd be devastated once the plant closed. He knew how deeply this would hurt her. And it tore at him.

His gaze shifted to the painting. His sister had once possessed a similar personality to Kristin; long ago, she'd been a free spirit, too. A free spirit crushed was a horrible thing. That wouldn't happen to Kristin—not if he could help it.

Damn it. He paced his small, window-lined office, tearing his hands through his hair. He hated that Kristin had affected him, hated that he'd let himself get close to her, and that the thought of her had prevented him from doing his job with his normal, brutal efficiency.

He was being tested, literally, and his feelings for her were making him fail.

He picked up the letter and placed it in the front pocket of his dress shirt, beside his necktie. He had come up with a solution to his problem, and the letter was it. By now, she would have learned the news. She wouldn't see it—people never did—but the closure would be the best thing for her.

Kristin was talented. She was smart. And she wasn't fulfilled where she was—even he could see that, and he'd only known her for one day. His proposal would nudge her into doing something better for herself. Bring her out into the wide world.

And he could help her with that.

He pressed his palms into fists. He hated *needing* this so much—this desire to see her do well. It wasn't safe for him. It was a threat.

But, the smile on her face when he'd recited the Burns poem to her couldn't be forgotten. That little moan in her throat when he'd kissed her had stayed with him.

The sweetest hours. He returned to them again and again. In his life, he didn't have a whole lot of times like that to rest with and think of.

He retrieved his suit jacket from the back of the chair and shrugged into it. Even on a Friday afternoon, Malcolm had a long stretch of meetings ahead. He pulled together a folder containing the financial reports that the company officers had requested of him. It would be another extended evening of discussing numbers with his uncle. The discussion would eventually be carried to a restaurant in the Old Town, but all would be business.

There would be no more "sweetest hours" for him, unless, maybe, his letter could convince Kristin to forgive him. Now that the deal was closed and he could speak truthfully with Kristin, he'd swing by the mail room on the way to his meeting and see that his letter to her got off safely. That was the best that he could do for her within the rules of his business dealings.

"Mr. MacDowall?" One of the pool secretaries met him in his doorway. Malcolm didn't use secretaries; he took care of all his own administrative work and travel arrangements. Confidentialities were better kept that way.

"Yes?" he said, walking around her and down the hallway as he spoke.

The secretary hastened after him. "Sir, I've been asked to make an appointment in your calendar for Monday."

He glanced sharply at her. "What about?"

"Ah…you were recently in America, correct? At the Aura Botanicals plant?"

His feet slowed, stopped. He turned to her. She was smiling nervously. He had a terrible foreboding about this.

"Who is asking?" he said.

"There's a lady…an engineer, Jean says…in the reception area asking to schedule some time with you."

For a long moment, Malcolm couldn't move. Didn't dare to breathe.

But it couldn't be Kristin. She didn't yet know his real name, for one thing.

He thrust the folder containing the financials for the meeting with his uncle into the secretary's hands. "Please, take this to the fourth floor conference room and give it to Mr. Sage's assistant. Tell the group I'm delayed, but will meet with them shortly."

"Yes, sir."

Malcolm kept walking. He strode through the "sheep's pen," the field of cubicles containing their support staff. He marched into the reception area, hoping upon hope—

It was her.

Kristin Hart's curling, rich blond hair was the first thing he saw, because her back was to him. He swallowed, his heart seeming to pulse in his chest.

She seemed thinner, or maybe that was just his recollection. She wore a heavy coat, but it was short, and he could see her legs from her knees down. Really nice legs.

She was just…beautiful to him. In his shirt pocket, he still had the letter he'd written her. He would have mailed it weeks ago, but there were agreements and red tape he'd had to go through in order to carry out his offer to her. He'd explained it all within the text, and now it was too late to mail.

The letter would have to be delivered in person.

He wiped a sweaty palm against his pants. This was what he'd been hoping to avoid. She might not take it well, not at first. He was more comfortable dealing with numbers than managing sensitive communications.

And, oh, bloody hell, he'd kissed this woman.

Without warning—with no time to figure out his strategy, Kristin turned to him. Maybe she'd known he was staring at her, because her first expression didn't seem to be shock.

A flicker of pleasure brightened her face.

He felt hope, because pleasure had been his first reaction, too. A huge part of him was damned happy to see her.

"George…?" Kristin's voice was throaty. Normally, it would have thrilled him, but…

I'm not George. If Malcolm never heard that damned name again, it wouldn't be too soon.

But he couldn't think of where to begin. How to say… everything he felt toward her? How had he phrased it in the letter? He suddenly couldn't remember a word he'd written.

She tilted her head toward him. Her eyes, so green and clear, stared into his. "What are you doing here, George?"

"I…was about to ask you the same thing," he said, stupidly so.

The receptionist hung up the phone she'd been speaking into and looked up at him brightly. "Hello, Mr.—"

Stop. Don't say another word. Don't speak my name. Malcolm shook his head at her.

The receptionist paused, her mouth pressing closed.

Malcolm strode forward and clasped Kristin's elbow. "Please," he murmured. "Come inside with me."

"But…I'm making an appointment to see a Mr. Mac-Dowall on Monday."

"Yes, I'll help you with that."

She nodded and followed him without question. He steered her inside, past the row of cubicles.

But the small conference room he'd had his eye on was occupied. He didn't want to bring her to his office, because a nameplate was clearly posted on his door, indicating just who he was.…

Kristin slowed, staring at him, confusion sinking in. She stepped back. "George, what's going on? I don't understand."

"I just want to talk in private with you."

"But…Jay said you had nothing at all to do with Sage. That you work for a consulting firm in New York."

So many agreements had been made between Malcolm and Jay. The lies they'd agreed to tell had all been related to security. Malcolm smiled nervously at Kristin even as he glanced toward the other conference room—the bigger one, with all the windows.

It appeared to be open. Maybe he could draw the blinds for privacy.

"Er…we'll discuss this in a moment," he said.

"Malcolm?" Their accounting assistant, a phone to her ear, beckoned to him from her desk. "Mr. McVicar is waiting for you in the boardroom. The call just came down from the fourth floor."

"Tell him I'm busy just now," Malcolm said.

He turned to Kristin, but her face had drained of color. She seemed to be breathing with difficulty. Her eyes were huge and glistening.

"Malcolm?" she whispered. "You're *Malcolm?*"

Oh, hell.

"Er, technically," he said.

"*Why* did you call yourself George?" she asked. "You lied to me. Why?"

He couldn't tell her the truth—not like this, not out here, with everyone gaping at them. "Kristin, please, let's…"

But she was blinking rapidly all of a sudden. She appeared to be swaying on her feet. He gripped her arm tighter.

One of the support staff stopped before him in passing. "Mr. MacDowall, I found a shop that will copy the large drawings for you." Without even glancing at Kristin, the busy assistant stretched out the two familiar, huge, blue schematics.

He shook his head at her, incredulous that this was happening to him now.

"You can take them with you to Byrne Glennie next week," the assistant chirped. "Here they are." She thrust them at him, pleased with herself.

This was why Malcolm usually handled such tasks himself—privacy and discretion were extremely important.

A strangled noise came from Kristin's throat. She pulled her arm away from him.

Malcolm put his hand to his head. He had no idea what to do.

Nothing could have gone worse for him. Nothing.

THOSE WERE HER BLUEPRINTS. *She* had made them, and not for him to steal. "What are you doing with my drawings?" Kristin demanded.

"I…er… Kristin…" He took her arm again, but she shook him off.

"Please, let me talk to you." He held open the door of an empty conference room, and Kristin followed him inside only because she needed answers.

Upset, still feeling the shock of the situation, she sank into a padded chair.

He walked to the windows and closed the blinds as if it was more important to hide her from everyone than it was to explain to her why he was at Sage Family Products and why people were calling *him* Malcolm.

"I thought you were helping us," she said. "George."

"I was," he muttered. "I am. Kristin, please, trust me."

He looked at her with panic etched on his face, and Kristin wanted to believe him, but how could she?

Then the door opened, and a beautiful blonde woman poked her head inside.

"Mr. MacDowall," the woman said, "I'm sorry, but your uncle is calling down from the fourth floor for you." She looked pointedly at Kristin. "Is everything all right here?"

"His *uncle?*" Kristin asked the woman, pointing to George…Malcolm…whoever he was. "Just who is *he,* exactly?"

A pinched line grew in the woman's smooth forehead. The model-like creature flicked a gaze at her, up and down her body as if judging her. She seemed to regard Kristin with pity.

Kristin bit her lip. Yes, she knew she appeared rumpled. She likely had dark circles under her eyes from the transatlantic flight, and she certainly wasn't dressed as well as the sophisticated city women in the Sage Family Products office. And then there was the fact that she'd been duped by George—or whoever he was.

"This is Malcolm MacDowall," the woman said calmly. She smiled brilliantly at him and then raised a brow at Kristin, as if Kristin was the one who was crazy.

Kristin glanced to George—to Malcolm. But Kristin had *trusted* him as George. She had brought him home to her *family* as George.

He had *kissed* Kristin as George.

So much for the magical day she'd spent with him. So much for the respect she thought he'd had for her. It had all turned out to be just another mistake on her part. An adventure with disastrous consequences.

"Kristin," Malcolm murmured. "Please, allow me to explain."

But her ears were buzzing harder. She couldn't hear so well anymore. Malcolm was saying something to the blonde woman, ushering her out, closing the door behind her.

"Tell me the truth," Kristin managed to whisper to him, once they were alone. "*Why* were you at Aura that Saturday? You were planning on buying us out and shutting us down all along, weren't you?"

His Adam's apple moved up and down. He sat heavily at the conference table, regarding her, pressing the back of his hand to his mouth before speaking. "John Sage is my uncle," he said quietly. "I work for the family."

She felt numb all over. Maybe she was in shock.

He really *had* betrayed her. He'd lied to her about who he was and why he was in her plant, and at her home. He had made a fool of her in front of everybody who mattered to her.

And then, he had kissed her. Stirring romantic feelings in her that were false on his part.

It always came back to that kiss....

She clutched her stomach. So many emotions rose in her that she was overwhelmed by them all. She had wanted to believe in him. She had always wanted to believe in everybody. She had wanted to believe that he was good and that people were good and that she was safe with him....

She was so naive. The tears were burning in her eyes. She couldn't control it any longer. They were going to come, betraying her, too, rolling down her cheeks if she wasn't careful.

No. She wouldn't let him have the satisfaction. In the past, no matter what had happened to Kristin, she had never cried in public about it. She had never lost control that way.

And she wouldn't now.

With her hand to her mouth, holding in the sobs, she got up and fled the conference room. Rushed out of the office and past the reception area. Pegged the button for the elevator until it came and then got in and headed down. She didn't stop until she was outside on the street.

The cold, damp air struck her face, invaded her lungs. Made her feel as crushed as *George* had.

She moved blindly. Clutching her purse across her coat, she ran to the big boulevard. She looked one way, toward the great castle up the hill over the city. Then the other way, down toward the blue sea in the distance.

Her decision made, she headed up the hill and around a winding corner. Almost crashed into a huge, imposing man wearing a kilt and holding a set of bagpipes. "Be careful, love," he admonished.

But she pushed past the bagpiper. She didn't want to hear from any more Scotsmen who called women "love" and didn't even mean it.

Oh, God, George was a Scotsman. But he wasn't "George" anymore, he was "Malcolm." And he had played her for an utter fool.

She turned inside the closest shop, an ancient place with steps that led below street level to a business that sold tartans. It smelled like new wool. Rows and rows of colorful woolen kilts were displayed on industrial metal racks.

Plaid kilts reminded her of her Nanny, and thoughts of her Nanny comforted her, so Kristin stayed inside the cramped quarters, sniffling uncontrollably, her eyes burning.

Two female shoppers stared at her. Kristin must have been a sight—teary-eyed and snotty-faced, her makeup running—so she hurried into a back room that was currently empty.

Bolts of tartan fabric were stacked everywhere in rickety piles, making the place seem like a homey rabbit's warren.

Perfect. Kristin found a private back corner and sank to her knees, hidden from everyone. If only she had friends here, family. But she didn't. She was alone, in the big, bad world again. Just as she'd been alone those weeks, years ago, when she was in New York City. Yes, Arlene might still be her roommate tonight, but Arlene couldn't be let in on the secret with Sage. Kristin didn't want anyone from Vermont to get their hopes up that she might possibly have what it took to save the Aura factory.

And if she wanted to save the factory, she realized she had no choice: she *had* to work with this man. But how? How could she trust him, knowing that if he'd duped her once, he could easily try it again?

Kristin scrubbed her hand over her gritty eyes. Footsteps were approaching.

For the hundredth time, she wished she had never left home…

And then, she saw it. Directly before her, right in front of her eyes, at the very bottom of the towering stack of woolen plaids.

"Nanny," she whispered.

That familiar tartan that her Nanny had worn as a winter scarf. Red and green with a hint of gold and beige. Autumn colors. A hunting plaid, Nanny had called it.

With all her energy, Kristin focused on the bit of cloth, conjuring up the image of her Nanny, smiling at Kristin, encouraging her to be brave and have faith.

Nanny had been born here in Scotland, so in a sense, this was Kristin's home, too. Wasn't she entitled to be here, as well?

I am a McGunnert. I will not be afraid.

She ran her palm over the bolt of wool plaid and then wrestled it out of the towering pile. When she at last had it free, she held it to her nose and sniffed, as if to internalize and be part of all of its essence and the strength it represented.

The shopkeeper stood beside her. He was a pleasant-faced man with twinkling green eyes. "Well, miss, those colors do suit you."

Kristin smiled giddily at him. She stood, the bolt of fabric still clutched in her arms. "It does suit me, very much. Can you tell me the name of this plaid, please?"

"Let us see." The shopkeeper strode over and found a three-ring notebook binder on a side shelf.

Kristin followed him, peering over his shoulder as he flipped through the homemade pages, each encased in a protective plastic cover. The collection looked like years' worth of personal research on the shopkeeper's part.

"Ah. Here it is." He tapped on the image of the plaid she held. "McGunnert. A rare tartan to be sure, miss."

Kristin stared. On the page, along with an image of the plaid was a pencil drawing of a very distinctive bee.

She gasped, then opened her purse and dug through it until she found the box she'd brought containing Nanny's gold, bee-shaped brooch.

Exactly like the bee symbol on the clan's card.

"This is it," she said excitedly. She held out the bolt. "I would buy some of the cloth, but I don't sew well. Can you help me find something in exactly this McGunnert tartan?"

"Aye, miss, we sell custom-made kilts and ship them worldwide." He handed her a business card. "Now, where are you from?"

"Vermont," she said shyly.

"Ah. I knew you were not from Florida. You're not sunburned." The shopkeeper smiled, which encouraged Kristin to do the same.

"Rather than ordering something custom, do you have anything already made that I could buy now, and wear?" Kristin asked. "Maybe a scarf? I would dearly love a scarf." Just like Nanny.

"Come with me and we'll check together." The shopkeeper escorted her to the front room. On a counter, he spread out a shawl, larger than a scarf but smaller than a full-size blanket. "You'll not find many in the country," the shopkeeper said. "It's made for you, miss."

Kristin ran her hand over the fabric. "So soft."

"It's cashmere."

She winced and then lifted the price tag. Yes, it was out of her budget.

"Do you have a smaller scarf? Maybe something in lamb's wool?"

"Sorry, lass. As I said, it's not a popular tartan."

She gave the soft shawl a lingering glance, folded on the table. No matter the price, she had to take it.

She lifted the shawl and handed it to the shopkeeper. "Ring it up for me, please."

Five minutes later, Kristin exited the shop with her Nanny's beautiful shawl wrapped around her shoulders and her brooch pinned to her coat. If Malcolm was a Scottish clansman, then so was she. She had the weight of centuries of tradition behind her and flowing in her veins. She was brave. She was smart. She would not be kept down.

Outside, a flow of people walked on the sidewalks, and a succession of small cars and trucks drove past. Kristin aimed once again for the Sage Family Products headquarters building. This time, she held her chin in the air.

When she bumped into George—into *Malcolm*—dressed in his business suit with tie askew and hair blown about from the wind, and his face looking upset and bewildered, she only felt calm.

She could handle him.

With renewed determination and confidence, Kristin looked directly into Malcolm's eyes. She knew what she had to do.

CHAPTER SIX

MALCOLM WOULD NEVER forget the look on Kristin's face when she'd discovered that he wasn't who he'd said he was. As far as he was concerned, there wasn't a feeling worse than facing a person he'd hurt, even if he hadn't meant to do it.

But now, as Kristin stood before him, she seemed calm and resolved. The wind blew her blond curls around her face. She didn't smile to see him, just gave him a steady look.

"Are you okay?" he asked her. He'd been searching everywhere for her.

"I'm ready to talk to you." She pulled a tartan shawl closely around her shoulders. It looked good on her—brought out the green in her eyes and otherwise brightened what had been a lousy day for them both.

The sky was overcast now; another gray Scottish afternoon settling in, and he rubbed his arms, wishing he'd brought his overcoat with him. "Yeah, I want to talk to you, too."

She nodded. "Let's go inside, Malcolm." She indicated a coffee shop.

He patted the envelope in his shirt pocket. The letter was still there. "After you."

He opened the coffee shop door, the bell tinkling as she entered. Her turf, because she'd chosen the location. He'd actually never been inside this place before, had never even noticed it, despite its close proximity to his office. Maybe he'd driven by on his way into work, but Malcolm always had a driver with him. He never drove himself. It just wasn't safe for him.

Inside the coffee shop, about five or six tables were tucked among alcoves.

All were taken. Kristin aimed for the corner table, the most private one, in the best location. A solitary man had finished his cup and was staring into space. When he saw Kristin smile at him, he jumped to his feet and offered her his table.

Malcolm just shook his head. Obviously, Kristin had charmed him, too. She had that effect on people, like a sprite. How else had she gotten into Sage past the security guards?

He waited as Kristin sat, settling into the cushions on her wooden chair.

"What can I get you?" Malcolm asked.

"Earl Grey tea, please."

Malcolm preferred coffee. Dark, Italian espresso, as strong as possible.

He went to the counter and ordered their drinks, then brought them back. When he'd set his mug of coffee on the table, plus Kristin's steel teapot and empty cup and saucer, he sat and leaned forward. He would have reached for Kristin's hand, but he didn't feel like getting rejected again. It wasn't as if he went around holding women's hands, anyway.

"I'm sorry I couldn't use my real name. I wrote you a letter…and was just about to mail it when…" He pulled it from his jacket pocket and held it out to her. "It explains everything—best I could explain it, anyway."

She gazed at the envelope as she dipped her tea bag up and down inside the steel pot. Her brow was creased, and she seemed receptive to listening to him now. That was better than her previous cool remoteness, because it meant that she wouldn't run away from him.

But she looked away from the letter and shook her head. Her big green eyes tore at his heart. "You not only lied to me and my family, but you lied to Jay Astley. The man who hired you as a consultant in good faith to help us stay solvent."

"Jay knew that I worked for Sage Family Products," he said in a low voice, because people were at a table beside them, and not all of what he was about to say was public knowledge. "We'd already committed to buying Aura from him weeks prior, before I even met you. Jay wanted the news kept quiet while the details were finalized. Do you know what a nondisclosure agreement is, Kristin?"

She frowned as she poured her tea into the cup. "Yes, I guess."

"It means we signed a contract with Astley. As a result, we're obligated not to talk about certain things. Certain things that neither side wants known."

Why was he even saying this? He could get in trouble for breaking confidentialities.

"*Jay* knows what your real name is?" she asked. "He lied to me, too?"

Oh, hell. "Er…I can't speak to that. I can only tell you this—I would like to help you get a better job."

"*Me* get a job?" She put her hand to her chest.

"Yes." He felt so earnest. She just needed to read his letter and see how well he thought of her and how much he wanted her to stay. "Please, Kristin." He indicated the letter. "This is our formal offer. You've said that you love Scotland, and we would pay you well. You were undervalued at Aura. I know, because I saw your salary, and I think that we…"

Her eyes blazed at him.

What was wrong? Maybe he wasn't speaking as eloquently as he could, but she had to know he'd done his best for her. "Kristin?"

"Do you really think I want to move here and work for *you* after what you did to us? To my whole town?"

"What? No." He'd known this wouldn't be easy. "You're being stifled there, Kristin. Andrew…he's an ass, and frankly, I can't wait to terminate his position."

"*Andrew* has a new baby to support," she said crisply. "And what about Mindy, and Arlene, and Jeff?" Her forehead creased in outrage. "And Stephanie, my sister-in-law—you remember her? You ate in her house. Her livelihood is a sandwich shop that relies on the business of Aura employees. And then there's Stephanie's husband, my brother, who works in the accounting department at Aura? And my dad, who runs the Chamber of Commerce? You saw in person what Aura means to *all* of them."

"Companies are bought and sold every day," he protested. "You don't think I tried to save it? You told me Laura was your friend. Well, moving the production of her formulas to our Byrne Glennie plant is the only way to make sure her brand survives. Otherwise, Aura goes bankrupt and her legacy is gone forever. You know that."

She crossed her arms. "I have a better idea, Malcolm."

It occurred to him he hadn't asked her what she'd hoped to accomplish by coming to Edinburgh. He sighed. "Is that why you came here to Sage Family Products? To share with us this *great* idea?"

"Yes. I'm here to show Mr. Sage why he should keep the Vermont plant open," she said.

A laugh burst out of him before he could stop it.

She glared at him again. "How is that funny?"

If only she knew his uncle. "You're asking for impossible things."

She raised her chin. "Am I?"

"My uncle rarely even meets with people on his own staff, never mind staff from a company he's just purchased."

"Is that so?"

"Yes," he said calmly. If anyone knew his uncle, he did. "He doesn't even do television or public appearances. Never. He has no time and no inclination. He stays in the background, surrounded by his assistants and bodyguards. I doubt he would see the Queen if she so requested."

"Really?" she said again, raising her brow at him.

"Really." Malcolm tried to keep the bitterness from his voice. "Look, I'm the person he placed in charge of assimilating Aura. What happens to Aura is my call."

He didn't tell her that it was a test, that Malcolm's task was to acquire and integrate smaller companies that produced green and organic products. Aura was Malcolm's first acquisition, and if he failed—if he didn't have what it took—then another of his cousins would be tapped to someday run the family business.

"Interesting," she said dryly. "That's why 'George Smith' needed to steal my production diagrams."

He just sighed. "That was my security name, Kristin."

"Because we're so dangerous in Vermont, aren't we, Malcolm?"

How could he expect her to understand? She didn't understand security. Not the way he did.

It was visceral to him. He lived with the fallout every day. She didn't know what it was like to always be on guard, always wary.

Just this morning, his driver had turned on the radio in his car, and an old song had played. "Gloria." An obscure track from a Celtic rock band not yet famous. It was scary how music took a person back and put them right in the middle of a situation. *Tied up in the back of a van. Thugs screaming. Raining blows on his head.*

"You know nothing about safety," he said in a low voice.

Her eyes narrowed. "I most certainly do. And let me tell you, Malcolm, real safety is about people being secure with their own families, in their own towns. You ruined that for us. You came into my office, into our plant, and you took that away."

He sucked in his breath, stunned.

"Safety," she continued, "is keeping people employed, in the place that they know, doing what they know. Do you think your people in Scotland will care about Laura's bees the same way that we in Vermont do?"

"The plant in Vermont was hemorrhaging money," he said quietly. "It was imploding, and that is the truth."

"I'm done listening to your excuses, Malcolm. I came here," she said forcefully, "to discuss new plans for a new line. My goal is to show you how to save the Vermont plant."

"Kristin, I want to help but I can't give you that."

"I have solid plans that will keep the Vermont plant open *and* make it profitable."

"It's not possible."

"Everything is possible."

He shook his head, sorry for her. "It's a fairy tale to think so, love."

She flinched. He shouldn't have said that, and he knew it right away. Her green eyes bored into him. "We have to work together," Kristin insisted, "and we will, because your uncle, John Sage, directed me to meet with you on Monday. I already talked to him about it."

"You… What?"

"I talked to him."

He just stared at her. "What did you do, waltz up to him and tap him on the shoulder?"

"No, I shook his hand."

"And just like that, he said…?"

"He said that he wants me to work with you, and he had the receptionist make an appointment on your calendar for Monday." She nibbled her lip. "I'm sure he wants to see a presentation from us. *Both* of us."

"Did he actually say that?"

She crossed her arms. "Call him and see."

He would, but not yet. Not until he got something straight with her. "Kristin," he said gently, "I told you, Aura is dead. I ran the numbers every which way and—"

"*This* is for the Born in Vermont line." She opened her purse and shoved a copy of a bound report at him. "It's a new opportunity. New formulations that Laura developed. She tested it and got customer commitment. Read her plans and you'll see."

"Did you tell my uncle all this?"

"Not yet—not completely. That's where you come in. He wants us to confer, and then talk to him together."

Malcolm shook his head. He could not believe it. Then again, maybe he could—Kristin had a special way of charming people like no one he'd ever met.

Though he knew it wasn't smart or safe, he was half in love with Kristin already, and he definitely wanted her to stay. But she'd just made life so much more difficult for him.

He tore his hand through his hair. "I need to speak with my uncle first. We have meetings the rest of the afternoon, but not about this." He tapped her report. "We're a family-owned company, with responsibility to a lot of people, and we're juggling a lot of other projects at the moment—"

"You and I *are* working together on this, Malcolm," Kristin interrupted. "It's arranged. It's happening. And your uncle expects it."

"I need to talk with him first," he repeated.

"Do *not* try to talk him out of it," she warned.

"Do you think I want to send you home? Because I don't. I like having you here in Scotland, believe it or not."

She flinched. "I am not going to kiss you again, if that's what you're thinking. That's not why I'm here. In retrospect, that was actually a big mistake on my part."

A twinge of disappointment passed through him. Malcolm didn't want her to regret what they'd shared on Burns Night. It had meant something to him. Moments like that never happened to him, not in the careful, insulated life that he'd been forced to lead. The fact that he was falling for her was not normal for him.

She was special.

"Will you please read my letter?" he asked.

"If you champion my report," she said stubbornly.

Malcolm's phone rang, but he shut it off. The call was most likely to tell him that he had ten minutes to make it back upstairs to the fourth floor conference room. He didn't want to think about that right now.

"How did you travel to Edinburgh anyway? Who are you staying with?" he asked Kristin, changing the subject.

She looked down, taking a long sip from her tea. "I'm here with Arlene on the first leg of a tour of the British Isles," she finally admitted.

"So you have a hotel for tonight, then?"

"Yes. But tomorrow I plan to break from the tour group. At noon they're leaving in a coach bus for England." She stared at him, her expression a warning for him not to interfere. "Obviously, I've decided to stay in Scotland and work with you on preparing a presentation for your uncle. You *will not* stop that from happening, Malcolm."

Unfortunately, his concerns for her meant that it was in his best interest to keep her here in Scotland, close to him, for a while longer, too. But a presentation to his uncle? That was a bit much.

Still, he would not refuse her outright. Not just yet. "Why don't we take it one step at a time, okay? Right now I've got to head back to the office. I have afternoon meetings I'm already booked for, plus a dinner meeting to prepare for. Why don't we meet for breakfast tomorrow? It's the best I can do for now. And it's good for you, too, because Saturday is earlier than Monday."

She nodded slowly, seemingly pleased with her progress. "What time should we meet?"

"Ten o'clock," he said.

"Here. We'll meet here. And maybe it would be wise if you actually had a look at the Born in Vermont report before then," Kristin said.

He picked it up from the table and flipped through it quickly. Maybe twenty pages, mostly text, with very few numbers. His uncle required numbers. Income statements, balance sheets, cash flow analyses. Malcolm saw none of the above. Without those financials, the idea would be dismissed out of hand.

Tomorrow he would have to break the bad news to her about refusing her proposal. For now, he just folded the report in half and tucked it inside his suit jacket inner pocket. "Fine. I'll read it this evening. But I'd like you to read my letter, as well."

"Keep it for me," she said. "I promise I'll read it before I leave Scotland. But right now I'm concentrating on this presentation."

He stared into his coffee, considering. He could see

where that would be a positive for him that she not learn about his offer, or his feelings, just yet. He could wait and see how things went, hedge his bets with her.

Part of his letter was a formal job offer to her from Sage. The other part...

Well, it was personal. Intensely personal, at least for him.

And he was starting to see that maybe he'd been caught up in her magic, temporarily infected by their evening together in Vermont. Maybe it was only silliness on his part to imagine anything more between them.

This way, he could be sure. More careful about what he offered and promised.

He placed the letter back in his pocket. "Here is my business card," he said to her, and took one from his wallet. "Just in case you need to contact me before tomorrow."

She held his card to the light, squinting at it. "You're Vice President of Sage Family Enterprises?"

"One of them." He sighed at her. "Kristin, don't get your hopes up over this project."

"DON'T GET MY..." She scrubbed at her eyes, suddenly angry. How was Malcolm being any different from her family, telling her that she was crazy to believe in things that they knew nothing about? She'd been foolish to think he was any different from the rest of them.

"I know you want to break away and travel in your life, find some adventure," Malcolm said to her. "So why don't you take the afternoon and the evening to sightsee with your group, rather than worrying about this?"

"Sightsee? You're telling me to *sightsee?*" Was that his response to her plans—was he dismissing this as part of a silly adventure on her part?

"You like castles," Malcolm said. "Well, we have castles in Scotland."

"Castles," she repeated. Like McGunnert Castle? Everybody making fun of her dreams and interests. Patronizing her.

Something in Kristin snapped. She was tired of people refusing to believe in her or take her seriously. Hadn't they been wrong about her—about Nanny's plaid?

They were probably wrong about Nanny's castle, too.

Maybe the whole point of this trip was to show her that what she knew in her heart was what was right for her. Take the plaid, for example. Kristin had been told her entire life that this mythical tartan did not exist. That the McGunnert clan did not exist. That she was making things up in her mind.

"It's not possible," her family had said to her.

And then…here in Scotland, she'd actually seen with her own eyes what she'd always believed. She had material proof of the very tartan that she had found while researching her family history on the internet—the tartan that everyone had told her was only a fantasy. A mirage.

And yet, that so-called mirage now sat on her shoulders.

The experience back in the woolens shop had been a sign. It was as if her Nanny—her grandmother, the woman she barely remembered—was telling Kristin that she was *right*. That she would be okay.

Kristin knew exactly what she was going to do now.

Malcolm was behaving no differently from her family—he doubted her. He hadn't believed that she'd dared to talk with John Sage. She could see it in the way Malcolm had only glanced at the report, dismissing it on the surface without even reading it. He'd told her to sightsee. Oh, she would sightsee all right. She would see the ultimate site—the final pull to prove to herself that she was okay. She was going to prove them all wrong, including him.

If Malcolm insisted on making her wait until tomorrow morning to discuss Born in Vermont, then she would bide her time and wait. But she would make good use of that time in-between.

Leaning over to the empty seat beside her, Kristin opened her purse and pulled out her guidebook. "I'll see you here tomorrow at ten o'clock," she said, carefully not looking at Malcolm's handsome face. His Scottish good looks were only a distraction from what she really needed.

"Kristin—"

"Unless you're ready to talk about Born in Vermont, then we have nothing more to say for now."

He drummed his fingers on the table. "So, are…you going to meet up with your tour guide?"

Why was he so concerned with how she was going to spend her time? Perhaps he had some sightseeing spots he'd like to recommend!

She sighed and continued to stare at her guidebook. "Please, just go, Malcolm."

Malcolm hesitated, but finally, she sensed the weight in the table shift as he rose from his seat. His chair scraped back. In silence, he walked away from her and out of the coffee shop, the bell on the door ringing behind him.

She closed her eyes. She hoped she hadn't made a mistake. But his physical presence was just too unnerving to her.

If only she could take back that kiss—that moment—they'd shared on her porch in the January snow. But she couldn't. Ever.

MALCOLM STOOD ON the pavement, crowds rushing around him. Kristin had come here to visit his company, but he had upset her and he felt some responsibility for that. How could he leave her alone, not knowing whether she was really okay or not?

Cursing softly, he ran a hand through his hair. Until now, Kristin had never owned a passport. Obviously, she wasn't travel-savvy. What if she didn't go back with the tour group this afternoon and something happened to her, alone in Edinburgh? How could he stand it?

But, he'd delayed his uncle long enough; Malcolm glanced at his watch and groaned. They had rescheduled the meeting for him, and Malcolm only had a couple minutes to get back.

But he couldn't help it; he kept his eye glued to the coffee shop window. Inside, he could just see her pretty blond hair, bent over the table. He had to wait for just a moment and make sure Kristin rejoined her tour group.

He didn't feel the same responsibility toward the rest of the people in Aura—yes, it was sad that they would be losing their jobs, but that was life, it was business. If not Sage, then some other company would have bought their brands and shut them down. No matter what Kristin said, he just didn't see how there was any salvaging the Vermont plant. Nothing remained to be done except the route that he'd recommended, and his uncle had already approved.

Malcolm was responsible for the people in Sage, too, and he would not do to them what Jay Astley had done to his people—bankrupted them with his poor decisions.

Malcolm leaned against a lamppost, his attention focused on all directions at once. Periodically, he changed his position so that his back wasn't exposed for long periods of time, but he always kept Kristin's face in his sight through the coffee shop window.

After a while, she came outside, her purse slung over

her shoulder. He waited until she rounded the street and headed into a car-hire business.

He paused, his breath roaring in his lungs.

What the hell? She was hiring a *car?* By *herself?* In Edinburgh?

His mobile phone rang. Malcolm glanced at the display. His uncle. *Damn it.*

Malcolm had to take the call. There was no refusing his uncle.

As he pressed the phone to his ear, he kept his gaze glued to the door of the car rental store. He could only hope there was no other way out of the shop. "Yes," he said into the phone.

"Malcolm, where are you?" His uncle's assistant spoke in a measured and calm tone. "We're waiting to start."

Malcolm closed his eyes. He could either abandon Kristin, or he could please his uncle. There was no doing both.

He would undoubtedly regret this, but…

"I have to cancel. Tell my uncle…that something urgent requires my attention."

A pause stretched on the other end of the line. "Mr. Sage wants to know…is this regarding the Aura buyout?"

"No," Malcolm said quickly. "It's…er…personal."

His uncle chuckled. Malcolm heard him clearly in the background. They must have had him on speakerphone, the bastards.

His uncle's voice came on the line. "Is it regarding the American woman I met earlier, Malcolm?"

Damn. Damn, damn, damn. "Yes," he gritted out.

"Good. I like her. She has courage."

Malcolm exhaled. Wonderful. He'd known his uncle thought it past time for him to settle down and begin raising the next generation. But *Kristin?* Clearly, his uncle was playing matchmaker.

"Take all the time you need this weekend," his uncle continued. "The rest will keep until Monday." The call disconnected.

Dumbfounded, Malcolm stared at the phone in his palm. He'd just been given the go-ahead to follow Kristin. This was his opportunity to make sure she would be okay.

Shoving his phone in his front pocket, he entered the car rental shop to see what she was up to.

Kristin stood at the counter, her elbows on top of it and her palms splayed flat, as if she were grounding herself there. A determined but giddy smile was on her face.

Trouble. Involuntarily Malcolm's palms clenched into fists. The back of his neck prickled.

A desk clerk returned with Kristin's credit card. "Here you go, miss."

"Thank you." Kristin replaced the card in her purse. "Where may I pick up my car, please?"

Malcolm's back had been turned for five minutes, and she'd already hired a car?

"Just a minute," Malcolm said to the desk clerk. He intercepted the rental agreement as it came from the printer and studied the black-and-white paper. Kristin had ordered the cheapest car possible. Good Lord.

"Hey!" Kristin said, grabbing the agreement from him. "Are you following me, George? I mean, *Malcolm.*"

"Somebody has to," he said. "You're a one-woman demolition team. Where were you planning on going? This is Scotland—we drive on the other side of the road from you lot, you know."

"Got it covered," she said. But her smile faltered.

A manager came from the back room to join them. "Oh!" he said. "Mr. MacDowall."

Malcolm ground his teeth and nodded curtly at the stranger.

"Can, we, er, interest you in leasing something sporty, sir?"

Kristin turned to glare at Malcolm—warning him off, he supposed. And while Malcolm was off guard for that split second, she grabbed the rental agreement from him and signed it. "May I have a map, please?" she said to the counter clerk.

A high-level, one-page summary map of the country? She had no idea what she was getting into at all.

But he kept his mouth closed. Stood back and waited for her to conduct her own transaction and accept the car keys. When she left, he followed her to the street, and then to a small lot. He kept back enough that he wasn't on top of her.

He caught up to her as she was inspecting the car panels and windshield, apparently, for dings and scratches. She glanced at the rental contract and then back, circling the vehicle.

He nearly choked. The damn thing was little more than a golf cart, in size and in horsepower. If she had to outrun someone, she would never make it.

"Where are you going?" he asked.

"Sightseeing," she said sweetly. "Just like you said."

"How far do you intend to drive?"

"Why? Would you like to come with me? We can discuss our joint presentation for Born in Vermont."

"No," he said quickly. "I just…think I should know your plans. For safety reasons, of course."

"Born in Vermont *is* my safety, Malcolm."

"We have a meeting scheduled together for tomorrow morning," he pointed out. "That's still on."

"Fine. Until then, I'm going to drive to my hotel and leave a note for my roommate as to where, exactly, I am going."

"And where is that?" he asked. "*Where* are you going?"

"You're not my tour guide or my roommate, Malcolm."

He crossed his arms. "You're right. You're smart and capable. I know—I saw you in action back in Vermont."

She didn't answer him. He'd forgotten, flattery did not work with this woman.

He sighed. "Go ahead. Get in and drive out of the lot and then across one city block. If you can manage that, then I'll go away and leave you in peace until tomorrow morning."

"That's big of you." But she ignored him, opening the passenger-side door and stepping inside. Then she got out again, her face flushed. She walked around to the other side. Opened the driver's-side door—the *true* driver's side—sat inside the vehicle, and closed the door.

He stood beside the door and waited. He was hoping she was like most Americans he'd met, as far as her driving skills were concerned. It wasn't a knock on her—he was sure she was an excellent driver back home—but he'd grown up in both cultures, and he knew the vehicles and the people.

She climbed back out of the vehicle—red-faced again—and shut the door. "Excuse me. I need to go back inside and change my car from one that isn't a manual transmission."

"*Or,* I can chauffeur you where you need to go," he said quietly, not moving from where he stood. "Strictly as a sightseeing escort."

She crossed her arms. "Malcolm, no offense, but unless you want to talk Born in Vermont, I'm not interested."

He swallowed at her barb, though rationally, she was right to be cool with him. He could take it. Anything would be worth it not to see her in harm's way. "Please, just don't go running off without thinking your journey through. At least tell me where you are going."

"It's none of your business," she said. "If I tell you anything concrete, you'll only try to talk me out of it."

But her face was pink. Why would she be embarrassed? Did she have something to hide?

He glanced at her guidebook with its picture of a castle on the cover. "You're taking my advice and going to see castles, aren't you? That's great, but why can't you stay here, in the city? We have castles in Edinburgh, too."

"It's a day trip, Malcolm. People do take day trips."

"Yes, and they bring guides with them. They go on group tours. At the very least, they travel with a friend."

She tilted her head. "What is this really about? If you cared about my well-being, then you'd keep Aura open."

"All I'm saying is that it's not safe for you to go alone."

"Why?" she asked, laughing. "Is Scotland so danger-ous? Are the sheep violent? And the cows? I'm going to the country, Malcolm, not a city vice den. Besides, I'm tired of being safe. Weren't you the one who said that I was naturally adventurous? That you hoped I found my castle one day?"

He'd been so damn wrong for saying that. But he'd been affected by her kiss, by the *spell* of her. "You don't know Scotland," he insisted. He knew he sounded stubborn, but if she knew the truth…

"You really do think the Scottish countryside is unsafe, don't you?" She stared at him, her head tilted, seemingly curious. "*Why* are you so convinced of that?"

"Because it's true. Bad things can happen anywhere."

"I know, but really…"

His breath exhaled. *Don't tell her.* "And people get kid-napped sometimes."

"Kidnapped?" She laughed and shook her head. "Why would you even consider that? It's crazy."

"Is it?" He grabbed his phone from his pocket and thrust it at her. "Look it up. Go ahead, do an internet search of my name. *M-A-C-D-O-W-A-L-L.* Find out what everyone in Scotland already knows. Maybe it will give you some caution."

He shoved the phone into her hands, so she had no choice but to hold it or let it drop. She didn't let it drop, which gave him a small spot of comfort.

She also did not open the phone's web browser. Instead, she looked up at him with those big green eyes.

"You were kidnapped?" she asked in a low voice.

He dragged in a breath. Exhaled again. "Yes."

"Because you're rich?"

"Because my family is rich. I was ten years old." The anger burned in him, not for himself, but for Rhiannon, his younger sister.

"Oh." Kristin cupped the phone more tightly in her hands. Brought it up to her heart. "I'm sorry, Malcolm."

"I…" He didn't know how to respond. This had never happened to him before. He just did not speak of his past to people.

Twenty years ago, for one thing, news hadn't made it across the globe the way it did today, with the prevalence of the internet and twenty-four-hour television channels. Today, the kidnapping story of an industrialist's young niece and nephew might be news in America as well as in Britain.

He'd been lucky, he supposed. Malcolm had gone through twenty years of schooling in America without his ordeal being common knowledge. He crossed his arms. "In any event, do you see my concern?"

She nodded. She still gripped his phone to her heart.

"Yes, well, never mind all that." He swept his hand toward the car door. "May I please drive you? Just humor me."

She nibbled her lip. "Is that why you use a false name when you travel?"

He stilled. He hadn't really considered that. Not as a direct result, anyway. He thought he'd been using the security name in order to keep the acquisition plans secret and safe.

She looked back at him with those big green eyes. It was as if she saw all. All the pain buried in him, like a well beneath his skin, covered over with a scab on the surface.

Please don't ask me any more questions.

She didn't. She just handed his phone back to him. "I'm sorry about what happened to you," she said quietly. "But if you're not going to talk to me about Born in Vermont yet, then this is a trip that I need to take for myself." She stared down at her toes. "Honestly, you shook my confidence today, when I learned I'd been lied to and hadn't realized it. I need to prove to myself that I'm not a fool— that I'm still okay. And that I *will* be okay."

A million things sprang to mind to reassure her with, but he remained silent. He nodded, thinking of Rhiannon. "Please, let me drive you anyway."

"No, I'm going to switch cars now." She left and went back inside the storefront. He leaned against the hood of the car and waited.

When she came back, she had a glum look on her face. Obviously, no automatic transmissions were available.

"I can drive," he said. "It's just for the afternoon."

"No. I think I'll ask the men to give me an impromptu lesson."

Malcolm held one ace in his hand, and it was time to play it. "If you let me go with you, I can promise to hold off packing up your Vermont factory for a week or two longer than we'd planned. That would mean an extra paycheck for all of your work colleagues, which is more than we'd budgeted for or agreed to. But decide now, Kristin, because my good faith offer to you expires in five minutes."

Her head snapped up. "And you'll promise you'll keep the Sage people away from the plant until I get home in two weeks' time?"

"Yes. Fine. But no more discussion about your Born in Vermont report today, or I cancel everything."

"Done," she said. "Because we're still discussing it on schedule, tomorrow. You won't change that, right?"

How was it that she constantly got him to do things he had never planned in the first place? "Right," he said. And breathed a sigh of relief as she handed him the car keys.

Hefting the weight in his hand, he kept his smile to himself. Because now he had a bigger problem…

"Please, stop at my hotel," she directed him as she opened the passenger-side door. "I'd like to pick up some things and leave a note for Arlene."

He nodded curtly. "First, let me just check the equipment before we leave." He strode over and inspected the vehicle's tires. Opened the hatchback and checked for a tire-changing kit. Went round to the front and opened the bonnet. Tested the headlights. Adjusted the mirrors.

It was a dumpy, ugly little car, but it appeared to be in working order. He got inside the driver's seat and started the engine. It didn't sound too bad. "So. Where's your hotel?"

"Um…" She opened her purse and pulled out a business card, handing it to him. Her tour group was staying at a small, budget inn.

He handed her back the card, then gripped the stick shift and depressed the pedal. He'd driven a stick in America—had learned to drive in America, actually—but had never driven a stick in his native country. The problem being that it was on the other side of the steering wheel than he was used to.

Just brilliant. But he smiled brightly at her. "Don't judge me if I'm a bit rusty."

"Being rich and all," she said, teasing him, "I suppose you are chauffeured more often than you chauffeur others?"

"Er, yes. Something like that." And crossing his fingers, he threw the midget clown car into gear.

CHAPTER SEVEN

KRISTIN PRESSED TWO fingers to her lips as the car bumped down the street, her body jerked forward, then backward by Malcolm's unskilled driving.

Malcolm's face was red, and his mouth and eyes tight with concentration. The only reason Kristin didn't snicker aloud was because she knew she could do no better, and probably a whole lot worse. She had never driven a stick shift in her life. She didn't know anybody who owned a vehicle that didn't have an automatic transmission.

Honestly, she was thankful he'd been there to help. But still, she would be wise to stay wary of him. She'd bought his "George Smith" act hook, line and sinker, and she still felt duped.

Why hadn't she trusted her own instincts better? From the beginning, she'd sensed that he was Scottish, that he wasn't who he said he was. He'd called George Smith his "security name." At first, that had felt like a slap in the face to her. Now, it made a little more sense.

Kidnapped at ten years of age—she couldn't imagine a child going through that, and honestly, she didn't want to. It was just too upsetting, too painful to think of. It was never wise to allow herself to enter into that mind-set.

She tapped her coat pocket, but it was empty, nothing inside—no flashlight. Once she had it with her, at hand again, she'd feel better—which was partly why she wanted to return to her hotel to retrieve her whole suitcase, as opposed to just fishing out the more detailed map she'd packed inside the front pouch. The map that the car rental shop had given her was of no help at all.

She glanced at Malcolm, now more comfortable controlling the car's stick shift. The stoplight at the end of the street had turned red, and they idled behind a small truck. Malcolm must have felt her gaze on his face, because he turned to her and smiled.

He looked great when he was relaxed. He wore a gray business suit that couldn't hide his firm thighs or his crotch, which the light wool cupped as he sat in the driver seat. Adding to his accidental sexiness, his tie was loosened and the top button of his blue shirt, the color of his eyes, was undone.

Her cheeks felt warm. She jerked her gaze away, her hands twisting in her lap. What was going on with her? It could be very dangerous being cooped up in this tiny automobile together for a few more hours. She needed to take care not to fall under his spell again. She was not jeopardizing the reason she was in Scotland, even if she had agreed not to mention those three words *Born in Vermont,* at least until tomorrow morning.

She wrapped her shawl more tightly around herself.

"It's Friday afternoon," she remarked, staring forward through the windshield to the city traffic before them. "Don't you have plans tonight, George? A big date, maybe?"

He raised a brow. "Looks like you're it," he teased. "Lucky you."

Yes, lucky her. Kristin clenched her hands in her lap.

"Bear with me," Malcolm said, as he checked both directions before exiting into traffic. They drove "the wrong way"—on the left side of the road—and it felt strange to her. Sitting to the left of the driver was also a new expe-

rience. She would have eventually figured it out for herself—if she had survived engineering school and a stint
away from home in a strange city then she could handle
driving a stick shift on the wrong side of the road. But still,
it made her nervous.

Malcolm laughed at himself, fumbling with the stick
shift as the car bumped along up a hill. "I haven't driven
myself anywhere in I can't remember how long."

Working a manual transmission was a skill she definitely would work on learning once she returned home.
It might help her avoid this sort of trouble in the future.

Malcolm pulled into the alley, or "close," as the Scots
called it, where her hotel was located.

"I'll be right out." Kristin opened the door but, on second thought, turned and held out her palm to him. "May
I have my car keys with me, please?"

"Why? We're parked here illegally. Someone might ask
me to move the vehicle, and then what will we do?"

"Tell them I'll be right out," she said sweetly, and kept
her palm turned upward.

A frown line appeared on his forehead. "Kristin, do you
really think I'm going to drive off and leave you here?"

She nodded. "It's a concern, yes."

He made a small smile. Looked into her eyes, completely unnerving her. "I won't leave you, Kristy. I promise."

Oh, that sexy Scottish accent. She shivered. This could
be big trouble.

More shaken than before, she slammed the door and
went into the small building with the gray stone facade
and a brass-handled door. Inside, she quickly completed
her business. Retrieved her small, carry-on suitcase from
the desk clerk she'd checked it with. Left a note for Arlene that she'd met up with a "friend" and would not be

back until late, but not to worry about her; she would call the hotel and leave a message for her if she wasn't back by eight or nine o'clock.

When she wheeled her luggage back to the car, Malcolm climbed out and lifted the suitcase into the open hatchback. Standing beside him, she unzipped the front pouch and pulled out her folder full of research on the McGunnert castle.

"Where to?" he asked, once they were buckled inside the car again.

Determined to remain calm, she unfolded the large map and spread it over the dashboard. She pressed a finger to the *x* she'd drawn on the village where the castle was said to be located.

He raised a brow at her. "This is a joke, right?"

"I'm very serious." She pointed to the key ring, swinging back and forth from the ignition switch. "You wanted to drive, now, drive."

He laughed at her. "Kristy, if we drive all the way up there and back..." He traced the route with his finger. "Then we'll be driving into the wee hours. Can't you find a closer castle to visit? There are nice ones here." He indicated an imaginary arc on the map, in an area closer to Edinburgh.

"No," she said. "I want this one." She pressed her *x* again.

"Did you hear what I said, Kristy?"

She stretched the beaded bracelet on her wrist. *Damn.* "I worked out the mathematics of the trip. With the speed limit and the distance we'll be driving, I don't see how it can possibly take that long."

"Kristin," he said, flustered now. "This is Scotland. Rural Scotland. Do you see any motorways on that route? No. These are twisty, mountainous roads, and on some parts of your route, we'll most likely be driving on one-lane roads for both directions."

Shoot, shoot, shoot. She hadn't anticipated this problem. "But...I looked at satellite photos on the internet. It seemed perfectly doable."

He leaned back in his seat and smiled at her. It didn't come off as patronizing, not in the least. He looked...sexy, actually. He'd loosened his tie further and removed his suit jacket. It was folded and laying across the backseat.

He caught her looking him over, and, irritated with herself, she stared down at the folder in her lap. It contained all the internet research she'd found in the past few weeks since Burns Night, the bulk of it completed in the past three days, ever since she'd known she'd be flying into Edinburgh.

Yes, presenting her Born in Vermont proposal to Sage was the "do or die" item on her agenda. But, the opportunity to be in Scotland was also too tempting to pass up. She hadn't been sure if there would be time to squeeze in such a side trip, but if there was, she'd been determined to be prepared.

And now, here she was. Nothing was going to stop her. Especially not *him*.

"Drive," she insisted.

He ran his hand over the steering wheel. "Hear me out, Kristy. You might not like it, but I have an idea." He tapped his thumb against the wheel. "There's a hotel property I know about three quarters of the way north. It's decent. I've stayed there before while on business. Just to be safe, I can call and book us two rooms now, so we'll have the reservation as a fallback."

She squeezed her palms over her knees. She should have changed out of this too-revealing-for-comfort skirt and into her plain old jeans while she'd had the chance. "Is a hotel really necessary, Malcolm?"

"Aye. I think it is." He nodded, his expression serious, but his Scottish burr was in full exposure now, shaking up her nerves.

He spoke on, oblivious to her discomfort. "You're lucky it's light out fairly late in this country. We should be able to get to your castle before nightfall, if I press the engine on this midget car, and pray it holds up." He frowned. "But I'm not sure how safe it will be on the way back, driving the twisting roads in the dark. If conditions aren't the best for driving, we can decide whether to use the hotel reservation or not." He turned in the seat to peer into her eyes. "Is all this worth it to you, Kristy?"

It was her choice? Cancel her mission and remain safely in Edinburgh with Arlene and the tour group, or find her castle and be stuck in close quarters with him for the night?

She shivered. No way could she let anything physical happen with this man who was the key to Born in Vermont being implemented.

"Keep driving," she said.

She heard his soft exhale of breath. He wasn't pleased with her decision. So be it. He wasn't pleased with Born in Vermont either, but she would work on that, too.

"Very well," he said. "I'll take the fastest route, though it might not be the most scenic."

"That's fine," she said crisply. She glanced at him again. "Remind me why you're doing this for me?"

"I'm a nice guy," he said in his American voice.

"No, you're not, *George*."

He smiled sadly. "Maybe I'm hoping you'll agree to work for us over here. The company could use your expertise with Aura."

"Not happening, George."

"Maybe you'll change your mind when you see what good company I am." He said it matter-of-factly, which made her breathe a bit easier.

"Never, George," she said lightly.

He chuckled. "So…" He reached for his phone in the car's console. "Do I have your permission to make that hotel reservation? And could you please call me Malcolm, Kristin?"

She chewed inside her cheek. He *had* said two rooms. This was something she would insist upon, at a minimum. "How expensive is it, *Malcolm?*"

"That's my worry."

"No, it's mine, because I don't want to be beholden to you. For *anything,*" she emphasized.

He shrugged, nonchalant. "Don't you think I owe you for the hospitality you showed me when I was in Vermont? I'd have been lost without your help." He glanced at her. "So. May I make the call?"

Her hackles were up. She could express her irritation—give him a list of all the complications that his lies in Vermont had made for her, but why bother? It was done and over with now. The lesson she would take out of it, however, was to remain on guard with him. Especially where it came to the physical attraction she'd been starting to so obviously feel toward him again.

"Fine," she snapped, staring forward through the windshield. "You pay for everything." But she made a face at him. "However, I will be clear. I am not sharing a room with you. This will be strictly business between us. You won't charm me otherwise, so don't be getting any ideas."

"That's the first time anyone has ever suggested that I might be charming," he said.

"Because you're not," she retorted. "You don't smile enough, for one thing."

He gave her a broad grin, one that showed two dimples. She stared for a moment, fascinated. Malcolm was even showing his teeth. It was the first time she'd really seen them. One of his teeth was chipped, very slightly, and it gave him a rakish look.

She gazed up, into his sky-blue eyes. And darn it if something didn't stir in her again. He was so good-looking when he smiled like that. His whole being lit up.

Now that she thought of it, it was *lucky* for her that he so rarely smiled.

She crossed her legs. "Please, let's leave."

He started the engine. The clunky little jalopy sputtered and purred to life. "Put on your seat belt," he directed.

She buckled herself in. And as Malcolm drove them out of Edinburgh and across the bridge over the pretty firth to the north of the city, he switched to a tour guide's narration of the sights they zoomed past.

Gradually, she relaxed a bit. As promised, he avoided talking about Sage to her. His little stories and anecdotes contained no innuendo, nothing inappropriate that she needed to worry about, just a pleasant pride in his country that was comforting to her.

And she *was* interested in Scotland—in the pretty sea sparkling in the sun, the boats on the firth, and once they were out of the city, the green everywhere, especially among the rolling hills. Malcolm's voice was gentle and modulated, deep and rich. And strangely, the longer they drove through the countryside, the more of a soft burr his voice took on, gently lilting.

It lulled her. Her eyelids drifted closed once or twice, but each time she managed to jerk them back open. Yes, she was jet-lagged—she hadn't slept in nearly a day—but she was in Scotland, at long last. She'd waited her whole life for this, and she wanted to see everything.

There was no time for sleep.

"KRISTY?" MALCOLM ASKED SOFTLY.

He took his eyes off the road and glanced to his left. Kristin's head bobbed forward and then snapped back. She was dozing. Jet lag, probably. He wanted to let her rest, but she needed to see the magnificent castle they were passing on their left.

He touched her arm. "Kristy?"

Immediately, she jerked awake. "Malcolm!"

"Look." He tilted his head toward the window on her side. "Don't you want to stop and see it?"

"Your accent…" She blinked at him, smiling, still on the brink of sleep. "It's so nice."

It was the Scottish talk she liked. He should speak to her more often in his native tongue; it gave excellent results. "Is that castle not enough for you?" He pointed out the window. "Do you wish to take a look?"

Her head on the back of the seat cushion, she gazed sleepily at Malcolm, still smiling. The castle on the hill outside didn't seem to interest her at all.

He drummed his fingers on the steering wheel and asked her a question he should've clarified before they'd left Edinburgh. "*Why* do you want to go so far north, Kristy? What's so special about *this* castle we're going to see?"

She was silent for a moment. He glanced at her. That dreamy smile had been erased from her face. "You'll see when we get there."

He gripped the steering wheel tighter. "I don't like surprises, Kristy."

"I know. So consider this good for you."

This was not reassuring to him. He liked to be in control.

He frowned and focused on the road ahead. The engine protested and whined as he pressed harder on the accelerator; they were climbing up, into the mountains.

But the road suddenly curved, dipping down, and Malcolm eased his foot off the gas pedal. He was getting better at balancing the gas with the clutch, and with his left hand, he shifted into a lower gear. He couldn't see around the outcropping farther on. Probably just more sheep, possibly a Highland cow.

It was actually kind of funny, if he thought about how his day had turned out. When he'd left for work this morning, he'd no idea he would end up with Kristin Hart on an expedition to the Highlands. Not a bad bargain for him overall, though it was becoming more and more apparent that this was a woman who was meant to march to her own drummer.

Constantly, she surprised him.

As they turned the corner, he slowed. He heard a distinctive noise.

Bagpipes.

Kristin sat up in her seat, excitement lighting her face like fireworks. "Do you hear that? Pull over, Malcolm!"

He steered the wee midget car across to the other side of the road, to a front-row position to watch the piper, decked out in his full kit: kilt, sporran, formal Bonnie Prince Charlie jacket, and of course, his caterwauling bagpipes. Not a chance was Malcolm rolling down his window to amplify the volume.

"It's a sign," she breathed.

"Not really. They do this sometimes, for the tourists. There must be an attraction close by."

Kristin turned and looked past him, squeezing his biceps in the process. He liked the warm feel of her hand on his body.

"Which clan tartan is he wearing?" she asked, oblivious to her effect on him, her face alighted as she watched over his shoulder.

"I…" *Have no idea.*

Realizing what she was doing at last, she drew her hand back from him as if she'd been touching fire.

"Er, I have a kilt," he said, solely to impress her. "Did I tell you that?"

Her expression perked up. But she sat carefully on top of her hands. "Which clan? MacDowall?"

"Hmm? Yes." He was staring at her legs. Her skirt had inched up over her knees. She had very bonnie legs.

"I suppose I'm entitled to wear the McGunnert clan for my mother's side," she said, "and also, I believe, Ross and Stewart on my father's side. McDonald is in there somewhere, too."

"The Lords of the Isles," he remarked.

"Who, McDonald?"

"Aye."

"I'd like to see these Lords of the Isles. Is that far to—"

"No, we cannot drive to the Hebrides, Kristin. There are ferries involved. That would require a few more days, not mere hours."

"Of course." She nodded.

Interesting. He was beginning to see that appealing to her sense of adventure was key to interesting Kristin in anything.

"Since you've the blood of the ancient Highlands in you," he hinted, "you should tell your tour guide to show you the Culloden Battlefield."

She frowned. "Unfortunately, the tour group will be spending most of their time in England."

"That's sacrilege," he said.

She turned to him. "What other clans' plaids are you entitled to wear? Do you own kilts representing all the families in your bloodline?"

"No, lass. You choose only one. You must be loyal, you see."

"In that case, I choose McGunnert. It's rare, but…I actually knew one of them."

"Your grandmother?" he asked. He glanced to her shawl. "Is that the McGunnert plaid?"

She nodded. "It is. I bought it in Edinburgh."

Most likely after she'd run from his office. "Ah, Kristy," he murmured.

But she didn't let on that she knew what he referred to. Defiant, she turned to the bagpiper outside the car and sighed at his music. "Can you feel it in you, Malcolm? The sound of the bagpipes just…does something to me."

He thought of a saying his father sometimes proclaimed: "If the call of the pipes doesn't stir your blood, then you can't be Scottish."

She smiled at him.

The bagpiper abruptly stopped playing. He strode over to the car and tapped on Malcolm's window. Malcolm rolled it down.

"Are you looking for a bed-and-breakfast?" the piper asked.

"Er…no."

"Because there's a guesthouse over yonder." The piper pointed toward a road that forked off to the right. "It's new."

"Are we far from McGunnert Castle?" Kristin asked him.

The piper scratched his head. "Never heard of it, lass."

Wait a minute.

The piper left them and Malcolm stared at Kristin. "Mc-Gunnert Castle? Is *that* where we're going?"

She lifted her chin. "It certainly is."

"I thought your family said there is no such thing?"

"That's what they said, but it doesn't mean it's true. Look at my shawl, for example. They also said that the McGunnert plaid didn't exist. But it does, and I found it."

"So...bottom line, you're directing us to a castle that doesn't exist?"

She looked hurt. "Be fair, Malcolm. I've done a lot of research since Burns Night, and I'm now certain there's something to the story."

He groaned. He should have guessed this was what she'd had up her sleeve. "Kristy," he began.

"Why is this sounding like you don't believe in me?"

"I do believe in you. But I also believe in being practical."

And just then, the skies opened up. Literally. The rain started slowly, in fat, loud drops on the windshield, which, within a minute, had turned into a steady pattering.

"Shall we continue on to my castle?" she said brightly.

Malcolm sighed, but he turned on the engine and then flicked on the windshield wipers.

Except nothing happened with the wipers.

He tried again. Lifted the lever up. Pushed the lever down. Tried to wiggle it side to side, even.

Still, the wipers refused to move.

Maybe he was doing it wrong. "Kristy, could you check in the glove box for an instruction book?"

She opened the lid and peered inside. "There is nothing here."

He dipped his head. Studied the instrument panel. Yes, he'd been pushing the proper lever. And the wipers were present, too, on the outside of the car window. They just weren't *working.*

"And in bloody Scotland," he muttered. "Where it rains more often than it *doesn't* rain."

"So, what are you saying?" Blinking, she bit her lip.

He didn't want to transfer his concerns to her, but she deserved to be told the truth. He gestured to the front window, sheeted with the heavy rainfall. It was impossible to see a thing in front of them, and they weren't even moving yet.

"Bottom line, Kristy, we're stuck here, at least until the rain passes."

"How long do you guess that will be?" she asked nervously.

"In Scotland?" he deadpanned. "It could be until June."

AN HOUR LATER they were still sitting in the car. Malcolm had called for roadside assistance, but the operator told him that they were beyond the zone of service. He and Kristin had no choice but to wait for the heaviest part of the rain to pass.

They waited. And they waited.

And they waited some more.

Kristin had turned silent now, which made it worse for him, because he'd always loved her free spirit and free chatter. Maybe she was piqued about his lack of faith in the mythical McGunnert Castle, but on this matter, he definitely sided with her family.

Real castle owners did not send scam letters abroad, searching for heirs. Neither did every clan name possess a functioning castle.

But rather than push the matter, he'd backed off. He didn't want to argue with her. Besides, she seemed exhausted.

With the rain drumming on the car's roof, she drifted to sleep. Malcolm pulled out his phone and GPS and attempted to figure out exactly where they were and what services were nearby.

Like the piper had said, Malcolm found a listing for a bed-and-breakfast located just over the glen. Besides that, he saw nothing else. The bed-and-breakfast was so small—and perhaps, new—that there weren't any ratings or reviews Malcolm could check; no website or photos he could find. It was a mystery as to what could turn up there, and Malcolm detested mysteries. He was a man who needed data points.

But, the temperature was fast dropping and Kristin was shivering, so he took his jacket and tucked it around her to keep her warm. When his hand accidentally brushed her waist, she blinked her eyes open. He paused, leaning over her body. When she saw his coat covering her, her green eyes softened.

He waited, her acceptance of his jacket—of him—meaning more than was probably good for him.

"You're tired," he said.

"Just a bit jet-lagged." She sat up. "We should check out that B&B."

"I never sleep in strange places. It could be dirty... dangerous."

"Then maybe this is an opportunity to bring you out from your shell a bit."

This *whole* day had been about her bringing him out from his "shell." "At least let me check it out first, will you?" he asked.

"Certainly, Mr. Safety Conscious. I'll rest here while you do." She turned aside, her lips curving upward. Sighing with what he hoped was contentment, she curled the collar of his coat inside her fingers and pulled it to her nose. Her eyelids drifted shut. Her lashes were long against her cheek.

She just…did something to him. Being with her put him in heaven, and in hell, too. She was so unconcerned with their predicament, and that was maddening to him. He should not want to help her or take care of her so badly.

And yet there was more to it—much more to it—than just keeping her safe. She *intrigued* him. She drew him to her and fascinated him to the point that he'd be content to be with her for hours, just to see what she would do next. He knew he was more interested in her than was wise. If she had her way, she'd be leaving for home soon, he suspected—once he evaluated the proposal that he assumed to be as unfeasible as Aura had been, without Laura at the helm.

Still, he couldn't tell Kristin that. He did not want to discuss her plan, not yet. Rather, he should work on getting her acclimated to him and to the country. Only then might he get her to consider staying on in Scotland.

But the Scottish weather was not cooperating. It kept getting worse: the rain drummed harder instead of letting up. Malcolm called his road services account again, but they couldn't promise service tonight. He phoned the car rental place—a veritable junk shop—and only ended up losing his patience and shouting at them.

Not good. He scanned the web browser again for a garage close by, but the closest one wasn't picking up their phone. He and Kristin were in the country, and he was mainly a city person. He was out of his comfort zone, and he didn't know what to do.

He glanced at Kristin, still sleeping. Part of him should be happy. She was with him, and they were in this together. He was glad he'd driven her—if she'd been alone, then she would have been facing this problem alone. Yes, she was capable, but it was better to have him with her than not with her.

Find a safe place for us to stay. He opened the door and rushed into the rain, matting his shirt to his skin before he was able to huddle again under the open hatchback. A portable umbrella poked out of the sleeve of Kristin's suitcase, so he borrowed that and opened it.

They weren't going anywhere tonight, was his guess. He might as well inquire if the bed-and-breakfast had two rooms open. Malcolm at least wanted to find Kristin a place to sleep comfortably while they waited out the storm.

First, he made sure the vehicle's doors were all locked. He'd pulled the car far enough off of the road that it was out of danger of being hit by another car, or even being seen, for that matter. He gently closed the hatchback, and, facing into the sting of the biting rain, he followed the direction the piper had taken up the hill, heading straight toward what appeared to be a small Highland croft house, rural in character. Completely out of Malcolm's element.

He rang the bell, and a plump landlady answered, informing him in a heavy Highland accent that, yes, this was a bed-and-breakfast, and, no, the local garage wasn't presently open and wouldn't be until morning. She offered to place a call for him, and he accepted her offer, waiting while she left a message. In the meantime, she informed him that she had one room available. In exchange for cash—no credit accepted—she gave him a key.

Kristin was not going to be happy with one room. But at least she could stretch out and rest more comfortably than sitting in that cramped, cold passenger seat.

He opened the wet umbrella he'd left in the entry, then dodged the mud patches as he made his way back to the car.

When he unlocked the door, Kristin woke with a start.

"I checked it out," he said, jumping inside, out of the drenching rain. The drum of it was loud on the metal roof, and he needed to raise his voice to be heard over it. "It seems safe enough. Follow me. Take the umbrella, and I'll carry your suitcase."

"Thank you, Malcolm. I know how hard this is for you."

"If it's still raining in the morning," he said, "then the bed-and-breakfast people will drive me to a garage when it opens."

"That sounds like a plan."

"Right." He nodded. "Brilliant."

She laid her head back on the seat and grinned at him. "When is the last time you had an adventure like this?"

He thought for a moment. "Burns Night."

Her cheeks grew pink. "Well…we should get going. It will be good to get some rest if we're going to find Mc-Gunnert Castle once the rain stops."

"Kristin…what if there is no McGunnert Castle?"

"Malcolm, I saw a listing for it on the internet. After Burns Night, I checked."

Oh, and everything on the internet is true, isn't it? But he bit his tongue.

"Are you doubting me?" she asked.

"If all you found is the one mention, then, yes, Kristy, I am."

"In that case, tomorrow morning I'll go on without you. Maybe the garage can arrange for a rental car for you, and I'll keep mine for myself." She took the wet end of the umbrella, but he kept his grip on the dry end.

"Kristy, be reasonable."

She glared, exasperated with him. "This time, I'm choosing to trust in my gut. And my gut tells me that my castle is *there*. No, I don't have a lot of supporting information right now.

"But I will find McGunnert Castle before I leave Scotland. And if you don't want to come with me or believe in me, that's perfectly fine."

She leaned over and withdrew the key from the ignition. Tugged her umbrella firmly until he released it. Then, she went out her door, stomped through the driving rain, opened the hatchback and yanked out her suitcase. All without giving him so much as a second glance.

He closed his eyes. The woman drove him daft. And when it did come to pass that there was no mythical, shining castle for her at the end of the rainbow—because *all* castles in Scotland were well documented, everyone knew that—then he would need to be there to pick up the pieces for her. It was the story of his life, and he did not want to do it with her. He'd wanted her to be different.

Who was he kidding, she *was* different. Smart, capable, resilient. At heart, he'd seen that in her. Maybe this crazy trip was his fault—he'd betrayed her, after all, and maybe the shock over that had affected her. Everybody had their way of living, their way of coping with the world. He supposed hers was changing.

But this…flight of fancy…would not end well. He could see it happening, unfolding as if in slow motion, as he saw most disasters, and he was powerless to stop it.

Plus, practically speaking, after it was all over, she'd need to get back to Edinburgh, and he was her ride. Yes, if nothing else, he was dedicated to being her chauffeur for this expedition, whether he approved of her motivations or not. And he wouldn't abandon her—or anyone else in such a situation, for that matter.

Damn it.

He got out, slammed the door behind him. In the space of a breath, he was soaking wet. He had no suitcase, no spare clothing. His shoes squished in the mud, his hair matted to his head.

He retraced his steps to the bed-and-breakfast, and with his long strides, he quickly caught up to Kristin. He fell in step beside her. At the front door to the whitewashed croft, the landlady "tsked" him when she saw their sorry state.

That's when he recalled not having been entirely nice to the landlady earlier; maybe he had snapped at her a bit when she'd said she only had the one room available instead of two, and then again when she'd wanted cash, not credit card.

He just was on edge. His patience stretched to the limit.

He stayed behind with the landlady, smoothing her ruffled feathers and inquiring about getting his clothing cleaned and finding a toothbrush. He'd left Edinburgh with none of this planned ahead; normally he would have stopped at his flat to at least have changed into jeans. What was Kristin *doing* to him?

He went into the front parlor, where Kristin sat on a settee beside a stout man with weathered, red skin, who—judging from his work boots and attire—appeared to be a dairy farmer, maybe the husband of the owner. He and Kristin had their heads buried together inside a large, colorful research book titled *Highland Clans*.

Malcolm groaned.

It was clear he needed a new strategy for changing the way he dealt with Kristin.

CHAPTER EIGHT

"Niver gae tae bed angry, lass."

Kristin sat at a small table in the kitchen of the quaint, homey bed-and-breakfast. Alistair—the B&B owner's husband—had enthusiastically shared a library of his wife's—Eileen's—research books.

Presently, Eileen was helping Kristin to "tea," as she called it, but which really was just a light supper that didn't involve tea of any sort.

Kristin munched happily from a packet of "crisps"—potato chips, to her—and tried to decipher what Eileen was saying. "Could you repeat that, please?" Kristin asked.

"Niver gae tae bed angry."

Kristin smiled and nodded. She still didn't have a clue, but Eileen's accent was so interesting, it should be called a different language altogether. Kristin's brain needed to slow down and back up just to catch what Eileen what saying.

"Oh, my gosh," she finally realized. "'Never go to bed angry.' You think George Smith and I are *together?*"

"Aye, lass."

At last she and Eileen understood one another. "No, you see, George Smith and I are not romantic partners. We're just…work acquaintances who got caught in the rain with car trouble."

"'Tis spring," Eileen insisted. "Maybe a romance will blossom."

"No." Kristin emphatically shook her head. "It won't. In fact, if you can make sure that our two rooms are as far apart as possible from one another, that would be best."

"No, there's just the one bed, lass."

"One bed." Kristin put down her bag of crisps. "Do you mean, as in one room?"

"Aye." The landlady smiled and leaned in closer. "And I wouldn't toss him from my bed, were I you. He is a handsome braw one, ken what I mean?" She winked.

Kristin's mind was swimming; she didn't understand the last bit of what Eileen had just said. *"Ken what I mean?"* she repeated helplessly. "What's that…?"

"She's saying, 'Do you know what I mean?'" Malcolm said, walking up behind her.

Kristin jerked her head up. Great, he'd overheard them discussing her sleeping with him. She felt the blush creeping over her face.

Malcolm smirked at her, the maddening man. He passed her a bottle of water and half a sandwich from his plate, then leaned his backside against the counter, casually crossing his feet as if he enjoyed this conversation immensely. "Go on. Don't stop your talk on my account."

"George and I will *not* be sharing a bed tonight," Kristin announced. "Is that understood by all?"

"Well, that's me." Eileen pushed herself up from the table and winked at them both.

"That means she's finished and is leaving," Malcolm explained to Kristin before she got a chance to ask.

"Oh," Kristin said. "Good night, Eileen."

"Good night, Kristy. Good night, George." Eileen motioned to the sandwiches on Malcolm's plate. "Put the wrappers in the bin when you are done."

"Aye," Malcolm agreed.

"And watch the wee beasties," Eileen said.

"Right-o," Malcolm said. "Er...don't forget what we discussed earlier, Eileen."

"Oh, aye, give me a wee bit." Eileen waved her hand back at him and shuffled from the kitchen.

"What was all that about?" Kristin demanded to him.

"Nice lady." Malcolm sat down at the table. "She said to give her a bit of time." He nodded. "Yes, I think I smoothed everything over very well with her."

"What exactly are wee beasties?"

He gave Kristin a "Don't ask" look, then just shrugged. "Ants. Mites. A couple of silly little dogs. Could be anything. Could be nothing. Next time, I'll get you a room in the Four Seasons."

"*Next* time?"

"Oh, and thank you for using the George Smith name. I know it must burn a hole in you to have to say it aloud again."

She sighed at him. "I'm fine, *George*."

"Aye, that you are. You're a princess among women."

"Never mind your flattery, I meant what I said about the bed," she insisted.

He gave her a smile. "I checked the satellite imagery software and the 3D maps on my smartphone. I found something very interesting. Did you know that no castles whatsoever are showing up on your *x*-marks-the-spot map?"

She saw what he was doing. "Then your technology is wrong," she retorted. "Because Alistair found me a research book that clearly lists McGunnert Castle as located in the very village where I said it would be."

"Maybe his book is wrong."

"Maybe your smartphone is wrong."

He raised a brow at her. The man was maddening. And

sexy. But at least they weren't raising their voices at each other anymore.

"Do you know what, George?" she said sweetly. "I think I've been understanding about you and your security name. Now, I think it's your turn to be understanding of me—I don't want my goals and my dreams stomped on anymore." Her hand went up like a stop sign. "No more stomping on me. I won't tolerate it. Do you get it?"

"Okay," he said, quickly enough to make her suspicious. "I get it."

She crossed her arms. "You do? Really?"

"Sure." He gave her a charming, lopsided smile. "Believe it or not, you make sense to me, Kristy. Now I know why you were so happy to have the Burns Night celebration. You love Scotland. It's obvious—it's in your blood. And I also know why you—and not one of your managers—were alone in the factory on that Saturday to begin with."

"And why is that?"

"Simple," he said, his face the picture of innocence. "People take advantage of you, and you let them—or at least you used to. You don't want that kind of life for yourself anymore. No more people telling you what to do, how you should live, what you should say or not say. I think you've had enough of your old life, and that's one of the reasons why you're here in Scotland, whether you realize it or not."

It was all true. "Okay…" So he sort of understood her— she still wasn't sharing a bed with him.

He pushed his cell phone across the table to her. "Go ahead and use my phone to call Arlene about your delay in getting back to Edinburgh. I don't mind."

She sat there, holding his phone while he gathered up

the rubbish from their make-do meal and then dumped it all in the trash receptacle.

He glanced at her. "Is everything fine with you, lass?"

"I'm…trying to decide whether I'm being trampled or not."

"Oh, Kristy." He gave her a look. "You'll *know*."

She shivered. There was an undercurrent that was just… drawing her to him again. And making her very nervous at the same time.

His gaze met hers and held it. "Do you know what my next big job is, Kristy?" he said in a murmur.

"Why…don't you tell me?"

He smiled slightly. "It's getting you back to Edinburgh safely so we can have that meeting and evaluate our next steps together. And I do promise to accomplish it without trampling you. Is that an agreement, then?"

Her heart pounding, she nodded.

For a long moment, they just stood there, looking at one another, eye to eye.

At last she took a breath. "Thank you for letting me borrow your phone."

"Aye." His voice was still very low. Then he added, "Tell Arlene that George Smith says hello."

He walked away and left her alone in the kitchen.

MALCOLM GAVE KRISTIN time to settle in and then headed up the stairs with a tray Eileen had given him, holding two tumblers each containing a finger of apricot-flavored brandy. An interesting choice, but he'd been grateful to Eileen for the hospitality.

He balanced the tray on one side and knocked on the door.

"I'm decent," Kristin called from inside.

Too bad. He would rather enjoy seeing her indecent. But

he turned the door handle, whistling, determined to stay on course. He'd said he would believe in her—a tall order, for someone naturally skeptical. Then, he'd promised not to "trample" her. Though frankly, he considered himself the one person who would never do anything of the sort.

Immediately, he noticed that the air in the room was damp and warm, and smelled like a pine and birch forest. Must be the potions she'd showered with. Nice.

Kristin gazed up at him from her position sitting up in the only bed, which took up most of the small room. Her hair was wet and combed back. Pillows were propped behind her against the headboard, and she was burrowed under the covers, with the sheets pulled up over her breasts. One of those research books Alistair had given her was open in her lap.

No, he wasn't going to get sidetracked into a discussion about castles right now.

He placed the tray on the bedside table. What he really felt like doing was climbing into bed and burrowing under the sheets with her, but from the way she eyed him, the answer was a definite no. And her attire communicated the same message. She had on a flannel, long-sleeved, high-necked nightgown, like somebody's granny might wear—not a hot young woman who rocked a short skirt and a tight sweater as she did.

He took the measure of the bed with one glance. Large and comfortable-looking, with plenty of room for both of them. But Kristin had established herself in the center, staking out her turf, and her turf appeared to include the entire property.

He sprawled on the lone, ancient chair in the room instead, and immediately sank low into the cushions. No possibility of getting a good night's rest there.

She went back to her research book and ignored him.

He untied his laces, dropped one wet shoe, which landed with a loud plunk, and then the other.

Slowly, she turned a page. "Did you ask Eileen for a blanket for yourself?"

"No, lassie, but 'tis good of you to worry about me."

She smirked at him.

He took a taste from the snifter and immediately bared his teeth. Eileen's homemade brandy was stronger than it smelled. A bit sweet, but not too much. "Would you like a wee dram?"

"No, Malcolm." She said "no" like "nae" and turned another page. "There's a couch in the sitting room that should accommodate your big, Highlander body pretty well. Do ye ken what I mean?" she said in her Scottish voice.

He "kenned" that she'd noticed his body. He smiled to himself. "For someone who is busting out and declaring her freedom, you're playing it awfully safe tonight, love."

She turned another page of her book. "Nothing is going to happen between us, Malcolm. Don't even try."

"You think I sleep with strange women I barely know? The nerve." Little did she know, but he didn't sleep with women he actually *did* know. He was a monk in service to his family. "Which brings me back to you. I thought *you* were the adventurous one, and *I* was the careful person. And yet, look how cautious you are tonight. Granny-neck gown and all."

She crossed her arms. "It's how I stay warm. Scotland is cold in spring. And Alistair hasn't exactly turned up the heat very high, has he?"

Malcolm didn't want to talk about Alistair. He wanted to talk about her. "I'll bet your mother wears granny-necks."

"She does."

"Your sister-in-law. Your niece."

Kristin pursed her lips. "Yup." She smiled brightly at him. "Must be a Vermont thing."

He leaned forward. "I don't think so. I think it's a Hart-family thing."

"And your point is?"

"Did your grandmother wear granny-necks?"

Kristin frowned. "I don't remember that. She died when I was small."

"And yet, you've idolized her into a role model."

Slowly, Kristin shut her book. "Okay, I don't see what this—"

"Allow me." He leaned forward, offering her a snifter one last time, but she declined. "Love, I've met your family. And if I may remind you, they thought I was just grand."

"Easily fooled, I suppose," she said breezily.

"You're not like them. Your parents are safe and cautious. I would imagine that they never really encouraged you or your brothers to venture out into the world or go very far," he said. "So there you all are, still living steps from the house you grew up in."

"Malcolm—"

"That night, when I said to find your castle, I meant it figuratively. Not like this." He laughed dryly. "Anybody could tell that you long for freedom, and yet, this is your first time away from home, isn't it? You didn't even own a passport."

She gathered her wet hair in one hand, then let it go. "Actually, you're wrong about that. I lived in New York City for a while."

He blinked but did not let on that he was surprised. "And?"

"And, I got a better job at Aura." She pursed her lips at him. "I liked Aura, very much." She reached over to the bedside table on the other side, and unzipped a kit. Opened a pot of something-or-other, honey-scented, and rubbed it on her hands. "It made me feel healed, working there. The bees healed me."

"Healed you from what?"

One shoulder lifted, then dropped. "I don't know. Maybe it was hard being the only girl in the middle of all those boys growing up," she said.

He laced his hands behind his head and leaned back, letting her continue.

"I *like* to have fun." She rubbed that hand cream in vigorously. "I wasn't always so serious in my life, you know."

He thought of her dancing the Highland Fling with her niece. She'd seemed like a different person in that moment. "What happened to you?"

"Nothing happened, Malcolm. Just drop it." She narrowed her eyes at him. "Anyway, I'm not here so you can analyze me, or dig deeper into my psyche. I'm here in Scotland because your business put my company *out of* business. I'm here to save my factory and my town. My main purpose on this trip is to convince you of the legitimacy of my proposal—which we *will* discuss tomorrow. For tonight, though, you can walk away from me at any time. I'm not holding you here in this bedroom."

"No," he said quietly. "You are not."

He leaned his head back again. They both knew he was lying. There was just something about her, something maddening to him.

She *did* hold him there, like a sun held a planet in its orbit.

She attracted him. She fascinated him. She infuriated him.

He couldn't put his finger on it. She was a mixture of cautious and reckless, high and low, out-of-control and scared. But there was something he was missing, something vital about her that he didn't understand.

And yet, she seemed to understand him very well. She may not like him much; she hadn't liked his security name or his job requirements, that was for sure. But when she'd found out about *the kidnapping* she had looked at him with empathy, though she hadn't asked a thing about it or even attempted to coo over him or "mother the hurt away."

I'm sorry, she'd said, and she'd meant it. But that was all she'd said.

It was the perfect response, to his mind. Maybe he'd been looking for this response all his life.

And in that respect, *she* was perfect.

If he was honest with himself, a big reason he didn't date his countrywomen in general was because everyone he'd met who was his age already knew about him—or at least thought they did. Once they heard his name, they all knew. Even the women in his office. Sometimes, he caught them gazing at him with sadness and sympathy, but it was a sympathy that wanted to question him, to hear the details that were never made public. To get an inside scoop and to elicit emotion from a man who did not give it.

Maybe there was a twisted power in that, in uncovering a man's wounds and then being the only person allowed to peel that bandage on and off at will.

And it sickened him. Whenever he'd dropped the drape and allowed himself to be himself, he'd always seemed to attract that type of woman. Hovering, protective, solicitous.

Until Kristin. She'd had him from that moment at the car rental shop, when he'd blurted out the truth and she'd reacted in exactly the way that he'd needed.

He wanted to keep her with him, in Scotland, at least for a while longer. Maybe that was selfish of him. Right

now, she still seemed a bit stressed and out of sorts. She'd
lost her job at Aura. She'd lost her way. She seemed to be
looking for something to believe in, and so maybe that was
why she'd latched on to this new scheme to save Aura. A
scheme that was impossible, because it was a money-loser.
It was also a scheme she did not need.

Kristin Hart was smart and important and kind. She was
so much better than Aura Botanicals—that fading, hope-
less factory—and the skeptical, rigid family who clung
to her in the snowy, cold town whose industries had seen
better days.

"Malcolm?"

He lifted his head. "Kristy?"

"You should go downstairs and find a blanket."

"I know," he said quietly.

He went downstairs and searched out Alistair. Their
B&B host was watching a Formula One race on his television in the sitting room. Malcolm kicked back in a chair
beside him.

"Is she from Florida?" Alistair asked.

"Kristin? No. Why do you ask?"

"Always wanted to visit Florida."

Malcolm nodded. "Aye." He turned his head. "Has she
found anything regarding the castle?"

"No, but sometimes the ruins are only listed in the old
maps."

"Ruins?"

"Aye. We've thousands of ruins in the Highlands. Some
not very old. The mountains reclaim them when they're
abandoned, you ken. All that's left are the foundation
stones."

"Where can I find these old maps?"

Alistair pointed to the shelves.

"Have you shown her any yet?"

"She didn't ask."

Malcolm tried not to smile. "Do you have any Ordinance Maps?"

"Oh, aye."

Malcolm retrieved what he needed. Then, ten minutes later, after a visit to Eileen and her electric clothes washer, he headed back to the suite wearing a borrowed bathrobe. This time, he just used his key and quietly opened the door.

The light was on, and Kristin was asleep. She'd blockaded herself with a row of pillows lined down the center of the bed like a wall, splitting the mattress in half as if they were an Amish couple.

Maybe she'd decided to relent on chasing him away. He could wake her and ask.

Or, he could just quietly and unobtrusively stretch out in the chair in the corner and try to sleep as well as he could since he had another long day of driving ahead.

He placed the book full of maps on the table beside him and settled into the chair. He shut off the lamp, but the damn belt on his robe was bunching into his stomach, making him uncomfortable.

He raised his head to check on her. Her chest was rising and falling; she was definitely asleep. If he had his druthers, he would strip off the robe. He was a red-blooded Scot at heart, and that is what Scots wore under their kilts, too.

But he was pushing her enough by sharing the same room with her. How Kristin dealt with him when she woke in the morning would tell the tale.

CHAPTER NINE

THE NEXT MORNING, Kristin rolled over and rubbed her eyes. For a moment, she had trouble remembering where she was. The bedsheets smelled unfamiliar and felt crisper against her skin than she was used to.

I'm in Scotland. She bolted upright and smiled.

But right beside her, Malcolm was asleep on the chair. His arms were thrown over his head. A lap-blanket was wrapped around his hips.

From the chest up, he was naked. Very, very naked.

The smile drained from her face. *Oh, no.* She wanted to glance away, but she couldn't.

Her heart pounded. She thought back to the evening before, trying to remember.

She'd worn her flannel nightgown, which was still on her body. Her hair had been wet from the shower and now was a mess—the result of sleeping on it damp. Malcolm had left for the public rooms, and she had arranged the pillows as a barrier in case he returned to get his things and would receive the reminder that they were here together on business only.

And then somehow, after all her preparations, she'd gone from feeling nervous to falling into a dead sleep, probably because of yesterday's jet lag. She had a slight headache from not drinking enough water and being dehydrated, and she hadn't eaten much of the supper they'd shared.

She glanced back at him in the chair. From the bare skin at his hips, it seemed that Malcolm wore nothing, not even underwear. She felt suspicious from the way the light blanket clung to him.

Swallowing, her gaze followed the muscles of his chest and shoulders, the strong biceps bracketing either side of his head, his hands beneath.

His chest rose and fell with every breath from his lungs. Of course Malcolm had to be perfect. Fit. With a strong torso. Slightly tousled hair. Stubble from a day's growth of beard on his chin.

She couldn't see his bottom half because it was beneath the blanket.

By instinct, she hugged herself. Then she got up, wheeled her suitcase into the en-suite bathroom and closed the door as soundlessly as she could. Her hands shaking, she dressed in her jeans and a fresh sweater. Brushed her teeth. Washed her face, still creased from lying facedown on the pillowcase, and combed out the tangles in her hair as best she could.

Her pallor was pale, as if she'd been spooked. She'd packed a small pouch with the bare minimum in cosmetics, and she rooted for the pot of blush, her lipstick, and a quick coat of mascara.

Gah! It was no use. She looked as if she'd seen a ghost.

When she came out of the bathroom, Malcolm was awake, rubbing his face with his hands. He saw her and smiled, a transformation that sent him from gruff-looking to Highlander-Adonis. She froze, shocked all over again. She would never get used to that.

"Good morning, Kristy," he murmured in his sleep-roughened Scots' voice.

She caught her breath; she couldn't help it. "I...wasn't expecting you here."

"I know." He shrugged sheepishly. "Sorry. They wouldn't let me sleep in the parlor."

"I thought I'd been clear." She stared at his chest, mostly smooth, but with a smattering of dark hair in the center. What would it feel like to run her fingers through it?

"I, er, tried to sleep with just the robe on," he said, following her gaze, "but it was too damned uncomfortable."

"Right. Well, what's done is done, and I'll go now—"

"Didn't you see? I found something last night." He reached over and picked up an open book from the table beside him. "I wanted you to see it first thing. You didn't notice it?"

No, she had gawked and stared at him, instead.

Striding toward him, she took the soft-sided notebook, realizing it was a set of Ordinance maps for the county—very detailed, down to the level of footpaths, it seemed.

He'd bookmarked one particular page with a yellow sticky note. It didn't mean much to her—she knew virtually nothing about this landscape.

"Do you see what that is?" he asked. "*X* marks the spot."

She followed his finger and squinted at the fine, italicized print he pointed out. "McGunnert Castle Ruins," the map clearly read.

"Ruins! That's why we couldn't find it."

"I owe you an apology, Kristy," he said quietly. "There *is* a McGunnert Castle."

More than the apology, this was the first solid confirmation she'd seen as to the specific location of her castle. With a whoop, she jumped up and down.

He raised his palm and slapped her hand with a joyous high five.

"Since when are you buying into my castle quest?" she asked, careful to stare into his eyes, and not, um, at his bare, muscled chest.

But his eyes seemed to catch on to hers, and it was easy to get lost in their depths. They really were beautiful. Sky-blue. Or, as blue as the sky she was used to, in Vermont. In Scotland, it seemed rare.

Except on Malcolm's face.

Still grinning, he picked up the digital clock, also on the table, and squinted at it. "If we go downstairs now, we'll be first at breakfast, and we can get an early start on our drive." He smiled at her. "Have you ever eaten a proper Scottish breakfast?"

"No." She stared at him, wondering, ah, where his clothes were? He made a move to swing his legs to the floor, and she yelled, "Stop!"

His brow knit. "Kristy?"

"Let me, ah, leave you, and then you can get dressed."

A dimple formed in his cheek. He seemed to be holding in a smile. "A bit prudish, are we?"

She turned away, exasperated.

"It's okay," he said. "I'm just having some fun with you. Eileen washed my clothes and promised to find me some jeans and trainers—for a price, of course." He pointed to the door. "Can you be a love and fetch what she's found for me? Eileen said she'd leave it just outside."

She opened the door, but nothing was there. She stepped out into the corridor and looked around. Checked the door-knobs facing the hallway. All were empty. Kristin could smell bacon cooking, so obviously, somebody was awake.

She went back into the bedroom. "Your clothes aren't here, Malcolm."

"Well, isn't this a pickle?" He stretched to get up.

"No, stop!"

He tilted his head and grinned at her. To her, he seemed unconcerned with his current state of near-nudity. It flabbergasted her. He was uptight in every other way; this did not compute.

She, on the other hand, was a quivering mass of jelly inside. She turned for the door without looking at him. "I'll go find Eileen."

Behind her, she heard the floor creak, likely from him stepping out of the chair…and from beneath the blanket.

With an exhale, she closed the door firmly behind her and hotfooted it downstairs to the dining room, past a side table spread with a cold buffet. Fleetingly, she saw cereal. Muesli. Milk in jugs. Berries and chopped fruits of various forms set out in serving bowls.

Not what she'd expected for breakfast in Scotland, but her immediate mission was to find Eileen.

Her hostess was dressed in gray sweatpants and a pink sweater with a Scottish thistle embroidered on the front. She spoke into the telephone, and from what little English Kristin could pick out, it sounded as if she was giving blow-by-blow directions to a lost tourist.

Kristin stood in the corner, catching her breath.

Alistair came round the corner holding a spatula and wearing a "Kiss the Chef" apron. A big set of lips was located over his…

No. Just, no.

Kristin went over to Eileen and crossed her arms, waiting for the call to finish. She knew she was overreacting, but she just felt…uneasy.

Eileen noticed, and bless her, waved Kristin with her into the private part of the house where she and Alistair lived, into a kitchen with a small—tiny, really—clothes dryer, still running its cycle.

Eileen covered the phone and then opened the mini-appliance. "George's clothes are inside. His suit's hanging on the back of the door."

Then Eileen uncovered the phone and continued talking into the mouthpiece to her lost customer.

Kristin's head was spinning. She bent to the clothes dryer. Inside was a man's underwear. T-shirt. One sock. The other sock.

She seemed to freeze inside. This was too intimate, more than she was comfortable with.

What was going on with her? She had brothers, for heaven's sake. Her family chore as a kid had been to fold the family's clothes. A few times a week, her mom had taken the load out of the electric dryer and then piled everything into a yellow plastic laundry basket left on the dining room table for Kristin to fold and put away when she'd arrived home from school on the bus.

It had been no big deal to Kristin. Everybody had a communal chore in her family; that was just hers. As a result, Kristin had handled more pairs of men's white BVD briefs and Hanes undershirts than probably even a department store salesperson. She matched socks like a pro. Each brother's was color-coded. Really, how was this any different?

It's a lot different, something inside her said. *Because you're different now than you were back then.* And Malcolm was...he was...

Definitely not her brother.

So? She'd had boyfriends before, she'd...

Kristin put her hand to her mouth. It had never occurred to her that maybe her failure at living away from home *had* changed her. She hadn't dated since then. She'd felt like such an overwhelming failure at being unable to assimilate, that she hadn't wanted to think about her sheltered existence.

But Malcolm had brought it back last night—with his presence, and with all his talk—and maybe her need to feel safe and sheltered with her family in Vermont still lingered, fresh inside her.

Kristin exhaled. She retrieved Malcolm's clothes for him. She carted the bundle and his suit hanger upstairs, and when she got to the room—to *their* room—she listened through the door. The shower was running. *Good.* She went inside, and steam envoloped her. She left Malcolm's clothes in a pile on the bed and then headed back down to the breakfast room.

Enough. She had only a few more hours to endure until ten o'clock. Then she could go back to concentrating on her factory. Her people. Her future.

MALCOLM SAT BESIDE Kristin at a rustic, communal dining table while Eileen served them a hot Scottish country breakfast like he only received when he was home visiting his family.

Two eggs, sunny-side up. Scottish-style bacon. Oatmeal, cooked the way he liked it. Coffee in his own individual press.

The food was definitely the best part of the B&B experience, in Malcolm's opinion. Four other people joined him and Kristin: two backpacker couples consisting of Canadians, an Australian and a New Zealander. All spoke English, and the conversation centered on the sightseeing they had lined up for the day. Just innocent small talk, nothing controversial to worry about.

Except Kristin. She kept her eyes on her plate and said little, acting strangely withdrawn.

Malcolm bit into a potato cake. Where had Kristin's naturally enthusiastic self gone? He'd become used to it, and frankly, he missed it this morning. He was caring more and more about her, no doubt about that. And her crazy zest for life seemed to be rubbing off on him, too.

He was pretty proud of the job he'd done with his research skills last night—and he'd loved watching Kristin dance around the room when she'd seen the result. Yeah, he'd taken some pride in the fact that, thanks to the clue he'd found, she was closer to pinpointing McGunnert Castle than she'd ever been. They both would be chasing her dream today, after all.

The woman to the left of Kristin asked her a question, and Kristin turned to answer her politely while barely picking at her egg.

"What do you think of the blood pudding?" Malcolm asked when she turned back, hoping to play on her love of all things Scottish, or at least, get a rise out of her. To the uninitiated, the round patty was often mistaken for a common sausage or salami. But the Scottish version really was made with blood.

"It's nice," Kristin murmured.

"Nice?" he repeated.

She nodded, lost in her own thoughts, not even looking at Malcolm.

And she'd been this way since...

Hell. He put down his fork. *This* had started with the clothes situation. Yes, he had slept in the buff because it was comfortable for him. But he'd slept in the chair and hadn't dared touch her. Plus, she hadn't seen anything of him—his lighthearted clowning that he was going to get up and fetch his own clothes hadn't been serious—she had to have known that.

But she was definitely upset. She was more squeamish that he would have expected, given her personality. Besides, Scots were known to be...

Well...

Like Robert Burns himself, sometimes his people had the reputation of being a bit earthy. Funny about it, too.

He glanced at their host, Alistair, wearing his daft apron as he ladled out a second helping of eggs, whistling the tune to a well-known bawdy song.

But Malcolm didn't have the chance to talk to Kristin alone again to ask her about it until they were shoehorned back inside their wee knee-scraper of a car.

As Eileen had promised, a man from the local garage had shown up to repair their faulty windshield wipers, and as a result, they were travel-worthy again. Kristin's suitcase was packed inside the boot—trunk—beneath the hatchback. His suit—jacket and trousers—was hanging from a hook in the backseat.

Eileen had sold him a pair of her son's left-behind jeans, a worn blue raincoat and a new pair of trainers, still in the box. The jeans were an inch too short and lower in the hips than Malcolm preferred, but it was better than wearing the damn business suit. If he'd known he would end up in the Highlands, he never would've left his office without rain gear and a change of clothes at the minimum.

Still, he started up the engine, happy to be on the road again with Kristin. He waited until they were down the hill and into new territory before he asked her.

"Kristin…?" he began.

She seemed to sense what he was going to say and intercepted him: "I'm tired, Malcolm."

He glanced at her, assessing her mood. She was closed inward. He needed to tread softly.

"I just wanted to say that I'm sorry about the thing with the clothes this morning."

"Don't be," she said, "it's not necessary."

To him it was.

She sighed at him. "Can't we just forget about it?" She looked out the window, a furrow in her brow. "I've decided that I need to consider the whole experience as just part of the adventure."

"The whole experience? You've…not much experience with men?"

"Oh, please, Malcolm, it's not like I haven't dated—I've even had a few serious relationships. I'm just…used to my life in Vermont, that's all. I'm not used to being here."

"I've lived both places, Kristy," he said quietly. "More time in your country than in mine. We're not that different, you know."

She pressed her lips together harder. She was hugging herself as if she was upset.

Something was bothering her. It was killing him not knowing what it was.

"I want us to be honest with each other," he said. "We didn't start off on the right foot, me being deceptive to you with my security name, but I'm hoping that can change."

"I'm fine, Malcolm." She showed her teeth in a smile to him, but it came out like a grimace. "I really am."

He nodded, letting the silence stretch out as the wee car coughed and sputtered its way up the hilly road.

She reached for a radio knob, but the whole kit was missing from the car; just a gaping hole remained, so she gave up and snatched her hand to her lap, where she twisted her fingers.

He said nothing. Just waited some more. After a time, she drummed her fingers on her knees. Outside, they passed more Highland cows and bleak Highland moors, but she'd seen herds and stretches of green rolling hills like this yesterday, and so the novelty had worn off. The questions had subsided.

But that was not the reason for her drumming.

Kristy glanced sideways at him. "I do like men, Malcolm, if that's what you're thinking about me."

He mashed his lips together, holding in a guffaw. "I was not thinking that, lass, but 'tis good to know."

"And I'm really not a prude."

"I should not have said that you were."

"It's just… We barely know each other," she said.

True. He drummed his own fingers on the steering wheel. "Ten questions. What's your favorite dessert?"

She paused, leaning her head back on the seat. "Um, anything with chocolate," she said tentatively.

"What day is your birthday?" he asked.

She smiled at him. "June eleventh."

"I'm January twenty-fourth."

She sat up straighter. "That was the day before Burns Night."

"Aye."

"So…you spent your birthday night in a hotel in Vermont?" she asked, curious again. "Did you even celebrate it?"

He laughed. "No. And that's exactly what my sister said to me when she called me that morning in your factory to chide me about it."

"Get out!" Kristin twisted in her seat and grinned at him. "*That's* what the phone call I overheard was about?"

"Aye." He nodded. "Being in Scotland, she was five hours ahead of us, and so waited to call, thinking she'd be teasing me about having a hangover. She clearly has the wrong idea about me, you see."

"Why?"

He shrugged. "Why? Well, I don't know. I haven't seen her much lately. Most of my life, I haven't lived in Scotland. I only moved back recently, and now I live in a flat in Edinburgh."

She nodded, digesting it all. He was still working on the assumption that he could convince her to move here.

But if he brought it up again too quickly and in the wrong way, he might push her further away. He didn't want to do that. He liked that they were getting closer.

After a time, Kristin opened the book of Ordinance maps Malcolm had borrowed from Alistair, having promised the B&B owner upon pain of death that he would mail it back to him on Monday, when he returned to the office.

He let the silence sit. When they came to a petrol station at a roundabout, Malcolm pulled the car over and went inside, buying some chocolate bars and two water bottles for the rest of their journey. When he came outside again, Kristin was stretching her legs and twisting her lower back to and fro. He knew how she felt.

He handed her one of the waters and a chocolate bar.

She stared at it, biting her lip in wonder.

No, Kristy, he thought. *I am not a man who forgets things, once learned.*

"Thank you," she said quietly. "You're a kind person at heart, Malcolm."

No, he wasn't. Depending upon the situation, he could be brutal.

But Kristin affected him. She made him relax his defenses and want to be kind to her.

"Are you feeling better now?" he asked.

"Yes." When they were back in the car, buckled in, she turned to him. "You wanted me to be honest with you. Well, okay, here it is. I'm not…looking for a hookup." She coughed, embarrassed. "I don't want you to get the wrong idea about me. When I first heard you talking on the phone that day in my office at Aura—especially when I overheard your accent—a hookup with you was actually the first thing I thought of."

Her cheeks turned pink, and she laughed self-consciously, tucking her hair behind her ear and looking away from him.

"But…that's really not my personality at heart. And I don't think that's yours, either," she said hurriedly, daring to glance at him. "Besides, we have this…conflict between us regarding Born in Vermont, and I don't want to fool myself into thinking that a hookup might be able to influence you into implementing my proposal, because that would cause all sorts of additional problems that would haunt me when I got home…."

She let her words trail away. Her hometown back in Vermont, the fate of the factory, was the big excuse she was leaning on, he saw that now.

But was that the whole story? There seemed to be something more he wasn't seeing, and that she wasn't showing him.

Playing ten questions with her, feeding her chocolate, hunting down her castle—none of those things were going to bring it out of her, whatever it was.

He reached over and adjusted the mirror. "For today, we're a team. We're castle-hunting. How about we leave it at that?"

"What's in it for you?" she asked.

Time spent with her. *Kristin* was in it for him, and the promise of more in the future, if he didn't screw it up. But he just smiled at her.

"Malcolm, today is also the day we talk about Born in Vermont. Ten o'clock. You know that."

"Yes," he said. "I promised I'd discuss it with you, and I will."

THE DETAILED SCHEMATICS on the Ordinance map didn't always translate into what they were seeing on the road ahead of them. And the internet directions made everything seem even more confused.

Malcolm scratched the back of his neck. Eileen had used

some kind of itchy detergent on his collar—she'd shrunk the shirt, too. In frustration, he peeled the damn thing off, wadded it and tossed it into the backseat, so he was left wearing his white T-shirt. Kristin didn't seem to notice.

"Go here," she told him for the tenth time that morning, turning around and pointing to a fork in the road behind them.

He swore they'd circled the same two mile radius at least three times, from different directions. He felt tired and cross. "You're not even looking at the map," he protested. He pulled over and turned it in her lap so he could see what she meant.

"Listen to me, I'm serious," she said, "my intuition is telling me that the ruins are *that* way." She pointed again.

"We've been down that road before."

"No, we haven't."

"Don't you remember that cow?" he asked.

"We've seen dozen of cows, but not him," she insisted. "He's a new one. See the weird twist on his right horn?"

Malcolm couldn't help it; he laughed.

"I am *deathly* serious," she said, but she was giggling, too.

"All right, I'll do what you say." *Always listen to the woman,* that's what Malcolm's father would counsel.

"I'm telling you," she repeated again. "I just have a feeling."

"I know, I know. Look, I'm turning the wheel for you," he grumbled.

A sheep farmer was headed toward them on the narrow single-car lane, and riding some kind of off-road vehicle that Malcolm doubted was properly licensed for the roadways. A sheepdog trotted along beside him.

Malcolm pulled over into a farmer's driveway, rolled down his window and beckoned the farmer to them.

"Aye?" the farmer said.

"We're looking for—"

The dog broke into a conniption fit of barking.

"Hold your wheesht!" the farmer said to the sheepdog. *Be silent,* it meant. The dog quieted down.

"We're looking for McGunnert Castle," Malcolm continued, using his "Scottish voice." "It may be a ruin, or even just a cellar."

"Aye," the farmer agreed in an equally heavy vernacular. "'Tis a small ruin."

Malcolm's heart sped up. "Is it nearby?"

"Of course it is," Kristin piped in. She pointed past the back window. "It's down that lane behind us, isn't it, sir?"

"Aye, 'tis," the farmer replied. "Another small way. Off to the right, in the trees. Where a grove of pine trees should not be."

At least Kristin didn't say, "I told you so."

Malcolm executed a turn, then did as he was bade. He was through second-guessing.

"There it is!" Kristin shouted. "There! There!"

He drove the short distance, and over the rolling green hill was a stand of pine trees, and beneath that, a shadow....

He braked to a stop, and before he could ask Kristin to wait for him, she opened the door and jumped out, running—her gait easy, hair bouncing in the wind, elbows gracefully pumping. Over the boggy field and into the distance.

Malcolm watched for a moment, feeling the anticipation himself. Still, by habit, he gazed around them. Other than himself and Kristin, he didn't see a soul.

He locked the vehicle and followed her across a green moor still damp and cool from a passing rain shower. His unfamiliar shoes sank into a few squishy spots. Overhead, a large raven cawed and called.

He passed into the stand of trees with wide-spreading branches and plenty of room to walk beneath and jogged to catch up to her.

"Malcolm, look!"

There were indeed ruins, and she stood atop a low wall, looking upward at a higher, broken wall. The section of wooded area had seemed to grow over the stacked stones, consuming them. True to what they'd been told earlier, the roof was missing from the structure.

"Do you see?" she said. "I was right, wasn't I?"

"Aye." He stood beside her. "But how do you know it's yours?"

"Because it said McGunnert Castle right on the map."

"True, and your grandmother was a McGunnert, but how do you know this was hers by right? Did she live here? Was this her village? Or did the letter-writer just pluck her name out of the U.S. phone directories, looking for a person to fool?"

"Here is the proof that she at least knew what this place was." Kristin stepped onto a low wall and began to climb the crumbling stones higher. "There, in the upper right corner. Do you see?"

Malcolm squinted. And just as he squinted, a shaft of sunlight glowed down upon a square in the stone, illuminating an inlaid carving of a bee in flight.

"Compare that to my grandmother's brooch." She unpinned it from her shirt and jumped down to show him the likeness.

Their heads bowed together. Malcolm inspected the bit of carved gold. "It's the same sketch of a bee."

Kristin nodded, her face shining. "This small ruin isn't the whole, fully functioning structure I was hoping for, but it's a castle nonetheless, and to me, it's beautiful. Even if somebody else owns it, which I'm sure is true, it doesn't matter. In my heart, this was my Nanny's, and now it's mine. I'm the one who believed in it."

Malcolm gazed up at the castle wall turret. An eerie feeling came over him, as if he was standing in a place almost…holy. Kristin was meant to be here, and he was meant to be here, too, in this spot, in this moment.

But moments were fleeting, and sadness passed over him. Unless he convinced her otherwise, Kristin would leave soon—gone from his life forever.

It's not as though he could ever go back to Vermont with her. He was the man who'd destroyed her town's livelihood. Kristin's beloved bee potions.

But for the next few minutes at least, they were still together. He bent to the spongy, squishy earth, and pocketed a polished black stone, loosened from the castle wall at some point. Silly and sentimental of him, maybe, but he would keep it on his desk as a reminder.

No. Who was he kidding? He tossed the stone away. "What are you going to do now?" he asked her.

Kristin pulled a small digital camera from her back pocket and walked around the low structure, clicking photos of the ruins from several angles. He leaned against a boulder, watching her. Without warning, she turned and took a quick photo of him.

Nobody took pictures of him. He didn't like it and normally didn't let people do it. "What's that for?" he asked.

"For me. Just me and nobody else." Her cheeks were flushed.

Oh, Kristy. Malcolm couldn't move.

"Will you…take a picture of me with my castle in the background?" she asked, her voice shaking.

Nodding, he accepted the camera from her and backed up.

Through the lens she was blinking at him, her hands

clasped. He paused, holding the image in the viewfinder, memorizing it for himself. With the dew and light hitting the castle wall behind her, she looked beautiful.

A pain in his chest, he snapped the photo.

Her smile faded. "It's sad, isn't it? We had a good adventure together."

"Yeah." He couldn't even pretend that he didn't know what she meant. It seemed as if neither one of them wanted the moment to end.

He took out his own phone and snapped another photo of her. This was for himself. Lowering his head, he turned the camera off. A fat raindrop landed on the screen. Another one hit his head.

"I'll get the umbrella," he said, handing Kristin her camera. "Wait here, under the trees."

By the time he got to the road, the rain was falling at a steady clip. The moor misted and fogged pretty quickly.

"I'm coming!" she called. "I don't mind the rain!"

He looked back and saw her running toward him as fast as she could, laughing.

What was it about her? She always lightened his mood. The woman was just what he needed in his life.

Together they raced to the car. Inside, he opened the glove box and pulled out the minibottle of whisky he'd brought from the B&B. He unscrewed the top and held it to her.

"You first," she said, smiling.

"To castles in Scotland." He tipped the bottle to his mouth and took a taste. It burned a warm trail down his throat. Wiping his lips with the back of his hand, he passed it to her.

With her eyes on his, she accepted the bottle. She leaned her head on the headrest. "To castles in Scotland," she whispered.

Her eyes never leaving his and, without wiping the bottle first, she put her mouth where his had just been and drank deeply.

He couldn't stop watching her.

She took the bottle away, wiping her mouth. Her eyes were bright and shining. And her lips…

Her mouth parted, and her gaze lowered to his lips.

"Malcolm…" Her voice was low and husky and struck just the right chord in him.

He lowered his head to kiss her at the same time that she moved toward him.

She kissed him so sweetly.

HE TASTED OF the whisky. The stubble on his cheek from not shaving this morning brushed her cheek, but Kristin would have it no other way. If she'd learned anything from her experience castle-hunting with him, it was to trust herself and do things on her terms. Kissing him just…felt right.

She made a little noise in her throat and leaned back on the seat again, just gazing into his brilliant blue eyes and his handsome face. He leaned his head against the seat back, too, gazing at her and saying nothing.

Apparently she was starved from not being kissed by him, ever since he'd left Vermont. Until now, she hadn't realized.

This time was different from Burns Night, though. This time she'd gone out on a limb with him, and he with her, just a little bit more. Baby steps, the way she needed it. Maybe the way they both needed it.

She tilted her head toward him for another kiss. "More…" she whispered to him. "Please. Just like the first time."

He understood. He didn't reach to touch her with his hands.

The warmth of his large body, close enough for her to be aware of his chest rising and falling, but not making contact with her—not at all—made her feel safe. He was sensual but controlled.

He kissed her again. Slowly, drinking her in. Both their heads leaning against the seat back, only their mouths touching.

The drum of the rain on the roof intensified her heartbeat. The scent of their wet, woolen clothes and the humidity in the air of their private hideaway increased her tenderness toward him.

The fact that Malcolm had stayed with her through all the highs and the lows of this crazy drive to find her castle just made her want him more.

She placed her palm flat on his chest, her fingertips brushing that sexy indent below his Adam's apple and down over his hot skin, to the edge of his shirt. Breaking all her own rules...

His head dropped back. "I have an idea," he said gruffly.

No. No ideas. "Kissing you just feels good," she said. "Can't we keep it at that?"

CHAPTER TEN

OH, KRISTY. MALCOLM reached up and caressed the edge of her smooth cheek with the back of his knuckle.

"I'm just…not looking to be part of a relationship right now," Kristin said, shivering involuntarily.

He stilled. Withdrew his hand from her. There *was* something there. He hadn't imagined it.

"We still have to discuss Born in Vermont, Malcolm," she said.

"I know. It's just about ten o'clock." And he'd promised to bring her back to Edinburgh, too. Somehow, though, his priorities had shifted. He wasn't keen on letting her go just yet.

"Why don't you take more time, another day or two here?" Maybe then he could figure her out more fully. "You're in Scotland now. From the day I met you, you were in love with this place. You wanted me to talk to you like this." He gave her his best brogue, really rolled those *r*'s. "To talk to you, love, in that Sean Connery voice."

"I'll make a recording and bring it home with me," she said, laughing.

"Ah, but it's not the same. Can a recording kiss you?"

"In my imagination, when I want it to. And when I don't want it to, it won't."

So, that was her secret. "I thought you were adventurous," he said.

She held up her camera. "I am. Look what I just did."

"Yes, and did you know that there are real, fully functioning castles that you haven't seen yet? And…have you seen a Scotsman dance the Highland Fling? Or been to a real Scottish pub and…eaten…haggis in Scotland? Plus, we have islands and firths and the Loch Ness monster…."

Now he was getting silly. "And golf and whisky tours and Burns readings."

Stupid and hokey, but it was working. Her lips were parted, and the spark was in her eyes.

Kristin laughed and shook her head. "*Why* are you tempting me? Do you think that will make Born in Vermont go away?"

"No." It was because when he kissed her, he wanted to keep going, to make love to her, even in this tiny, creaky, ridiculous little car. With the rain drumming on the roof and the smell of the wool from her damp shawl against his nose, the scent of that amazing shampoo she used in her hair.

Man, he would never get Aura out of his life.

"When I met you, you stayed so close to home, working in that closed-in factory, and you didn't seem happy about it, to tell the truth, but there you stayed anyway. And here, just now…" He glanced toward the castle ruins. "Running through the fields, you seemed happy. You were free."

"You're psychoanalyzing me again."

"Yes," Malcolm said. "And I'll stop now, because I hate it when people talk about me as if they know me, too."

Curious, she glanced at him. "Well…" She was wavering. "Where would I stay? If I did decide to extend my time, that is?"

He was thinking on the fly. None of this was planned out—which was a completely new way of living for him. He usually plotted his life ten steps ahead. But with Kristin's presence, everything had changed. He felt refreshed.

"In my flat in Edinburgh." He held up his hand before she could protest. "The flat next to mine is empty at the moment, and since I know the landlord, I could ask him—"

The shrill ringing of a phone sounded. His phone, with a very distinctive ringtone. Malcolm stilled.

"Who is it?" she asked.

"My uncle." He reached over and shut off the phone.

"You should take his call."

"No," he said. "I'm talking to you."

"It might be about Born in Vermont."

He stared at her. "Why would you think that?"

"Because he seemed very interested in what I had to say about it."

"You…had an extended conversation with him about Born in Vermont?"

"Of course. Why else would he have told me to work with *Malcolm*." She peered at him. "You see, I can psycho-analyze you, too. Did you know that your whole expression changed at his ringtone? You became fierce-looking. How do you work with him, anyway? What kind of arrange-ment do you two have?"

"Okay. I'll have to look into this on Monday," he sud-denly realized, groaning. "We don't know who owns the rights to Born in Vermont, us or Jay. That's the first thing my uncle is going to want to know. If it is us, are we leav-ing money on the table? If not, do we want to buy the rights from Jay? These are the things my uncle will be concerned about."

She bit her lip, as if debating whether to tell him some-thing.

"Kristy?" he asked. "What is it? Is there something you're not saying?"

Finally, she sighed. "Hear me out for a minute, okay?

Did Jay Astley get a large sum of money from Sage in the Aura buyout?"

"Ah…he sold his brands to us," Malcolm said. "And he's a consultant on our payroll, so he's been well compensated. I can't tell you details, but…why do you ask?"

"Because here's my problem, Malcolm. No matter who owns the formulations, I need to figure out something to do with the old Aura building so that we can keep people employed. You said you're putting it up for sale. Well, I originally came to Edinburgh because I wanted to talk with John Sage about that. Like I told you, Laura was working on a new product line she called Born in Vermont, something she felt was outside the branding of Aura. The hallmark is that everything about that product needs to be made in Vermont, because of the way it's branded. So, if it turns out that Sage owns it but isn't interested in the line, then I'll need you to offer it back to Jay." She looked at him hopefully.

First of all, Jay Astley was so much in debt, he wouldn't have the capital to buy much of anything from anyone. But he couldn't tell Kristin that. "Have you talked with him about your ideas?" he asked.

"Well, yes, but he thinks you own it. So my plan now is to explain Born in Vermont to Sage. That's why I came to Scotland in the first place."

"I see," he said.

"For the past twenty-four hours I've been playing by your rules, Malcolm. I've been very good—you have to admit." She smiled at him. "And since I've found my castle, I'm feeling even more empowered. I'm up for taking a few days beyond Monday to stay with you, but only if that stay includes working on the Born in Vermont proposal."

She shrugged. "And, if you ascertain that you don't own the brand…then I can go home and tell Jay that he has the rights to it. Besides, you promised not to pack up the plant equipment until I got home, and I can't imagine you'd go back on your word now."

She had him there. Between a rock and a hard place.

Malcolm crossed his arms, thinking it over. Listening to the rain patter on the roof.

There was still no way he could recommend that his family invest in Born in Vermont. But, if she stayed a few more days, then at least he'd have the opportunity to spend more time with her.

"Tell me more about this Edinburgh flat of yours," she prodded.

"You'd be staying with me, essentially," he said.

She nodded slowly. "I'm just having a hard time seeing you in a flat." She cocked her head and laughed, showing her dimples. "I expected something totally different for you."

"Like what?" he asked, curious.

"Well, you're so hyped up on security…" She tapped a finger to her lips. "I pictured you in a stone fortress of a Highland castle, very remote, with twenty-four-hour armed guards and security for the laird."

"You just described my family's home in Inverness," he said, shaking his head. Leave it to her and her romantic imagination.

Her eyes bugged out. "Your family lives in a castle in Inverness? Seriously?"

He grinned at her. "Glad to finally impress you."

"It's always been my dream to stay in a real castle in Scotland." A giddy smile spread over her face. "It's not a ruin, is it, Malcolm?"

"No, it's real. It's livable."

"Could I possibly stay there instead?" she begged. "I'll keep this little car nearby—" she patted the glove compartment "—and stay, just as a guest, at least until we go to your office on Monday to meet with your uncle."

"But my family lives there."

"So? You met my family. It's only fair."

"But…" His mouth moved, but he couldn't find the words. Emotion, dread and fear invaded him. "I'm very protective of them. I don't just…let…" He let his voice trail off.

"Don't you *ever* bring friends home?" she asked gently.

"No. Of course not. My sister lives there," he blurted. She tilted her head to him.

Great. "My sister is an artist," he explained. She was reclusive, but that was none of Kristin's business. "She paints landscapes. She just needs…peace and quiet."

Kristin's eyes widened further. She seemed even more interested than before.

"You don't want to stay there," he said hurriedly. "Trust me."

"Actually, I do want to. Very much. You intrigue me, Malcolm." She smiled at him. "And if I'm to assist you with making your recommendation to your uncle, and entice you with the Born in Vermont products, then what better way to do so than to get to know you better? The real you." She wrapped her tartan shawl around her shoulders and smiled at him harder.

The unfortunate part was, Malcolm could totally understand what she wanted, because he understood her. In addition to deciding to bewitch him over Born in Vermont—which would not happen—she also wanted to stay in his authentic Highland castle and use her treacherous death-trap car to zoom around the countryside, visiting the Culloden battlefield and driving along the lochs and seeking Loch Nessie—doing the things that tourists flocked to his home country to see.

"Yes," she mused, "I feel much more empowered, and I think this is what I prefer to do until Monday." She nodded. "In any event, Malcolm, here are our choices—I stay in your family's castle, or, you drop me off in Edinburgh and meet me in your office on Monday morning, like your uncle said."

He felt his teeth clenching. The helplessness rising in him.

But then an idea occurred to him. If Kristin stayed with him even a few days longer than Monday, then he could take her to the Byrne Glennie plant, just so she could see, firsthand, the possibilities for her future if she decided to stay and work with him.

Yes, she had already turned him down, but that was because she hadn't seen the facilities for herself. This time, he would drag her kicking and screaming if he had to.

"Is that a yes on the castle?" She smiled at him.

He noticed that the rain had stopped. There was a bittersweet feeling to him. He really did want her with him, for just a while longer.

But at what cost?

To bring her home to his family was to bring her awfully close to him. Closer than he'd ever let anyone. So close that there would be no turning back.

Isn't that what he'd wanted, though? What better way to understand Kristin than to show her the truth of his world.

"Okay, we'll give it a try, but just for a day or two," he agreed reluctantly.

She gifted him with a smile. "One more question. Could you also teach me to drive this left-handed stick-shift? It's a safety issue," she said, wide-eyed. "You never know when I might need the skill."

"Aye. Right," he said sarcastically.

Because Kristin would do what Kristin would do. And

he would rather be the man who showed her how to do it than be the man who left it for another to do the job.

No matter how much it hurt, because the other option would hurt worse.

THEY DROVE THREE hours to get to the MacDowall castle, over winding single-lane roads that skirted the edge of a loch with deep blue water.

The castle itself was approached by a long driveway. Gray stone walls and a turret stood in the middle of a green spongy field atop a hill with a long view of a valley.

It looked like a fairy tale to Kristin. And at the entrance to the drive there was even a guardhouse with a security person working inside. Kristin had been joking when she'd suggested it to Malcolm. But it was true.

She wrapped the soft cashmere McGunnert shawl around her and gazed at the serious Highlander sitting beside her, one hand guiding the steering wheel, the other settled on his lap.

Everything was going her way, at last. For the first time in a long time, Kristin felt hope. If she put her mind to it and believed in herself, then she could accomplish miracles. Already she'd achieved more than she'd dreamed she could.

She had traveled to Edinburgh. She had met with Mr. Sage. Together with Malcolm, she had found her grandmother's castle, and now, with him again, they would find a solution to keeping the factory open by implementing Born in Vermont.

Yes, there was something about first seeking out and then finding that castle—when nobody had believed in her—that gave her renewed confidence in herself. Kristin hadn't felt this free and capable since, well, she had left college and gone to New York.

She needed to keep this feeling going. The only complication was Malcolm. She had kissed him again, and there was no going back and erasing that from either of their minds.

She wriggled in her seat, sighing. She had enjoyed it immensely, though. That man just knew how to kiss her. He also understood that she didn't want a hookup or a relationship, so there was freedom there. He even knew she was leaving in a few days and had agreed to that.

The situation was perfectly safe, really. She didn't need to worry about getting in too deep with him.

She didn't *want* to get too deep. Through trial and error, she'd learned that about herself. As much as she might fantasize about finding a soul mate in her weaker moments, it just didn't seem to be in the stars for her.

What she needed to do was to focus on meeting his family and searching out and discovering anything that might help her strengthen her quest to convince Malcolm that Born in Vermont should be part of his company.

There had to be some way to help him relax his constant vigilance of the bottom line—it just couldn't be through a romantic interest in her, because that was the one commitment she could never give him. He lived in Scotland, and she lived in Vermont.

Malcolm drove the ugly white rental car up the crescent-shaped drive, stopping in front of the main doors to the castle. By now it was twilight, and the setting was utterly romantic. And utterly deserted.

Malcolm got out, took her suitcase from the hatchback and led the way inside.

He indicated that she walk before him. She'd expected a big, crumbling, drafty place, but instead, the main castle entry was nicely renovated and surprisingly homey and modern. An airy receiving room was before them, with comfortable-looking couches and a large stone fireplace, currently unlit.

"How long has your family lived here?" she asked.

"We moved in when I was young." Malcolm had turned gloomier and quieter. He picked up a coaster with a baronial shield on it, and then replaced it on the table.

"It's beautiful," she said, walking the length of the great mantelpiece, carved from mahogany. "Do people ever tour the castle? Is it open to the public?"

He laughed dryly. "No." At her questioning glance, he said, "It dates from the sixteen-hundreds, but was never open to the public. My uncle used to live here. He purchased it decades ago, but then moved to Edinburgh to be closer to our company headquarters."

Malcolm opened the telescoping handle on her luggage. "Come. I'll show you to a guest room upstairs." He didn't make eye contact with her, and she wasn't sure why. Curious, she followed him over beautiful tartan-patterned carpets and past a lush wall tapestry that looked like unicorns in a forest.

"Is anyone home this weekend?" she asked, hurrying after him up the beautiful, wide-curving stone staircase.

"Yes, my parents and my sister are here."

"Tell me about them. I'm looking forward to meeting your sister, in particular."

Malcolm stopped for a moment before leading her down one of the two hallways that joined at right angles. "Rhiannon is younger than me by two years," he said quietly, leading her down another tartan-patterned carpet. "Since she didn't greet us, I assume she's either walking the grounds or working in her studio."

"You said she was a painter?" Kristin remarked.

"Yes. She's really talented. Her oil landscapes sell to

collectors all over the world." He paused. "I have one hanging in my office in Edinburgh."

"I'd like to see it on Monday."

He glanced sharply at her. "We'll talk about it later."

One step at a time. She hadn't expected his total capitulation, but she would insist on traveling to the city with him. After work hours, maybe she could convince him to take her on a sightseeing drive, too. She would enjoy seeing all the landmarks.

"Sounds like a plan," she said.

Malcolm put his hand lightly on her shoulder and guided her to the bedroom she would be staying in. It was clean and welcoming with a beautifully ornate, carved four-poster bed. She felt very lucky.

"It looks like Paul made the room up for you," Malcolm remarked.

She'd heard Malcolm place a phone call while they'd been en route, but she hadn't known to whom. "Paul?" she asked.

"My parents' butler." Malcolm smiled slightly at her expression. "Don't get too excited. Paul is the only full-time staff they have. And he's been with us forever." He glanced at his watch. "He's probably serving my parents their afternoon tea now."

Sure enough, Malcolm led Kristin downstairs again, this time to the back of the castle through a dining area with windows overlooking a garden and a small yew maze. They came to another sitting room, where the butler, Paul—a middle-aged man dressed in a black suit and tie—poured tea in a china set and served it beside another fireplace.

Though the castle was pleasant and new inside, the traditions were apparently old. Seeming to brace himself, Malcolm formally introduced his mother and father to

Kristin. The four of them sat in comfortable wing chairs and sipped their tea from delicate teacups and saucers, which they placed in their laps. A far cry from dinner with her own boisterous family. Malcolm's parents were polite and formal, by Kristin's family's standards.

Malcolm introduced her as "my friend from America who I invited to stay with us this week."

That pleased Kristin. It also seemed to put his parents at ease, too. Malcolm's father nodded to her. To Kristin, he seemed pleasant, but aristocratic in bearing. For a Saturday evening, presumably relaxing at home, he was dressed up, wearing wool pants, a collared shirt and a blue V-neck sweater the same color as his and Malcolm's eyes.

Once tea was poured, he idly scratched his dog's ears and chatted with Kristin about the history of the castle. He also talked to Malcolm about his gardening plans for the spring.

His mother kept smiling at Malcolm as if she wanted to get him alone. Otherwise, she was mildly pleasant to Kristin. Not overly familiar and not too distant, either. Just right.

Kristin breathed a huge sigh of relief. She didn't want anyone to get their expectations up—or down—about her and Malcolm. As far as the world was concerned, they were just friends. Yes, she would feel better, perhaps, if he made clear that they were work colleagues, but again, it was something she could work on.

After tea, Malcolm escorted Kristin on a tour of the rest of the castle. There were three levels, ranging from a basement with a rustic kitchen, to the ground floor with the common rooms, to the second floor with eight bedrooms.

She was curious, but she didn't ask Malcolm which bedroom was his, and he didn't volunteer the information, either.

It would be strange, she mused, being separated from him, after last evening's B&B bedroom share. And it was even odder that she didn't feel ecstatic about it.

Just one full day with him, and somehow, she now felt comfortable. Attached, as half of a pair, as strange as that seemed.

She glanced up at Malcolm's gruff expression, his hooded eyes. It was the same mask he'd worn throughout their tea with his parents. What had happened to the guy who had been so passionately kissing her, tempting her to stay longer in Scotland only a few hours ago?

"So, when can I meet your sister?" she asked brightly. She would like an ally, if she could find one. Maybe Kristin could show Malcolm's sister some of the Born in Vermont samples she'd brought with her in her suitcase. Maybe she would like the great smell and feel of Laura's creations, too?

Barring that, perhaps Kristin could persuade Rhiannon to be friends with her. Kristin would love someone to show her around and maybe give her some insight into Malcolm.

"I don't know where she is," he said.

"Hello," a soft voice said behind them on the stair landing.

They both turned.

"Er, Kristin, this is my sister, Rhiannon. Rhiannon, this is Kristin Hart." Malcolm's voice was clipped and he sounded off balance.

His sister was the opposite of what Kristin had expected.

Rhiannon wore trendy jeans and a pretty, pale purple blouse with tight-fitting sleeves, a loose neck with strings, and a flowing, peasant-style bottom. It gave her a bohemian look, and it conflicted with everything Malcolm had told her about Rhiannon on the drive here, warning Kristin about her shyness and her reclusiveness.

Kristin smiled at his younger sister. "Hello. It's nice to meet you."

Rhiannon ignored Kristin's outstretched hand and, instead, leaned in to give Kristin a hug. In a lilting, rolling accent she said, "So, you must be my brother's fiancée!"

Kristin gasped. "No!" She looked helplessly over Rhiannon's shoulder at Malcolm.

A muscle ticked in his jaw. Without amusement, he answered his sister. "Kristin is a friend."

Rhiannon cocked her head, a furrow in her brow. "Sorry, I just assumed."

"Why?" Kristin asked, genuinely curious.

Rhiannon smiled sheepishly at Malcolm. "Cousin Gerry's wedding is next weekend. I thought you were home for it."

Malcolm groaned and closed his eyes. "Damn it, I completely forgot."

Rhiannon turned to Kristin. "I apologize for my assumption, Kristin. But you see, my brother once told me that unless I saw him bring a woman to a family wedding, not to expect him to be getting married soon himself."

What should she say to that? "Well, that explains that. So, ah, do you have many cousins?" she politely asked, sidestepping the controversy.

"Mum has four brothers. All except Uncle John have kids." Rhiannon put her hands in her pockets. "So, yes, we do have a lot of cousins." She rolled her eyes. "Ask Malcolm to tell you about it sometime."

"I have four brothers, too," Kristin said.

Rhiannon smiled. "Then you and Mum have lots to talk about."

Kristin smiled back at Malcolm's sister. Kristin liked her already.

"Let's go take a walk on the grounds." Malcolm put his hand lightly on the small of Kristin's back and steered her toward the door.

His gesture seemed possessive, but not too much so. He kept his hand resting against her, and even through her thick sweater Kristin felt his touch. Admittedly it was nice, but…he was distracting her from what she was really interested in seeing. There seemed to be more to Malcolm's private life than she would've guessed, and it might be helpful to find out more about what exactly that was.

Kristin looked back at Rhiannon, only to find Rhiannon staring at her, too.

"Would you like to join us?" Kristin called to Rhiannon.

"Not now," Malcolm murmured.

"Tomorrow morning would be brilliant," Rhiannon replied. "Malcolm," she said to her brother, "*will* you be staying for the wedding?"

"Er…"

"Staying for the wedding sounds lovely," Kristin said breezily.

Malcolm raised his brows at her.

"Why not? My plane ticket home to Boston isn't for two more weeks. I'll just let Arlene know I won't be joining them when they go to England."

"Boston, did you say?" Rhiannon glanced to Malcolm. "Malcolm studied in Boston."

"Yes," Kristin replied. "I live nearby, in Vermont. It's a three-hour drive from Logan airport."

"And you traveled to Scotland by yourself?" Rhiannon looked surprised. Or impressed, Kristin couldn't tell.

"That's enough," Malcolm hissed before Kristin could answer his sister. He seemed distinctly uncomfortable, and Kristin did enjoy turning the tables on him for a change. It was amusing to cause him the same discomfort he'd caused her in her hometown. Of course, she wasn't overly serious about any of it. It was just that seeing him flustered also made him seem not quite so composed, with his emotions locked away. This way, he was more accessible. More human.

Teasing him, she patted his cheek. Such a masculine face he had. He hadn't shaved in the day and a half she'd been with him in the wilds of Scotland, and the dark stubble made him look that much more brooding and dangerous.

Not that she was frightened. In the short time she'd seen him interacting with his family, she'd become certain of two things—he was a good son and a caring brother. Add that to the fact that he was a fantastic kisser…and Kristin had to admit that Malcolm was becoming more and more attractive. She'd have to tread very carefully if she didn't want to fall for him.

His response to her pat on the cheek was to clamp his jaw tight and grind his teeth. He steered her in a more determined fashion away from his sister and down the stairs.

They passed the kitchen on the way out to the back door. Paul, the butler, stuck out his head. "Mr. MacDowall, sir, would you like a picnic box delivered on the grounds?"

"Really?" Kristin asked Paul. "You'll do that? Yes, please! The tea was very nice, but I was polite and didn't really eat much. I'd *love* to try those little ham sandwiches and some of those—"

"Send it," Malcolm growled to the butler.

"Very good, sir. I'll find you within…" Paul glanced at his watch. "The back of six, it looks like."

Malcolm nodded and grabbed a blanket and an umbrella from a cubbyhole in the coatroom. Holding Kristin's hand, he pulled her far enough away from the castle that they couldn't see the turret beyond the curve of the gentle slope they descended.

A faint pathway was visible in the pale green moor, and Malcolm followed it like a man who knew where he was going.

When they came to a dry glen protected by an overhang, and with an incredible view of the valley stretched before them, Malcolm spread the blanket. "After you," he said.

She plopped down, and he sat beside her, tearing his hand through his hair.

"Look, I'm sorry, Kristy. I just don't want to get Rhiannon's hopes up that you'll be staying around permanently if it's not going to happen."

"Well, I'm sorry, too. I was just having a bit of fun with you. Don't you think it's deserved?"

He leaned back on one elbow. "Wedding guest or no, it's an impossible situation. Rhiannon will get crushed if you get close to her and then leave. She's…different from most people, Kristin. She's very sensitive. I want to spare her any hurt."

"Okay. I can understand that." Kristin crossed her legs and watched two majestic hawks fly past in the distance. "I'll be clear to her that I'm not looking for anything romantic from you—temporary or long-term. I'll let her know that I'm here for Born in Vermont."

He nodded curtly. "If you don't mind, I'd like us to call a truce on it. A time-out with the Born in Vermont question, at least until Monday." He gazed at her. "I'll drive you to Edinburgh then. It'll take us three hours down, three hours back, but for a good part of it, we'll be on a fast, safe, dual-lane carriageway. Then, when I'm in the office, you can tour the Royal Mile and the museums. I'll find a top-notch guide to escort you, if you want, and we'll meet for lunch at midday."

"I'm here for Born in Vermont, not to sightsee, Malcolm," she said gently. "I will go to Edinburgh with you, but we need to discuss the particulars about Born in Vermont sometime, you know."

"I know. Lunch on Monday is what I prefer. After I've reviewed the confidential contract we signed with Jay Astley, then I'll have a better idea of how you and I should go forward." He closed his eyes and sighed. "With your permission, I'll bring my uncle to lunch with us."

Her heart beat faster. "You'll take me to a lunch meeting with your uncle?"

"Aye."

That, and the fact that Malcolm was pledging to review the contracts, meant that he was taking her idea seriously. She kicked off her boots, wiggled her toes and stretched out her legs. "That sounds excellent to me."

"Thought you would like that," he said wryly. But he leaned back on his elbows and stretched out his legs, too. He pulled out a whisky flask from his jacket pocket. "You must think I'm a lush. I'm not. It just seems appropriate at the moment."

He tipped back the flask and downed a sip. "Cheers." He passed it to her.

She drank a tiny amount, feeling herself getting used to the comfortable, peaty warmth that the real Scottish whisky gave her. "Cheers," she agreed. And to think that she'd thought she hadn't liked Scotch. Now, visiting the northern country with all its dampness, she understood the appeal of the blood-warming fire.

She passed his flask back, and noticed that the skin on his hands was rough...*hmm*. Feeling daring, she found the small pot of hand cream she kept in her pocket and unscrewed the lid. "May I?" she asked him, motioning to his hands. "It's made from shea butter and honey, mostly, with some essential oils mixed in. Smell it." She held it up to his nose.

He breathed in. "Nice."

"Do you mind if I rub it on your hands?"

His brow furrowed, but he held out his hands to her, palms down.

She took one of his hands. She had meant to begin gently teaching him about Born in Vermont, one small step at a time, but she'd miscalculated. Holding Malcolm's hand in hers and rubbing in the rich, sensuous cream was much more intimate than she'd expected.

His eyes hooded, he watched her. She could barely breathe. His hands were so much larger than hers. Rough. Those long fingers with short nails, bitten to the quick.

She swallowed and tried to think of Laura. Mimic the way that Laura spoke—the professional, enthusiastic cadence she employed.

"This…is my favorite healing cure." Kristin's voice sounded high; she was failing, utterly, getting distracted by the feel of his skin. She took Malcolm's other hand. "I know you don't want to talk about it," she said in a rush, "but at home in the plant, when I'd be having a bad day, the smell of the bees' products always made me feel better."

He put his hand to his nose. "I smell like you now."

"Pardon?"

"This cream, Kristy." He looked at her with those direct, clear blue eyes. "It reminds me of you."

"Oh." She was embarrassed. She put her palms to her cheeks; they felt warm.

Sighing, he leaned all the way back on the plaid wool blanket. Crossed his arms beneath his head and stared at the sky.

"The sweetest hours I ever spent," he murmured.

"That's from the Robert Burns poem, isn't it?"

He turned his head and looked at her. It reminded her of his body position just before the kiss they'd shared earlier, and for a moment, her mouth went dry.

But he did not move toward her; he stayed where he was, his hands behind his head, smiling slightly, his thoughts seeming far away. "This was my favorite spot when I was a lad."

"It seems like a great place to grow up."

He turned his head and looked back at the clouds. "Aye."

She rolled onto her stomach and picked a small purple flower blooming just beyond their blanket fringe. "Cousin Gerry is lucky to be getting married here."

Malcolm closed his eyes and smiled. "Gerry is an *idjit*."

She laughed. "How many cousins do you have?"

"On my mother's side?" He opened his eyes and appeared to be counting silently. "Dunno. Ten, maybe. Twelve?" He closed his eyes again. "My Uncle John is the only bachelor of all the siblings. He's the only one who didn't have any kids."

She rolled the purple flower between her fingers. "So… are you the heir apparent to John Sage's empire?"

He grunted. "You know how to ruin a Saturday evening, lass."

"I'm just trying to understand you."

He opened one eye. "Very possibly, but none of us knows for sure who will inherit it. One of my cousins is studying international finance in New York City. Much more ambitious than I am."

"Is he after your position as heir apparent?"

"*She*. She is."

"Who's winning, you or she?"

"I don't know. Does it really matter anyway? We're all in this together, Kristy. We live together as a family, or we die alone." He sat up and took a sip of whisky.

Was that bitterness or matter-of-factness, she wondered. She couldn't help asking him the question that was most on her mind. "Were you kidnapped and held for ransom because you are John Sage's nephew?" she asked bluntly.

He looked at her, his face stony. "Aye."

She hugged herself, arms around her knees. "What happened, Malcolm?"

He shook his head, laughing slightly. "I forgot you didn't know. I'm not used to that."

"Why not?"

He snorted. "They made a bloody television drama about it. Made every softhearted woman in the U.K. cry. They used a wee, pathetic boy actor. Changed the names and the order of things, of course, because it wasn't supposed to be me. The lawyers got involved, but still, everybody knew who it was based on."

"So…is that why you went to boarding school and college in the U.S.?"

"Yes. What choice did they have but to send me away? Safety reasons."

"Were you…hurt?"

He nodded. Took a drink from his flask. Didn't look at her.

"Rhiannon must have been devastated," she said.

Again, no response. Just a tightening of his jaw.

Poor Rhiannon. She must have been worried sick. No wonder she was sensitive to Malcolm's troubles.

"Did your uncle…pay the ransom?" she asked gently.

Malcolm focused his efforts on screwing the cap back on to the flask. "The family didn't have all that much money back then," he said carefully. "But now, we do, Kristy." He gazed at her. "And we will continue to, as long as I have breath in my body."

No money-losing deals, that's what he was telling her.

She put her forehead to her knees. There was a message in there for her. And suddenly, she understood him so much better.

She shivered, wiping the dampness in her eyes onto her jeans, hiding it from him. *Poor Malcolm. So young...* She hoped he didn't take it wrong, her showing him the Born in Vermont cream. She'd meant no disrespect.

There were so many more questions she could ask him, but it was just...sad. What good was it dwelling on past pain—and from his face just now, there'd been more than he wanted to tell her about. She should just cheer him up and be grateful for the "sweetest hours" on a rare, not too cold, sunny spring day in the Highlands.

It wasn't until they were walking back to the castle that, out of nowhere, what Malcolm had said hit her.

John Sage had not paid his nephew's ransom.

That meant that Malcolm had been with the kidnappers longer than he should have been.

CHAPTER ELEVEN

ON MONDAY MORNING, Malcolm picked through his nearly empty closet—a futile attempt. He didn't have many clothes up here at the castle, and he would just have to stop at his Edinburgh flat and fill up a suitcase before he and Kristin returned to Inverness this afternoon.

Malcolm groaned and tossed a jacket and trousers onto the bed. He was just so damned exhausted. Not even a hot shower had been able to wake him up. He stood in his dimly lit bedroom rubbing his face. How to solve the problem of Kristin's presence in his life?

Outside, it was dark; the sun hadn't risen. He and Kristin had a three-hour drive ahead of them, and though Malcolm had traveled the route often, it wasn't something he was looking forward to repeating again tomorrow. Yet for as long as Kristin stayed in the castle with him, he would be pleased, so he would have to speak with his uncle today about working remotely from his parents' home, just to make life easier.

On one level, the weekend with Kristin had been the best weekend Malcolm had spent in ages. Saturday night, they'd gone out to a small, intimate Italian restaurant by the river in Inverness for dinner, then to a local pub that friends of his parents owned, to listen to live music. Sunday had been bright and unseasonably warm, so they'd taken a long walk in the hills with Rhiannon.

Simply put, Kristin had a way of lightening his burdens.

She made Rhiannon smile, too, more than he'd seen in quite a while. Malcolm should be happier about it.

On the surface, everything was great, and it even seemed that Kristin and Rhiannon had much in common. The only problem was that it was marred by the nagging feeling that he needed to be more vigilant about letting Kristin get too close to them—part of the ongoing damage control over his decision to bring Kristin into the castle in the first place.

Ironic. The real problem was that he couldn't protect both Kristin *and* Rhiannon. At some point, Kristin would ask more questions about Rhiannon, and then something would have to give. Between the two women, Kristin was the stronger, and Rhiannon was by far the more vulnerable. His sister had rarely left their parents' property in twenty-some years. He could tell Kristin why, of course, but...

He wanted to. He wanted to be able to trust her completely.

That was the crux of the matter: how could he trust someone who might just up and fly out of their lives at any minute?

Malcolm knew the only reason Kristin was still with him—he didn't fool himself into thinking it was for his wit or his fine looks. No, it was for her Born in Vermont scheme.

When and if Kristin got the go-ahead from him, she would be gone from Scotland in a heartbeat. And he really was getting worried about himself—he was caring for her so rapidly that if she were inclined, she could use that power to charm him into a different recommendation toward Born in Vermont than was best for his family's business.

He could not let that happen. It was time for him to make plans to push harder with her.

Malcolm tossed his wet towel on the tiled bathroom floor and quickly got dressed. First, he needed to scope out the situation with Born in Vermont and figure out a plan before his uncle caught wind of it. There were schemes of his own he was still working on, and once in the office today, he could hopefully finalize them and work out a resolution that would be best for all of them.

WHEN KRISTIN ARRIVED downstairs in the castle breakfast room, Rhiannon was sitting with Paul in chairs facing the window. Both were sipping tea and watching a family of birds outside, though dawn had barely broken.

Rhiannon turned when she heard Kristin's footsteps. "Good morning." Rhiannon patted the chair beside her. "What would you like for breakfast, Kristy?"

"Just a quick bowl of cereal for me, please." Kristin set her purse and her work notebook on the table beside Malcolm's sister. Without asking, Paul reached over and poured her a cup of coffee and added a tiny bit of milk to the top. He had remembered her tastes perfectly. Wouldn't she love to bring him back with her to Vermont when her trip was over?

Kristin poured some cornflakes into an empty bowl. "Would you like to drive with Malcolm and me to Edinburgh this morning?" she asked Rhiannon.

"No, thank you." Rhiannon sipped from her tea and went back to gazing at the yellow finches outdoors.

Kristin waited, but Rhiannon didn't add anything more.

"Your Uncle John is joining us for lunch," Kristin remarked. "Why don't you come with us to the office? It could be fun."

"That sounds lovely," Rhiannon murmured. "But no, thank you."

Kristin drank her coffee, sighing happily as the much-needed caffeine seeped into her bloodstream. "Would you like me to pick you up anything in Edinburgh?"

Rhiannon shook her head. "I have a painting I want to finish today. My business manager is coming up from London tomorrow, and I'm making a final push before he arrives."

"That sounds exciting."

Rhiannon looked away from the window and smiled at Kristin. "Kristin, would you bring me back some photos from Edinburgh?" she asked. "I do love to see photos."

"Of course." Kristin nodded and dug into her cereal. She glanced up just as Malcolm strode into the room. Immediately, her heart drummed a bit faster.

He looked handsome, as always. Stern and serious, especially in his business clothes, but she was getting used to that in him. And when he saw her, his face brightened, and he broke out into that broad smile that just dazzled her.

She put down her spoon. Her hand unconsciously fluttered to her chest.

Malcolm winked covertly at her, but he bent over and kissed Rhiannon on the cheek. "Good morning, ladies." He waved away Paul's offer of breakfast, and instead, grabbed a pastry and filled a ceramic travel mug with black coffee.

"Are you ready, Kristin?" he asked, in that deep Scottish burr that always seemed to echo so deeply in her bones.

Her head dropped back, and she gazed into his eyes, sparkling more than they had a right to so early in the morning.

"I'm ready," she squeaked.

His knowing stare tugged at something inside her. He was freshly shaven, and a damp lock of hair fell over her brow. "Let's go, then. If we're to beat Edinburgh rush-hour traffic, then we're late already."

"Of course." She stood abruptly, reaching for her things.

When she glanced back, she caught Rhiannon observing them, a secret smile on her face.

"Go on ahead," Kristin said to Malcolm. He had tucked the pastry in his mouth as he used one hand to rummage through a board on the wall containing hooks that held sets of keys. His other hand gripped the mug of coffee. "I'll be right behind you in a moment," she said to him.

She turned to Rhiannon and whispered, "Will you be okay here today?" There was something about Rhiannon that drew Kristin into wanting to befriend her. In the two days she'd known Malcolm's sister, Kristin had sensed a gentleness and serenity in her that was greatly appealing.

"Oh, yes," Rhiannon murmured. "As long as the rain holds off, I'll do some walking, then I'll shower and settle in to paint."

That sounded like heaven, actually. Kristin sifted through her purse and pulled out a small plastic bottle. "This is shampoo that a lady from home made for me. If you decide to try it, I'm interested in hearing what you think. But don't tell Malcolm, because he thinks I'm trying to talk him into doing something that he doesn't want to do. And that's not my intent at all."

With a questioning look, Rhiannon opened the bottle and held it to her nose. A smile came over her face. "It's lovely."

Kristin nodded. "A dear friend of mine formulated it. It's all organic and hypoallergenic. Oh, and here—there's a conditioner that goes with it, too."

"Your friend is very talented."

"I know. She was. She passed away last autumn. I miss her so much."

"I'm sorry." Rhiannon's eyes, so like Malcolm's, gazed hauntingly at Kristin. "Are you asking Malcolm to invest in her company? Is that why you're here?"

"No," Kristin said firmly. "But I am asking him for his help in figuring out a way to keep my hometown plant open. That's what our mission today is, actually."

"And then you'll return home once everything is settled?"

"Yes, I suppose that's the plan. I live in Vermont, after all—it's my home." Kristin looked out at the birds. "Like this is your home."

"Of course." Rhiannon nodded. "I understand."

But Rhiannon's gaze followed Kristin as she waved at her and then dashed outside toward the driveway.

A damp, bone-chilling wind curled around her, and Kristin pulled the cashmere McGunnert shawl tighter around the shoulders and collar of her coat.

She didn't know why she'd just shared that confession with Rhiannon back in the house, except, somehow, she didn't want to lie to Rhiannon, or for her to get the wrong impression of Kristin's motivations with her brother. Besides, she'd promised Malcolm she'd be clear with his sister. She would not mislead her, or him.

And lately, Malcolm had been making it easier for Kristin to trust his intentions, too....

A gleaming silver sedan pulled up before her, the tires crunching over the gravel. Kristin jerked awake. This vehicle was much nicer than her rental, which Malcolm had wanted to have returned to Edinburgh, but she wasn't willing to give up her wheels—though she definitely wouldn't argue about riding in this car today. The engine idling, Malcolm leaned over and opened the door for her.

She jumped in, feeling bubbly and excited. She loved long drives. She had high hopes for their meeting with Malcolm's uncle and was anxious to discover if Sage owned the rights to Born in Vermont. If they did, that meant more time with Malcolm. More time to come up with a presentation to convince his uncle that the new venture was worthwhile for Sage.

The car smelled new. It was beautiful inside, spacious and roomy with leather seats and a polished wood dashboard. Her bottom felt warm, and she realized there was an electric seat warmer. She sighed, and sank deeper into the comfort.

"*This* is more like it," Malcolm said. "Are you ready to road-trip in style?"

"Aye," she agreed. "Floor it, driver."

THE DRIVE FROM Inverness to Edinburgh went relatively quickly—nothing like Friday's slow crawl through mountains and narrow, twisting lanes. In comparison to what Kristin was used to, this journey felt similar to the scenic ride from rural mountains in New Hampshire down to a sparkling, flatlander city on the coast. Portsmouth, say, or maybe even Boston.

She made the mistake of mentioning that to Malcolm.

"So," he said, as they waited at a roundabout's traffic light inside the Edinburgh city limits, "you do take trips away from home? You're not a recluse to your hometown?"

"Of course not," she said, wondering if she should feel insulted. "Why would you say that?"

He gave her a lazy grin, one hand on the top of the steering wheel, his thumb tapping to music on the satellite radio. "No reason."

"Do you think I'm like Rhiannon that way?"

A frown crossed his handsome face. "No." He glanced at her. "I was just noticing that your world in Vermont is safe for you. And yet, you crave adventure. It oozes from you. You can't hide it."

She laughed. "Maybe so, but…" She watched a white seabird fly past. Like a New Hampshire seagull, but smaller. "Well, maybe I am having a good time here despite everything else," she mused.

"That's good." The grin split his face. "Kristy, I would love to spend the morning with you—I would even invite you into the office with me, but it's illegal for me to break the nondisclosures. I know you want to be there, but…can you understand, and trust me with this step in the process?"

"Trust you?" she repeated dumbly.

"I need to meet with our lawyers first, but when I called them this morning, they reminded me that it's confidential. No one from outside the original agreements can be there while we review the contracts. I'm sorry, but I'll have more news for you at lunch."

"But didn't your uncle say that I should meet with you today?"

"He did. But he wants me to look into this first. And I will invite him to lunch with us."

Disappointment settling over her, she tried to think it through. What Malcolm said did have merit. "All right," she said grudgingly. "I'll give you the benefit of the doubt. But I warn you, I'd better meet you and your uncle at noon."

"You will." He gave her a relieved smile. "Until then I'll drop you off as close to Edinburgh Castle as I can get. Then we'll meet at lunch." He leaned over and opened the glove box, pulling out a cell phone. "I almost forgot. I got this for you. My number is programmed inside, as is my parents' number."

She took it from him, their fingers brushing, and held it to her heart, genuinely touched.

"Thank you, Malcolm." Maybe she could trust him to give Born in Vermont a fair consideration without her there to observe. "And thank you for looking into the Born in Vermont legalities for me. I do appreciate it."

His sad smile stayed with her. "I'll do what I can for you, Kristy. And you'll promise to keep an open mind with me. Aye?"

"Aye," she whispered.

The tenderness of his endearment for her stayed with Kristin for the next three hours. Three hours of a sunny, blue-sky morning at Edinburgh Castle, the great stone fortress on the rock that towered over the city.

Built on top of an extinct volcano, Kristin learned, the castle was filled with history. She spent the morning climbing battlements, peering inside chapels, visiting Queen Mary's bedroom and gawking at the crown jewels of Scotland.

But at the appointed time she was more than ready to meet Malcolm. She headed down the cobblestone, pedestrian-only street on the hillside—the famous Royal Mile—and into the doors of the pub that Malcolm had chosen for their lunch meeting.

He'd arrived before she did, and when she walked past the traditional brass bar with mirrors and stools inside the bustling, wood-paneled restaurant, Malcolm was already there. He immediately saw her, and he stood and waved her over.

With a calm expression, he passed her a luncheon menu. "How was your morning, Kristy?" He took her coat from her and hung it on a hook.

Her heart pounding, she ran her hand through her hair, raking the tangles she'd gotten from rushing along the windy streets to meet him on time.

"Edinburgh was great," she gushed. "I haven't had a vacation day like this in… I don't remember how long."

She took a breath. "But that's not the big reason we're

here, is it?" She peered at Malcolm, trying to gauge how the morning had gone, but couldn't tell from his expression if it had been favorable for her or not. "Tell me, because I'm on pins and needles. What happened with the lawyers?" She glanced around. "And where is your uncle? I thought he was meeting us."

Malcolm cleared his throat. "Well, we spent the early part of the morning meeting with our lawyers, attempting to gain an understanding of the contract terms regarding any new brands not covered under the original agreement."

"And?"

He tapped on the plastic menu, idly curling the corner of it with his finger. "And they're still looking into it."

Oh, no. Malcolm looked stern, not at all happy. She leaned forward. "What's wrong?"

"Nothing's wrong, but my uncle wants to fully understand the scope of this new development," he continued carefully. "He instructed that he doesn't want to let the Born in Vermont brand go back to Astley for nothing, *if* it turns out that we own it. My uncle might even prefer that we develop the product line ourselves. Either way, he requested to see more detailed financials from me on the projected numbers."

"That's…good news," she said. "Right?"

Malcolm's expression was carefully bland—she would hate to be on the other side of a negotiation with Malcolm. He had a great poker face.

"It'll take some work on my part," he said. "But essentially that's why he declined to attend lunch with us today—there are still too many unknowns with the proposal, and he wants us to work them out together first."

He paused, frowning. "Bottom line, can you stay a few days longer? I know you joked about it earlier, but it's serious now. He really does want to see something on Friday from us."

Her heart sped up. "He asked for a presentation?" This was great news. "Absolutely! You know that I can."

He nodded. "I can work from home—my family castle, that is. No need to travel to the office again."

"So…do you think I should stay at the castle, too?"

"Yes, you can stay at my parents' castle with me. And Rhiannon likes you, so it will be nice for her," he said finally.

Kristin couldn't tell for sure, but he seemed conflicted over that statement.

Malcolm reached for the seat beside him and, gazing down at it, carefully took an envelope he'd lain there, and then placed it on the polished wooden table before her.

For a moment there was silence between them until Kristin recognized the envelope. "That's…the copy of the report I gave your uncle last Friday."

Malcolm's lips were pressed together.

"Oh. You didn't know I'd given it to him, too…. I meant to tell you," she said. "Honestly, in the excitement, I just plain forgot."

He nodded tersely. "That's what I'd hoped, when my uncle showed it to me."

"Did that…cause problems for you?"

He took in a breath, as if hesitating to say so. Finally, he gazed into her eyes. She saw hurt there.

"I'm sorry," she said.

"I didn't say anything, Kristy. You don't know what you're sorry for."

"I can guess, though. I work in a corporation, too, Malcolm. Or at least, I used to." She ran her fingers along the edge of the binder. "My guess is that my report made you look bad. Like you weren't on top of the Aura integration the way that your uncle expects you to be."

He leaned back in his chair. He genuinely looked stunned.

"Am I right?" she asked.

He smiled slightly. "Yes."

"Why are you so surprised?"

"You." He shook his head, the grin spreading over his face. "You know more about business relations than you give yourself credit for. You constantly amaze me."

The person behind Malcolm attempted to scrape his chair back, and Malcolm had to stand so the man could exit. While Malcolm was standing, Kristin took the advantage to impulsively jump to her feet and bracket his head in her hands.

She firmly kissed him on the mouth.

His hands rested at her waist. "What was that for?" he murmured against her ear.

"You," she whispered, leaning her cheek against his scratchy cheek. "This is what I think about you."

And then she turned her head and kissed him again. He slashed his mouth over hers and kissed her more deeply. His fingers fanned across her lower back, and she felt sweet warmth spread through her. She sighed audibly and snuggled her hips closer to his body.

His tongue lightly swept the seam of her lips, a delicious invitation, and she opened her mouth to his, letting her tongue mingle with his. It felt amazing, even though she was fully aware that she was making out with him in public.

But inexplicably, she wasn't worried about that hurting their presentation. Malcolm was on her side. All the noise and the bustle seemed to fade into the background, until all that was left was her and Malcolm. She let her hands drift up, over his collar and feather through his hair. He smelled so good. And he tasted even better.

For a moment, she felt heavy with an ache, with a need for him....

"Are you ready to order?" A harried waitress interrupted them, a pen and a writing pad in hand.

Kristin jumped back, her hand instinctively covering her mouth.

Malcolm gripped her other hand in his, smoothly anchoring her beside him. "Do you mind if I order for you, Kristin?" he calmly asked her.

"I... No," she said to him. Truthfully, she hadn't even had a chance to look at the menu. "You go ahead, please. I trust you completely."

CHAPTER TWELVE

HE WAS FALLING head over heels in love with her, faster and harder than he'd expected. As if sucked into an ocean undertow that he had no control over, he had no choice but to go along, hoping for the best.

Tuesday morning, Malcolm knocked on the door to Kristin's guest room in the castle, knowing it was probably a futile gesture he had planned, but not knowing what else to do. It was time. He couldn't avoid it any longer.

Kristin opened the door and stuck her head out, blinking, likely surprised to see him here, rather than downstairs at breakfast as they'd planned. "Good morning, Malcolm," she said, smiling shyly.

He put his hand on the doorjamb, more to brace himself than anything else. After yesterday's hot, impulsive kiss she'd given him—in the middle of the day, in one of Edinburgh's trendiest office-worker haunts—he'd gone back to work, unable to concentrate. Useless for anything else but thinking of her.

"Good morning," he said in a low voice.

"Is everything okay?" she asked, pulling her hair back into a ponytail.

The curves of her face stood out clearly. She just bewitched him.

Honestly, he wasn't sure if he *was* okay. He wasn't himself, if that's what she meant. In the shower this morning, it had occurred to him that if they were successful in gaining approval with her Born in Vermont project, then she'd be going home and staying there, with no reason to visit Scotland again.

He could only think of one possibility to keep her in Scotland for a while longer and explore if what seemed to be starting between them could possibly have a future.

"I'm...scheduled to take a drive this morning," he said, jiggling his car keys. "I was wondering if you'd like to come with me." No, he needed to be clearer than that. "Actually, there's something I really need to show you."

Her brow creased. "I thought we were working on the Born in Vermont presentation for Friday today?"

"We are." He had flipped through the report last night in his bedroom, unable to sleep anyway. He'd estimated he would need two solid days, with her help, to flesh out and add the financial projections. "Just not this morning," he said. "I've had today's commitment set up for a while, and I can't cancel it. The trip won't take long."

"Where are we going?" she asked, still looking skeptical.

He smiled at her, because she looked as if she needed reassurance. "I'd rather surprise you."

She smiled and bit her lip. Kristin did love surprises. "Will I like it?"

He sure as hell hoped so. He had no idea what he would do if she didn't. "I know *I* like it."

"Hmm. Sounds like a plan, then." She opened the door wider. "Am I dressed appropriately?"

If she were in rags, she would look great to him. He gazed up and down at her, his body registering her formfitting pants, her boots, her long turtleneck sweater that just tantalizingly covered her hips from view. He kept thinking of yesterday, of what it had felt like to have her warm body pressed fully against him.

"Perfect," he murmured.

She smiled, pleased. Turning abruptly, she picked up her McGunnert shawl and wrapped it around her shoulders. Driving the final stake in his heart.

She *had* to stay longer.

And as she followed him down the stairs and outside to the car, it occurred to him what a risk he was taking. If he did this wrong, it could all end tonight.

KRISTIN LEANED BACK in Malcolm's car and hummed to the music on the sound system. They were zipping along past some of the most spectacular scenery she'd seen yet. A Scottish loch, so deep blue she could skim by it for hours. She watched what looked to be an eagle flying ahead of them, and it seemed to be leading them on a fortuitous path.

She couldn't help but believe that things were finally looking up for her. Malcolm had told her last night on the drive home that the lawyers had ascertained, after spending an afternoon reviewing documents, that Born in Vermont did belong to Sage Family Products, which meant that Malcolm was free to propose a business plan for it as part of his company. She'd barely been able to contain her excitement. She was closer than ever to getting what she'd come to Scotland for in the first place.

She leaned back in her seat, the belt snug across her shoulder, and gazed at Malcolm, driving in silence. In profile, she saw his strength. This was a man who got the job done: a capable man. He had rolled up his shirtsleeves, showing strong forearms with fine, light brown hair. He had strong biceps and shoulders, straining against the cotton broadcloth as he steered.

If she dared, she would love to snuggle up closer, run her fingers along his jawline and through his hair. She could envision herself curling up closer inside the curve of his embrace. He was just so damn sexy.

He felt her gazing at him, and he turned, smiling at her. A flush of warmth spread through her chest, and she looked away. Part of her still felt a bit skittish and conflicted. Yesterday, she'd loved kissing him in that restaurant, had hungered for him, had been amazed by how good she felt with him. But then she'd reminded herself: she had so much to lose in letting herself get too physically close to him. And just as quickly, the hunger had left her.

Thankfully, Malcolm had not pushed her, had let her sit in silence during the long, dark drive home to Inverness without nudging her to *talk* about it, and she had appreciated that, more than he'd ever know.

She was just so…afraid. Afraid of committing to too much, too quickly. Afraid of feeling trapped by her choices. But if she were honest, too, the major fear would be leaving the safety of the comfort zone she'd lived within for all these years. Malcolm had alluded to it on the drive to Edinburgh yesterday, but she hadn't really thought about it until now.

Unconsciously, she touched her throat. Loosened the shawl that had gotten too tight beneath the restraint of the seat belt, giving her freedom to breathe.

"Are you okay?" he asked.

"Are we almost there?"

"It's just over that hill." He gestured with his chin.

Where could they possibly be going? Malcolm turned the car onto a wider road, with two lanes in each direction, more like the highways she was used to at home rather than a rural country drive.

And then she saw it. "Sage Family Products," the sign read. "Byrne Glennie facility."

A chill shot through her body, and she felt her jaw drop open. What was Malcolm doing?

He turned the wheel so they headed down a long, pine tree–lined drive. Ahead was a huge, new facility at least five times the size of the Aura Botanicals plant.

Viscerally, she sensed a scream bubbling inside her, but she felt frozen in place.

Aura Botanicals didn't exist anymore. *This place* had swallowed it up.

She put her hand to her mouth. A huge employee parking lot surrounded the facility, and the spaces were packed full of the smaller, European-style compact cars she was getting used to seeing in Scotland.

"Why did you bring me here when I'd asked you not to?" she finally choked out, turning in her seat to face him.

Malcolm's face was slightly pale. He parked the car at a reserved space in the front and turned off the engine.

He didn't say anything, just looked at her, his poker-faced expression successfully masking his true designs.

"I told you already," she said, feeling something akin to hysteria growing inside her, "I don't want to work for Sage. Don't try to make me do something that I don't want to do. Don't *ever* try to make me do something I don't want to do!"

His mouth seemed to drop open. "That wasn't my intention, Kristy."

"But you are doing it!" She tore for the door handle, but the car door was locked from inside. Gasping, she fumbled for the lock, until she'd succeeded in opening the door and staggering to the pavement.

Outside, a blessedly cool breeze ripped through her, whipping her hair and the ends of her scarf. She clawed at her neckline, loosening the tight material. It felt so much better to have her feet planted free, on firm ground that she could run away over, if need be.

The door slammed behind her, and Malcolm was beside her in an instant. She backed away a step. "Stop trampling me," she said. "You're making me feel trapped."

"Kristin, I won't ever hurt you."

"I'm not *saying* you'll hurt me! I'm *saying* that you're... you're...trying to manipulate me and make me do what you want me to do instead of what I *want* to do."

His brows drew together, and his face darkened. Now he seemed peeved. "That is the last thing I would ever do to anyone. You must be mistaking me for somebody else."

When she didn't answer, his glare turned to a softer expression. "Is that what other people do to you?"

"No!" She crossed her arms. "There's just...a very strong reason why I am wary of being in relationships, Malcolm. I do have my comfort zone, but I'm also a person who needs to be free. I was born that way," she finished helplessly. "It's very confusing."

"I do see that in you," he said quietly. "You're a free spirit. You don't want to be trapped."

"Then why did you bring me here?"

"Because I thought you would be happy here once you saw it." He took in a ragged breath. Swiped his hand through his hair. "I thought of two main reasons," he said, not able to look her in the eye. "One, because you're talented—one of the most talented people I know—and they don't appreciate that in your hometown. And, two, yes, because I selfishly want you here and thought you might want to be with me, too." His gaze met hers, and stayed there. He seemed to be pleading with her.

"But why?" she whispered. "Why would you want *me?* I'm so flawed."

He bracketed her face lightly with his hands. "Flawed? You're amazing, Kristy," he whispered. "Flaws and all."

She backed away from him.

Oh, she wished she believed him. She wished she could be like other women and appreciate a great guy when she met one. But she couldn't....

Suddenly, she just felt so sad. "I can't, Malcolm," she said. "I wish, but, no, I can't."

"You can't what?"

"I can't go in there with you."

"You *won't* go in there with me, you mean," Malcolm said. "You don't even want to *try?*"

She shook her head. She really didn't.

He stared at her for a long time. His chest rising and falling. He looked as if he was giving up on her. Maybe he *had* given up on her; he just hadn't walked away yet.

Finally, he took the car keys he gripped in his hand and tossed them to her. She caught them, feeling their warmth transferred from his body.

"When you decide otherwise, you let me know, Kristy. But I have to go inside."

She hesitated, staring at him.

"So go ahead," he said, "you're free. Leave. Go see Loch Ness. Or Urquhart Castle. Or any other of a million places you could be besides here." He glanced at his watch. "I have work to do."

And then he turned and walked away. She watched him stride toward the glassed-in entry to the facility. Watched him disappear inside the building.

She waited, but Malcolm didn't come out again.

Now what? She shivered, leaning against his car, wearing just her shawl, not warm enough or waterproof enough to stand up to the wind that whipped her and the smattering of raindrops that fell from the gray-cloaked sky.

Tears stung her eyes, but she brushed them away. She had to do something. Anything but stand still and think. Or stay in place and feel pain.

Shakily, she held out his key ring and beeped herself inside his vehicle.

The driver's seat was pushed back much too far for her. She found the buttons that adjusted the seat for her shorter height. Then she rested her hands on the steering wheel.

She could drive away now—to anyplace she wanted. But somehow, it felt like she would be sabotaging herself if she did. If she ran from what had become of Aura, wouldn't that be hurting her chances for Born in Vermont?

She cared about Born in Vermont. She needed to fight harder for it.

Her eyes burned but she knew what she had to do. She *was* strong enough to face what needed to be faced, whether Malcolm understood that or not. She got out and locked the vehicle again. Girded herself to walk toward the entry that Malcolm had disappeared through.

A security guard greeted her from a front reception desk. He didn't seem surprised to see her in the least. It turned out that Malcolm had already signed her in and arranged for a name tag, reading just, "Kristin."

"I'll call ahead and tell him that you're here, miss," the guard said. "You can wait for him at the end of that corridor." The guard pointed.

Hesitantly, Kristin walked down a long, white hallway lined with windows on one side, overlooking the manufacturing facility. The plant below was fully automated, a huge, clean, frightening environment. The air didn't smell fresh and natural like at Aura, it just smelled…sterile.

Today, various creams and lotions were being disseminated into plastic bottles rolling along on fast conveyor belts, but even from this distance, she could tell that the formulations were inferior in quality to Aura's, with cheaper ingredients.

Bulk-produced and inexpensive. Mass-marketed and advertised on television. Everything that Laura had worked against. The very reason she'd started Aura Botanicals to begin with, she'd always said.

Kristin stopped and crossed her arms over her chest.

"Do you see that empty section over there?" Malcolm's voice was low and quiet to her ears. She jumped a bit to hear him behind her, but as much as her instincts wanted to, she didn't walk away from him.

"That's where the Aura Botanicals products will be produced," he continued, still explaining in a gentle tone. "The same packaging and formulations will be used as before, but we're planning to arrange the equipment and set up more efficient processes. What we need is a great industrial engineer, and that's what you can do here, Kristin, if you'd like. The job is yours if you want it."

Those were exactly the words that Laura had once said to Kristin. *Spread your wings and start fresh. Bring your vision here.*

Kristin put her hand to her mouth. "Oh, Laura," she whispered.

Back then, Jay's wife had hired Kristin and welcomed her into the Aura Botanicals family when she'd come back home from New York. She'd felt so shaken and beaten down, needing a job and a place to go where people believed in her, because Kristin wasn't sure she believed in herself anymore.

Kristin's eyes stung again. She blinked the moisture away. But she was failing; the waterworks were gathering anyway. She couldn't stop it....

A sob escaped from her. She clapped her hand over her mouth. Through blurred vision, she saw Malcolm peer at her. Saw him bring her close to him in an embrace.

His shirt was smooth and warm against her cheek, and he smelled comforting, like laundry soap and Malcolm. She squeezed her eyes shut and opened them again, the sobs catching her unaware, her chest heaving in and out in a staccato rhythm.

"It's all right," he murmured, gently rubbing her back. "Shh, Kristy, I understand."

Turning her head toward the hall window, she could see workers on the floor below them, gazing up at them and obviously observing them quite clearly, ogling the show.

Surely, the workers all knew Malcolm. Surely they were intensely curious about this—on the surface—most inappropriate display of emotion and affection in the workplace.

Abruptly she jerked away from his embrace. "I'm sorry, Malcolm, I can't do this. I need to go home."

His expression looked crushed. "All right," he said. He stepped back and rubbed his forehead. "I'll help you book a plane ticket tonight."

"No," she clarified. "What I mean is, I want to go back to your castle now. Maybe…Rhiannon is home."

Malcolm laughed, a short, dry laugh. "Of course she's home." He shook his head. "Sorry. I mean, yes, of course I'll drive you. Just wait here a minute while I reschedule my meeting."

"You don't have to change your schedule on my account," she said. "I'll…drive myself."

"Absolutely not." His mouth turned hard. "I'll drop you off to find Rhiannon, and then I'll come back here and do what I need to do. That's what *I* want. There are two of us in this mess, Kristin. You're not the only one."

TWENTY MINUTES LATER, Kristin watched Malcolm drive away. The silver sedan sped up the long, winding driveway toward the guardhouse and then turned onto the main road headed back toward Byrne Glennie.

She felt numb inside. Shocked and upset with herself.

Malcolm had barely said a word to her during the drive back. He'd seemed angry, lost in his thoughts, and she'd had no idea what to say to him, either.

Slumping, she turned and wandered back to the great room. Paul, the butler, must have laid the fire that glowed warm in the hearth grate. Kristin pulled up a stool and sat before it, warming herself, trying to keep from shivering to her bones.

The front door slammed, and Rhiannon breezed inside, bringing the clear, fresh air of the Highlands along with her, as well as Molly, Mrs. MacDowall's energetic golden retriever.

"Kristy," Rhiannon said, smiling, "I'm glad you're here." She pulled up another stool and settled in beside Kristin.

"I'm glad you're here, too. I'm having a really bad day."

"Maybe this will cheer you up. Smell my hair." Rhiannon fanned her long dark hair, the same color as Malcolm's, and held a section before Kristin's nose. "Can you tell I used your shampoo?"

"Born in Vermont," Kristin murmured, her heart sinking. "I would know that scent anywhere."

"Do you have any more?" Rhiannon asked.

She did, but…she'd been hoping to save it to convince Malcolm. But now it probably didn't matter.

"Would you like some hand cream?" Kristin asked. "I brought some of that, too."

"May I try it?"

Kristin smiled at her. "Are you sure you're not just saying this to cheer me up? Because I really do need cheering up right now."

Rhiannon grinned at Kristin, hooking her arm. "Okay, what did my brother do?"

"Nothing. What makes you think Malcolm did anything?"

"Because you're upset."

I'm upset with myself, Kristin thought, sighing. "Can you do me a huge favor?" She clasped her hands together. "*Please* come shopping with me. I need to get away and forget everything for a few hours."

"No, I'm sorry, but I really can't," Rhiannon said.

She did look sorry, and she probably had a painting to finish. Kristin nodded, understanding completely. "That's okay. It's not as if I know how to drive a stick shift, anyway." She made a short laugh.

Rhiannon regarded her. "Do you want to learn how? Because I can teach you. Colin has been giving me lessons."

"Colin?"

"My bodyguard," Rhiannon whispered behind her hand. She winked at Kristin. "Just don't tell Malcolm. You know how he'll react." She rolled her eyes. "Besides, I'd like to keep it private from everybody. It's still rather new for me."

How…lovely, Kristin thought. Malcolm's reclusive sister had found love. Smiling to herself, following along after Rhiannon, the two of them went outside and piled into Kristin's little white rental car.

With Rhiannon in the driver's seat and Kristin beside her, Rhiannon showed her how to press the clutch pedal in order to move the stick shift. Then she showed her how to balance the gas pedal with the clutch pedal.

Then they got out and switched seats, and Kristin faced the long, oval drive that ran along the front of the castle.

"You'd better buckle up," she only half joked to Rhiannon.

"Don't worry. I was terrible when I first learned. Just try your best, that's all you can do."

Kristin held her breath and took Rhiannon's advice.

At first, they had a bumpy ride, there was no doubt about that, though there was much giggling over it.

But after a few laps around the oval, Kristin started to get the feel of it.

"Okay, time to advance to the hill," Rhiannon said, and pointed up the drive toward the guardhouse.

"Are you *sure* you don't want to go into town with me?" Kristin asked as the tiny car puttered toward the main road.

"No," Rhiannon insisted. "Here, you can turn around at the guardhouse." She waved at the man on duty.

Kristin turned to stare, but the guard waving back at them had white hair and looked old enough to be Rhiannon's grandfather.

"Is that Colin?" Kristin asked cautiously.

Rhiannon burst into laughter. "No! Certainly not!"

Kristin giggled, too. She was feeling enough at ease with Rhiannon that it didn't seem too inquisitive to ask. "Why won't you leave the property?"

"I just don't want to." Rhiannon shrugged. "Agoraphobia, I suppose. Have you heard of it?" she asked, her tone matter-of-fact. "It's likely an aftereffect of the kidnapping."

"Of Malcolm's kidnapping?"

Rhiannon leaned her head close to Kristin's. "We were kidnapped together, Malcolm and I."

"You…you were kidnapped, too?" Kristin was sure her mouth had dropped open. "At the same time Malcolm was?"

"I assumed you knew."

"No." Kristin shook her head. "Malcolm told me that he was abducted, but he didn't say you were with him…." She let her words trail off, feeling helpless.

"I'm not surprised that he didn't say anything," Rhiannon said gently. "Malcolm feels responsible for me. I tell him not to, because he isn't, of course. But you know my brother."

Always so interested in safety. Always so hypervigilant with maintaining knowledge and control of everything going on around him.

"It does explain a lot of things about him," Kristin said slowly.

"Yes, it does," Rhiannon agreed.

"Thank you for telling me," Kristin said quietly.

"Enough of that." Rhiannon waved her hand. Kristin had noticed that Rhiannon liked to keep things as light as possible, which Kristin completely understood and respected—she preferred to do the same thing, herself. "Will you be staying for the wedding on Friday?" Rhiannon asked. "I hope so. I really do."

With that one question, Kristin felt as if she'd been centered and grounded. She needed to focus on the future, specifically, the rest of her week.

Whatever had happened between Malcolm and her, she needed to remember Born in Vermont. She needed to take care of what she'd come to Scotland to do.

"You are welcome to stay as long as you want, you know," Rhiannon said. "We don't stand much on formal ceremony here. In fact, I talked with my parents, and we would like you to attend the wedding, if you feel comfortable doing so. Then, for the reception, we're having a Ceilidh band come to play. Do you know what that is?"

Rhiannon pronounced it "kay-lee." Kristin had heard of the term. "Does that mean Celtic music and dancing?"

"It's Gaelic dancing. But, yes, I can teach you some of the jigs and reels if you don't know them. It's fun to watch. The band brings a 'caller' with them, and everyone dances. Some of my cousins are a raucous bunch, but don't let that worry you. Malcolm is quite polite. He's really a good dancer."

Malcolm, dancing? The vision brought a smile to her lips. She thought of what he'd told her about owning a kilt. "Oh, my gosh, if I do go to the wedding, then I'll get to see him in his kilt."

"Yes, you will."

But that brought up a new worry. "What do women wear to a Scottish wedding?"

"Nothing fancy. Most will be in regular cocktail dresses. Mum plans to wear a skirt and jacket."

"I didn't bring anything suitable," Kristin said. "Maybe it's best that I leave before then."

Not only did it seem inappropriate for her—Kristin didn't know the bride or the groom, nor the family very well—but today she had also effectively cut off whatever friendship or goodwill she'd been building with Malcolm.

"If you change your mind," Rhiannon said, "let me know, and I'll help you. With whatever you need."

AFTER KRISTIN DROPPED Rhiannon at the house, she aimed her car up the gravel drive and used the stick shift as best as she could to drive the route into nearby Inverness.

It was a fairly large town, with many traffic lights and roundabouts. Kristin felt overwhelmed and afraid at first, but after she'd made a few mistakes, she realized that nothing disastrous was going to happen, and she even started laughing at herself.

Finally, she stumbled—quite by accident—across the shopping district Rhiannon had mentioned. Kristin followed the blue P signs to a public parking space, paid her coins at the central meter, stuck her ticket on the dashboard and strolled into town.

She felt better just stretching her legs and walking past

the shop windows. In one boutique, she impulsively tried on and then purchased a pretty, mauve-colored blouse made of satiny material, with short cap sleeves, a deep V-neck and a sash that tied around her waist. It was now officially the sexiest top she owned.

Usually, Kristin dressed conservatively; this was something entirely new for her. But maybe there was something about learning to drive a stick shift—and in a busy town center—that warranted celebration.

Later that evening, Kristin borrowed a tablet computer from Rhiannon so she could make a video call to her sister-in-law. Kristin timed the call for the midafternoon lull between lunch and dinner at Cookie's Place. Kristin hadn't checked in with Stephanie since she'd arrived in Scotland, and just in case word had filtered back from Arlene that Kristin had abandoned her prepaid British Isles tour, she really should make sure that her family wasn't worried about her. Kristin hadn't wanted to think about what they were going through—the grief and worry over losing the Aura factory—but now, she was ready.

Stephanie picked up after only two rings. "Kristin! We've been thinking about you. How's your adventure going?"

"Hi, Aunty!" Lily piped in. On the screen, Kristin could just make out the top of Lily's auburn curls. "Where are you?"

Kristin blinked back the burning in her eyes. It was so good to see them. She took the tablet computer and curled into a comfortable, worn leather chair near the alcove window in her guest room. From this position, she could see over the back gardens and down the hill to the glen spread out below, like a beautiful panorama.

"Let me show you," she said to Lily. She turned the

tablet so Lily could see the view out her window. "I'm in Scotland."

Lily giggled and covered her mouth with her little hands. *Wow,* did Kristin miss her family.

"Here is my room." Kristin positioned the tablet so Lily could see Kristin's bed. "I'm actually in a castle right now. What do you think?"

"Are there knights in shining armor?" Lily asked.

That was too difficult a question to answer at the moment. Kristin put her hand to her throat. "When I'm done talking with your mom, I can take the computer with me and go on a walk through the castle. I'll show you the stone floors and the high ceilings and the big room where there's going to be a fancy wedding celebration."

"Oh, my gosh," Stephanie whispered into her computer's microphone. "You really did find a castle."

"Is everything okay there, Steph?" Kristin murmured. "I've been so worried, and I have so much to tell you."

"So do I," Stephanie said. "Wait, hang on a second." Her head disappeared from Kristin's screen, and Kristin instead saw the view inside Cookie's Place from behind the cash register. In the background, she heard muffled conversation and an Abba song—"Dancing Queen"—playing from the overhead radio.

So like Stephanie. The everyday reminder just made her feel more homesick.

Stephanie came into sight again. She had a pencil behind her ear, and she was eating what looked to be a peanut butter cookie this time. "Sorry, I needed to get Lily settled with her coloring book." She sighed. "It's spring vacation week. No school for the kids."

"I forgot about that," Kristin said.

Strange how life went on in the wake of something bad happening.

"So, I assume you met with John Sage," Stephanie said.

"Why would you assume that?"

"Because…" Stephanie leaned closer to the screen, and she was whispering now. "Everybody from Aura has been in here yesterday and today, and they've been talking about it nonstop. Did you know that the team from Scotland is being delayed? Evidently, they were supposed to show up Monday to start packing the machinery, but a directive went out, and they never came." Stephanie grinned at her. "Nobody seems to know how or why, but I do. I've been keeping your secret. You did that, didn't you?"

"I did!" Kristin did an impromptu dance in her chair. Stephanie's news meant Malcolm was keeping his word. Maybe she still had a chance to fix their rift. Maybe this partnership between them was salvageable. "Honestly, Steph? You heard them say all that?"

"So help me, God. I'd be an excellent corporate spy." Stephanie lowered her voice, leaning closer to the screen. "Speaking of corporate spies, you are amazing. I can't wait until everyone finds out how much you've been working your magic behind the scenes."

The magic hadn't come just from her, it had come from her and Malcolm together. Oh, God, she needed to see him.…

"Steph, I have to go. I have more to tell you, but not for a few more days. Friday, I'm hoping."

"You sound like you believe."

"It…hasn't been easy. There's a man…"

"A *man?*"

"Malcolm," she said helplessly. "And it turns out he's John Sage's nephew."

Stephanie whistled. "I'm not going to judge. But let me just say this…if you're able to pull off this Born in Vermont plan, then you'll be the hero of the century around here."

Kristin laughed. "Gee, no pressure from your end, is there?"

"Aunty!" Lily popped into view again. "Watch me do a cartwheel!"

"I didn't know you could do a cartwheel," Kristin said.

"She can't," Stephanie mouthed behind her.

"I just learned," Lily said with the wide-eyed expression of someone who believed in herself perfectly.

Kristin grinned at her. "I guess we're both learning something."

But just then there was a knock on her door. Probably Rhiannon. Or maybe even Paul—Rhiannon said he sometimes dropped by with tea at about this time. Stephanie would be tickled pink to hear that Kristin had use of a butler.

"Hold on," Kristin said. "Someone's at my door, and before I go I want you to meet them."

She sprang up and opened the bedroom door.

Malcolm stood on the threshold, wearing his wool overcoat, the smell of blustery weather on him. But his face brightened when he saw her.

She blinked, allowing herself to gaze at him for a moment. Her heart skipped in her chest at the sight of him.

Feeling flushed, she stood back and opened the door wider.

He dug his hands inside his coat pockets and stepped inside her bedroom.

"George!" Lily shrieked from the propped-up computer screen.

Oh, no, Kristin thought.

CHAPTER THIRTEEN

"Hi, Lily," Malcolm said to the little girl. "How are you doing?"

"Good!" Lily shrieked.

But Lily's face on the screen was quickly replaced by her mom's. Stephanie Hart leaned in closer—she looked dumbfounded. "George Smith? Is that you?" she demanded.

"Yes," he answered calmly.

Kristin rushed over and grabbed the tablet computer that was running the video conference. "Please don't tell anyone," she whispered into the screen at her sister-in-law. She glanced at Malcolm, darting him an apologetic look.

That had to bode well for him.

When he'd dropped Kristin off this morning, he'd assumed she would never speak to him again. In fact, upon returning from the long day of meetings with his Byrne Glennie people, he'd half expected not to find her at all. But when he'd seen that ugly, white, glorified golf cart still parked outside his family's castle, his hopes had soared.

How could he not help but grin at Kristin's sister-in-law now? "Hello, love," he crooned, laying the Highland accent on thick. "How's business with you this fine afternoon?"

"*This* is Malcolm," Kristin cut in hurriedly. Which made him believe she'd been discussing him with her sister-in-law.

Brilliant news.

Stephanie's eyes bugged like a bullfrog's. Her mouth snapped open and then shut.

He simply grinned at her.

"Um," Kristin said to Stephanie, "Malcolm and I have to go now. I think it's time we hang up."

"I'm going to pretend I heard none of this," Stephanie agreed. "But we will talk when you get home."

Lily poked her face into view on the computer screen.

"So, we're finished with our blethering, then?" he said in an exaggerated Scots' accent for the little girl.

She giggled hysterically.

"Good night, Lily." Kristin snapped off the iPad and tossed it on the chair. She put her hand to her mouth, too, and just stood staring at him.

KRISTIN FELT HER heart grow warm. And her eyes teary. "Thank you for that," she said to Malcolm. She meant it with all her heart. "That was kind of you to keep your word about delaying the Sage people from moving into the Vermont plant. You've helped Stephanie with her business, even if just in a small way."

Malcolm squirmed in his heavy coat. His smile seemed to vanish almost immediately. "Actually, I knocked on your door to let you know that I set aside tomorrow and Thursday to work on your Born in Vermont proposal. So…if you're still interested in working with me, my uncle is ready to hear from us this Friday afternoon, before the wedding."

"Of course, yes. That sounds great!"

He nodded, stiff and reserved. "Friday morning, my uncle will be arriving for the family's quarterly meeting. We'll give the presentation to him in the back sitting room, the one my mother normally uses."

"Thank you for coordinating with him, and for keeping

me informed," she said. "I want this to be the best presentation we can possibly give."

He shrugged. "I'm working here in the castle tomorrow anyway. You're welcome to drop in and out as you please."

"Sure. Thank you." She bit her lip, feeling as if she wanted to smooth things over. Everything was suddenly too formal between them.

"Malcolm," she blurted, "just because I don't want to work at the Sage plant doesn't mean that I don't want to work with you."

He dug his hands more deeply into his coat pockets. "Okay."

"So...can you accept that and still support me?"

He sighed heavily. "Kristy, it's my fault. I shouldn't have brought you to Byrne Glennie like I did." He withdrew an envelope from his pocket and handed it to her. "I saved this for you. It's sort of an apology."

Curious, she opened the envelope. Inside was a photograph of her and Laura Astley, walking the factory floor at Aura. Kristin had never seen the picture before, but from her short hair and baggier dress, it looked to have been taken the year that Kristin had first come to Aura. "Where did you get this?"

"It was tucked inside a box of files with the formulas that Jay shipped over. I found it by accident."

Kristin smiled to herself. Yes, Laura was a surprising pack rat that way. She was also quite old-school. Very few of her formula notes had been kept on the computer.

Kristin ran her finger over the photo. She was glad to have a picture of her old mentor. "This is the only picture I have of us together like that."

"Who is she?"

"Right, I forgot. You never knew Jay's wife."

"Ah." Malcolm sat cautiously at the end of her bed. The

only other chair in the room held Rhiannon's tablet computer. "Well, I'm glad I didn't keep the photo for myself. I was tempted, you see."

"Why? This is a six-year-old picture of me. I look nothing like that anymore."

Such a screwup, she had thought herself back then. She had been terrified all the time.

"I think you look beautiful," Malcolm said quietly. "Both then and now." His Adam's apple moved up and down. He just looked so vulnerable saying that to her that she couldn't stop staring at him.

"You do?" she whispered.

"Aye," he said, in that deep Scottish burr. "I do, Kristy."

Kristin put the photo down, a lump in her throat. From the way he gazed at her, she felt as if she was blushing all over.

He was sitting before her, so solid, so strong—all male. He was the one man who never seemed to take her exuberance or her quirkiness the wrong way. And he'd never made an unsolicited move on her, or even tried to kiss her when she didn't want it.

He did not scare her in the least, or even make her feel uncomfortable, and that was remarkable for her. She hadn't realized it until she'd seen this old photo of herself.

She moved the tablet computer aside and pulled the chair forward, facing Malcolm. Their knees were just barely touching, and it felt…nice.

Something inside her seemed to be melting. Was it her fear that was leaving her? Or the worry that often followed her around? Or her cautiousness that always kept her from taking chances? She put her hand over her mouth, trying to figure this out.

Malcolm was good to her. Kind. Handsome. And his kiss…

He smiled at her, that crooked smile she loved so much. "Am I forgiven for springing Byrne Glennie on you?"

"Y-y-yes."

His smile turned sad. "I can't promise you everything you want, Kristy. I don't know what will happen with Born in Vermont. It's not my call anymore."

"I know. But we can be a team, and make a great presentation together. That's all I can ask for."

On impulse, she jumped up and rummaged in a drawer. She'd unloaded her suitcase and put her clothes inside the dresser—it had made her feel more grounded.

She found her Born in Vermont kit and pulled out the bottle she was looking for. Then she pressed it into Malcolm's hand. "This is for you. Rhiannon asked me for more today, but I'd really been saving my last bottle for you. It's made from birch and a hint of pine—okay, that's proprietary, but we're both part of the same team now, right? Anyway, the point is, it's made for men as well as women...."

He unscrewed the cap and held it to his nose. A look of pleasure overtook him. "Kristy, that's your smell." He grinned at her. "It drives me wild."

"It... Really?"

"Oh, love." He threw back his head and laughed. "I'll have to finance the damn plant myself, just so I can have more to remember you after you're gone."

He looked sad all of a sudden.

She swallowed. She was pretty sure she'd miss him, too.

It was hard to know. She just was so different from other women when it came to relationships. She wished she could fall in love easily, relax and find her soul mate. Be like...Stephanie. See the man she wanted, go after him and then, *bam,* live happily ever after—whether he came from Vermont or Scotland.

But for her, allowing love in wasn't merely a quest, like

finding her castle had been. There was so much more to it. It was a mystery to her....

"What did you do today?" he asked. "I noticed that your white car is parked closer to the house than it was earlier."

"I spent some time with your sister." Kristin couldn't tell him about the driving lessons and Colin, because that would be a betrayal of the confidence she'd promised Rhiannon. She glanced at her hands.

She didn't particularly like keeping knowledge about Rhiannon from Malcolm. She didn't want there to be any more barriers, secrets between them. She wouldn't put herself in that position again.

"Anyway," she continued, "I took the car and went into town after that."

"What did you do there?" He seemed genuinely interested.

"Well..." She opened the closet and took out the satiny mauve blouse she'd purchased. It was clingier and lower cut than she usually wore for clothing, but...she'd liked it and it had called to her. And maybe she'd been ready for a change. "I went shopping and bought this blouse, for one thing."

She stood back and assessed it, pretty on its hanger. With the black skirt she'd brought from home—the one she'd worn to Sage the first day she'd landed in Edinburgh—it would make a great impromptu wedding outfit. She hadn't realized that until now.

"Also, Rhiannon invited me to stay for your cousin's wedding." She glanced at him, gauging his reaction. "What do you think about that? Are you going, too?"

"I think...you will look brilliant in that sexy blouse. And I think I'd be an idiot to miss seeing you in it."

She sat back down, but on the arm of the chair this time.

Just a tiny bit more distance between her knees and Malcolm's than before.

"I'm told you're a great dancer," she said.

He smiled. "Me? Maybe I am."

"I'm going to be at a disadvantage, aren't I?"

"Ah, the country reels. But not to worry, I can take it slow with you, lass."

She bit her lip, feeling the blush overtake her. They were no longer just talking about the wedding…. It made her a little nervous.

She stood. "Rhiannon already promised to teach me," she said lightly. "In fact," she babbled, "I guess I'll need shoes, too. I'll have to ask for her help with that."

"Kristy, love," he said patiently, "Rhiannon isn't going to be able to help you with wedding shoes."

"Why? Because she's agoraphobic because of the kidnapping?"

Malcolm blinked, physically seeming to back away from her.

Oh, no. She hadn't meant to blurt it out like that. "I'm sorry. Rhiannon told me today. I didn't mean to…"

"She *talked* with you about it?" He stared at her.

"She…just said…that you think it's your fault, but to her, it's not your fault at all. She thinks you blame yourself for what happened to her, and she doesn't want you to do that anymore."

"Really?" He stood. His face looked stricken.

"Malcolm, I am sorry."

He walked to the turreted window and looked outside to the darkening evening, the "gloaming," they called it. He braced his hands on either side of the window, his head down, and for a moment, he just stood there, alone.

She waited. She had a feeling he was gathering himself

and that he did not want her to leave him while he did so. She didn't want to leave him now, either.

"Kristy," he said, turning finally, "there is something I want you to know."

She braced herself, waiting.

MALCOLM RAN HIS tongue over his broken tooth. He had never gotten his tooth fixed, because he'd never wanted to forget.

Protect the ones that you love at all costs. That had been the major lesson he'd learned that week in his childhood, courtesy of the murderers who'd shoved him and his younger sister into a white van when Malcolm had been in charge of escorting Rhiannon to her weekly dance lesson.

Because of *his* ineptitude, *his* lack of judgment, his baby sister had been terrorized for eleven days. He still couldn't think about that time without wanting to destroy something—so he never thought about it.

He compensated, maybe. He knew that about himself. And he also took consolation in the fact that those three monsters had died a violent, bullet-ridden death, though not before they'd taken out two innocent police officers with them, one a mother with two young children.

Never, never, never was Malcolm letting anything like that happen again. Never would he allow his family or loved ones to fall in harm's way. Not in any way. Not in any form.

"Malcolm?" Kristin touched his hand.

He blew out a breath and faced her. *She* was not fragile. She was as strong a woman as he'd ever known. And who was he to desire to get close to her? Especially knowing all that he possibly could about her, when he didn't even have the guts to tell her the worst about himself?

"Kristy, I failed her."

"You were ten years old."

"*I* was responsible. When I should have grabbed her hand, pulled her out of there and run away with her, I engaged them instead. I thought that by talking, by reasoning honestly, that it would stop them from following us. When it was clear that it wouldn't, and it was too late to run, I punched one of them, but all it did was get me knocked out. And that was the worst thing that could have happened. Because that's when they terrorized her. And because I was out cold…" He raked his hand through his hair.

"I couldn't stop it from happening." His voice broke. "Kristy, she was just a little girl…."

"Malcolm, I'm sorry."

"I talk to her almost every day on the phone. Even now, I still do. You heard me that morning in your factory. But still, it doesn't help her, and it doesn't change anything… she's broken, and she got that way on my watch. Now, she doesn't go out. She hides away here. She paints her beautiful pictures and disengages from the world…."

He turned to her. "Have you been inside her studio yet?"

She shook her head.

"We'll go there tomorrow, you'll see. It's this fairy tale world that doesn't exist in reality…."

Kristin was looking pained for him, so he stopped. But *she* wasn't stopping him; she was letting him speak. She was just…listening to what came out of his mouth, without judgment, without telling him how he *should* be feeling. And he needed that, for once. It felt nice.

She was nice.

He was so hopelessly falling in love with her.

Maybe by telling her what had happened, he would drive her away. But he didn't see how much further he could push her—that damage was already done, he supposed. She had already shut him down, told him no. She wasn't going to move to Scotland. She wasn't ever going to sleep with him, never mind fall in love with him, too, no matter how much he might want it.

He looked at her again. She was still sitting on the bed. Waiting for him. Saying nothing. There was just understanding in her eyes. Empathy, as opposed to sympathy, and maybe that was the crucial difference that made him snap.

He just blurted it out. "I think she was molested."

Kristin looked at him, sadness on her face. Her hands were clasped tightly in her lap. Her head tilted, her eyes full of compassion.

He swallowed. So much pain he kept inside. He'd never dared tell anyone his suspicions. He had never even dared ask Rhiannon. He always stopped himself from thinking about it, or he would be driven mad.

He got up and paced, tearing his hands through his hair, wishing he could cut out the thought from his mind and erase it forever.

When he glanced up, Kristin was studying him.

He expelled a breath. "I shouldn't be talking to you about this. I don't know why I am. Forget what I just said."

"Malcolm, I was attacked, too. One night when I was walking home to my apartment in New York City."

He turned around. "Kristy?" he whispered.

"By a stranger. When I lived away from home those few months. He put a knife to my throat and robbed me—took my purse, phone, the watch I was wearing."

Kristin swallowed, rubbing her arms up and down. "I wasn't hurt physically. I never told anybody before, but if it helps you with your sister…I just want you to know that… well, to me…I feel like I understand her. After it happened, I retreated to my hometown, where it's safe for me. Where everyone is my family, and where the risks are low. And that's where I've stayed since.

"And just so you know," she said, "I don't think about it as often as I used to. It was so long ago. Maybe…Rhiannon keeps herself safe by drawing her beautiful pictures. I know that I have my scents and my shampoos I retreat to." She laughed hoarsely. Kristin had made such a muck of it—really, comparing a twenty-two-year-old to an eight-year-old.

"Oh, Kristy," Malcolm said in a low voice. He crossed the room to her. She could see, in the low light, that his eyes looked damp. Oh, she wished she had never said anything to compare a simple robbery to the horror of what Rhiannon had gone through. *Why* had she just said all that?

He cradled her cheeks with both hands. Just gazed into her eyes.

"I'm okay," she insisted. "I never needed to tell anyone about it. Not even Stephanie knows. Please don't make a big deal out of it. I'm just…well…scarred, I guess. That one experience has made me afraid of so many things—whether it be traveling to a strange country, or letting myself get close to people. Now you know." She swallowed and looked down at her hands, feeling miserable.

"No." Malcolm shook his head fiercely. His fingertips were gentle on her skin. "You are perfect," he said, in that lovely Scottish accent.

"I'm not. I'm a grown woman who's essentially afraid of the big, bad world."

"You are perfect to *me*."

Kristin looked up at him. Tears were stinging in the corner of her eyelids, and she needed to blink. She buried her head in his warm, broad shoulder.

"Kristy, you are the most perfect woman to me," he said, and his voice echoed to her very bones.

She closed her hand around his muscled back, his crisply ironed shirt bunching in her palm.

"Your magic and your zest for living just infects me," he murmured. "You say you're afraid of so many things, but what you've done to try to save your factory, your town, shows courage. I hope you see that."

"So…what should we do?"

"We'll do whatever you want, love."

With that, Kristin flung her arms around his neck. "Will you stay with me tonight? I want you to stay."

CHAPTER FOURTEEN

"ARE YOU SURE?" Malcolm murmured, nuzzling aside her top and kissing the tender spot at the base of her neck.

Kristin tightened her arms around him. Her heart was pounding so hard she could feel it in her eardrums. "Yes," she breathed. "Please."

His palms skimmed up the sides of her hips, beneath her loose tunic and to the bare skin on her waist. She wanted to close her eyes and moan.

How lucky was she? Malcolm had just told her that he accepted her as she was. Within her, it was as if a dam of worry had broken and rushed away, leaving her free to be herself.

Malcolm had asked her what she wanted. And what Kristin most wanted was him—all of him. For weeks and days and hours—sweet hours—she'd been in his company, desiring him. Even now, her nipples felt tight and her breasts full. She stretched upward on her toes, across his chest, longing for no layer of clothing between them. Just skin.

His hands slid over her backside. She wanted him inside her, so badly. And when he lowered his head and pressed a soft kiss to her throat, she almost lost it.

"Kristy," he whispered. "We…should find a condom."

"Yes. Um…inside my cosmetic case, I think." She was throbbing, all over. But somehow, her brain was managing to work again. "Do condoms go bad?"

"Show me it," he murmured. "I'll check."

"Don't you have any?" she asked, turning her head to look into his tender blue eyes.

"Er...no. Not here."

Scampering into the small bathroom, she left him on the bed, feet on the floor, back stretched out. When she returned, he looked dazed. He pulled her down to him with one hand and accepted the condom with the other.

He squinted at it, holding it to the light. Maybe the printing on the wrapper was a bit faded. It had been inside a pocket of her makeup bag for quite a while.

"It's good," he decided.

She breathed a sigh of relief.

A slow smile spread over his face. "Oh, love. You were worried."

He sat up and caught her face in his hands, smoothing back her hair.

"Please," she whispered again, and they fell back on the bed, limbs entangled.

She leaned over him and kissed him tenderly, lips barely touching him at first. His breathing grew heavy and labored. She ran her hands over his smooth, muscled back. He caressed her breasts, lifting her shirt off, over her head. With gentle hands, he explored her body, heating her, exciting her with his touch. He trailed featherlight sensations over her abdomen and between her legs. She couldn't see his expression clearly, but she felt the rhythm of his heartbeat, the heat in his breath.

She felt no fear. How could she? She was with Malcolm. She helped strip him of his suit, his work clothes, until he was naked and on top of the coverlet with her. She rolled over on top of that familiar chest, feeling deliciously happy, blessedly free, and he caressed her back, barely touching her.

Oh, she had never felt such desire. It didn't take an expert to see that maybe she'd been traumatized by her life, years ago, and maybe she'd been in denial about it. But now, no. All of that was swept away, and she was with only Malcolm in her head. No worries. No fears.

"Make love to me," she whispered.

"Kristy..." He caught her lips in a deep, soulful kiss, his strong hands bracketed on either side of her head. His tongue ran along the seam of her lips, stroking against hers.

The heat was building in her. She lifted her hips and rubbed against his erection. Groaning, he found her nub by touch and stroked her, softly caressing.

She moved on top of him, her lower back shifting and undulating. A soft rush of breath came from her.

He began to softly croon to her, using the full of his Scots' accent. No holding back. "Kristy, my sweet."

"I love when you call me that. Please never stop."

"I won't, Kristy."

She leaned forward, pressing her breasts to his chest, her nipples taut, and her forehead to his.

A CURTAIN OF HAIR, sweet-smelling hair, fanned Malcolm's shoulders. Tearing open the condom packet with one hand and his teeth, he quickly rolled it on. With a soft flutter of a moan, she didn't wait; she took him inside her. At first, he didn't move. He wanted to—God he wanted to. With one hand he was grabbing a fist of loose coverlet and gritting his teeth, but with his other hand, he kept up the soft stroking with his thumb.

She was just surrounding him. Maybe she was reclaiming a part of herself, through him. Heaven knew he had been coming alive through her all week long. Ever since the day he'd met her, actually.

He wanted her. She brightened his life by being in it. He wanted her however she gave herself to him. With whatever she had to give.

KRISTIN WAS ALMOST THERE. He was whispering in her ear, sweet nothings, touched with that Scottish burr. Her mind was softly, but quite thoroughly, being blown.

She needed this. She needed him. He understood her, and he didn't overpower her or patronize her. Even now, he let her lead.

"Malcolm." She turned her head and kissed him deeply. He shifted, moving his hand from between them and settling her hips down squarely to his, rocking her into him, in just the right place, with just the right touch. Instead of rubbing his hand, she was rubbing the length of his erection, inside her.

Stars exploded, and she cried out. On and on. It was the sweetest thing. Just…sweetness. Like a reclaiming of her soul.

He held her close to him, against his strong chest, entangled in his strong legs, the smattering of hair tickling her in the most pleasant sense. She squirmed in his arms, going in for a kiss, laughing slightly and running her tongue over that small chip in his tooth. The slight imperfection that kept him from being too perfect and that drew her to him.

Because he was wrong—she wasn't perfect. But it was nice that he thought so, even knowing exactly why she was not.

He's the only one who knows my fears.

She lay in Malcolm's arms, idly stroking his chest, thinking about what she'd just realized.

Ah, well, it didn't matter. Her body felt alive again, and that was what she was enjoying most.

WHERE HAD KRISTIN GONE?

The next morning the key ring for her white car was still hanging on the hook in the entry, so Malcolm knew she hadn't left the property.

He searched the castle from top to bottom. Inside her guest room everything looked tidy, and the bed was made. He stopped and touched her pillows and sheets. Earlier, the two of them had been tangled up in them together for hours. Maybe he should have waited until she'd woken up before he'd left. He just couldn't wait; he'd wanted to get as early a start on the day—and on their project together—as possible.

On impulse, he'd checked for the slip of paper on which he'd left a note for her, just in case it had fallen, but, no, he couldn't find it. She must have seen it. He trusted her and couldn't imagine what had happened.

He checked his watch again: nine-thirty. And yet, she hadn't met him at nine as they'd agreed on.

Malcolm shoved his feet into his boots, grabbed a raincoat and headed for the door to the garden. His last resort was to check the footpath that went along the edge of the glen. Because, well, security-minded person that he was, what if something had happened to her? The property was still fairly unfamiliar to Kristin, and it was windy, cold and raining outside. The boots that she'd been borrowing from Rhiannon were missing from the rack, so walking outdoors was his best guess as to where Kristin had headed.

"Malcolm," Paul called to him from the breakfast room. He gave Malcolm the "come-here" sign.

Malcolm strode across the carpeting still wearing his boots, laces flapping. "Yes?"

Paul handed a pen and a notebook to him. "Kristin left her notes here at breakfast. If you're going out to Rhiannon's studio, you'll save me a trip to bring them to her."

"You've seen Kristin this morning?"

"She was down early, and the two of them left together. From the sounds of it, I believe they're conspiring together about something."

Malcolm's heart slowed. He really was relieved. This just went to show him how important Kristin was becoming to him. And now, evidently, she was important to Rhiannon, too.

Smiling to himself, Malcolm took his time gathering his laptop and the report for Born in Vermont. Then he filled three travel coffee mugs, laced up his boots, and headed across the yard to the two-story outbuilding that held Rhiannon's art studio.

A gust of wind drenched him with near-icy sleet. So much for the unseasonably warm weather they'd been having. Inside the outbuilding, cold without heat, he hung up the raincoat and dumped the boots in the foyer, then jogged up the stairs.

He heard the music before he saw them. A raucous Highland reel.

He stood in the doorway and just grinned, watching something he'd never thought he would see.

Kristin and Rhiannon, dancing together. Rhiannon was even laughing about it, enjoying herself. Strangely, it looked as if Rhiannon was teaching Kristin how to do the jigs. What was especially remarkable was that Rhiannon, as far as he knew, had never attended a family wedding before.

Malcolm broke out in a bigger grin. The day could only get better.

"IT WAS SUPPOSED to be a surprise," Rhiannon was saying to Malcolm. "We'd only planned to practice for a few minutes, but we got carried away and forgot about the time. I'm really sorry."

"It's okay," Malcolm said to his sister, laughing, passing her a mug of coffee.

Kristin clasped her hands to her heart. She loved the light that spread over Malcolm's face when he was happy. Last night he'd been, well…amazing to her. Everything had changed between them. Everything had changed for *her*.

There was now one person on earth who knew the truth about her. And rather than blame her, or feel averse to her, Malcolm had understood. It was strange, but…she'd woken up, and she'd still felt free.

Her body still hot from learning the reel, Kristin walked over to the table near the door and gathered her purse, with her copy of the report she'd packed for Born in Vermont. She needed this proposal to be approved, now for a new, more personal reason than she'd had before: she wanted Malcolm to be able to travel to her, and to have a reason to spend time with her in her town, as well.

Kristin took the last mug of coffee Malcolm had brought and glanced at him over the top of the mug. Not for the last time that morning, their gazes tangled and then held.

His face was newly shaven, his hair damp. He wore old, comfortable-looking jeans, and they looked…really great on him.

She tucked her chin in to her collar, speechless for a moment. Malcolm's eyes were so blue, like the sky over Scotland on a rare, sunny day.

From across the room, he winked at her. He hadn't stopped smiling at her since he'd first walked in.

Now he strolled over and handed her the notebook she'd left in the breakfast room. His hand caught in hers, and their fingers interlaced. "Are you well today?" he asked in a low voice.

"Umm-hmm." She nodded, feeling breathless. The last she'd seen of him, he'd been asleep in her arms, his warm chest and steady breathing a comfort beneath her body.

"Thank you for last night," she said, suddenly feeling shy. She glanced over at Rhiannon, but Malcolm's sister had returned to her laptop stand, shutting down the computer she'd been using to show Kristin internet videos that demonstrated the overhead patterns of the dances. To Kristin's eyes, it had looked very similar to American square dancing.

Kristin glanced back at Malcolm, and he held her gaze. "Kristy, love, it was my pleasure." He said "pleasure" with a soft rolling *r,* like *playsurr.*

It meant the world to her that he still seemed to respect…and desire her, even more after last night. She'd been thinking about it in the shower this morning. Maybe her difficult time in New York had been a form of post-traumatic stress—in a small way, like a soldier returning from a battlefield. The only man she'd so much as hugged since then had been Malcolm.

Maybe this was not a bad thing, though. He'd been just the right person for her.

She actually felt *healed* in a sense, which was a great sensation. She hadn't wanted the night with him to end. And afterward, she'd slept so easily.

It made her trust him all that much more.

He reached out and moved a lock of hair out of her eyes. A small, intimate gesture, and Kristin didn't feel the slightest urge to flinch. On the contrary, it flushed her with desire. She caught Malcolm's hand and held it in hers.

"Are you ready, love?" he murmured in that low deep voice. "I want to get started."

"I do, too." She swung her hand in his and then stepped closer to him, between his legs. He drew his free hand lightly across her waist.

This is the sweetness of falling for someone who is good for me.

"Hey, you two," Rhiannon said from across the room. "Don't you have work to do today?"

"Sorry," Kristin said, dropping Malcolm's hand, feeling the flush cross her face.

Malcolm chuckled from deep in his throat. "Enough with the PDA," he agreed.

"Yeah," Kristin said. "I hate it when people do that, too."

"What's PDA?" Rhiannon asked.

"Public display of affection," Kristin answered. Rhiannon was so isolated here.

"What do you think of the studio?" Malcolm asked Kristin.

She had already spent an hour gawking at it. "This place is amazing."

"I paid her to say that," Rhiannon joked.

In Kristin's opinion, Rhiannon's studio *was* awe-inspiring—a large, airy space facing south with windows that opened up the length of one wall. The other three walls were covered with a mixture of murals and framed artwork. Even the floor was painted—parts of it to resemble a forest floor, other parts a pond and another section with a wide green field. Kristin and Malcolm currently stood in the field. Rhiannon knelt on a lily pad in the pond.

With the gentle, calming music Rhiannon now had playing in the background, Kristin would have to call this a haven of healing every bit as soothing as the beeswax and botanicals-scented storage closet that Kristin used to retreat to at Aura.

"Rhiannon, do you want to join us for lunch later?" Malcolm asked.

"Sure," Rhiannon said. "Where are you working today?"

"In the castle dining room," Malcolm answered.

Interesting. The dining room wasn't exactly private—there were no doors, and anybody could wander in and out to grab a cup of tea from the sideboard at any time.

As if reading her expression, Malcolm murmured to her, "We can't get distracted by each other today. There's a lot at stake for us with this report, Kristy."

He was right. When it came to…whatever it was that was happening between them, she and Malcolm had everything to gain for it to work.

And everything to lose if it didn't.

EIGHT HOURS LATER, Malcolm sat at the large, bare dining table, stretching his arms overhead. Papers were spread out over the table between him and Kristin, plus a portable printer. Malcolm had a spreadsheet set up on his computer—actually, several spreadsheets. He'd been in a nonstop, laptop-typing frenzy. He knew his uncle's tastes, and they tended toward numbers and graphs. Malcolm had grabbed everything he could find relating to data.

He'd spent all day creating spreadsheets and reports and filling in projected numbers for the Born in Vermont proposal. The document Kristin had brought to his uncle hadn't included forecasts—it contained mostly ingredients' lists, supplier costs and manufacturing costs. Malcolm was doing his best to fill in the blanks for expected sales and profits, coming up with something that would be useful in convincing his uncle.

Kristin was doing her part, too. Nobody could say they weren't giving it their all. They were moving through Laura's slim, bound original report, going product by product, deciding what should be included in an initial phase, and what should not.

Kristin was using an old laptop of his and was tapping in her own data that she'd uploaded from home on the Cloud.

He scrolled to the bottom of his screen and looked at his current set of summary totals.

The numbers, unfortunately, were bleeding red. Malcolm was coming up short on all counts, no matter what angle he tried changing.

Kristin took a sheet of paper from the printer. She frowned, too. Even she knew that, so far, it wasn't looking all that great.

"What are we missing?" she asked. "These numbers aren't showing a reason for your uncle to invest in this product line."

He forced a smile at her. No way was he giving her any reason to give up hope. It also didn't help him that it took everything he had to concentrate on what he was doing. "We'll just have to keep trying."

"You're invested in this as much as I am," she noted.

"Sure. Why not?"

"No reason." She had a goofy smile on her face. Again, she held his gaze. Her lips parted, and she leaned back in her chair.

He closed his eyes and scrubbed his hand over his face. He wanted so damn badly to make love to her again. For half the day he'd been aroused. And she was…well…

Her nipples were hard under her thin shirt. Her eyelids were hooded.

But instead of the answers he needed coming to him, his gaze kept drifting back to her. Then when he looked at her, he would find her doing the same to him. Kristin would blush and turn back to the pages. The pattern would be repeated.

For the hundredth time that day, he closed his eyes. "I am so far gone," he said aloud.

"Malcolm?"

He hadn't meant to say that. For one thing, it made no sense for him. He worked at *Sage*. His allegiance was to his family.

But, if Aura were kept open, even in a smaller capacity, then he would have reason to visit Kristin in America.

The thought slammed him like a ton of bricks.

He glanced up at her again. She was gazing thoughtfully at him, too.

He *needed* to make this work, for both parties.

"We're really a team," she asked him, "aren't we?"

He smiled at her, just as Rhiannon breezed inside. "How is the Lord of the Spreadsheet doing?"

Kristin snickered.

"Paul said to move you two along," Rhiannon said cheerily. "He wants to set the table for formal dinner. All five of us tonight."

Malcolm glanced at Rhiannon. "We're actually kind of busy."

"No," Rhiannon insisted. "You need to bring Kristin to eat with Mum and Dad, Malcolm."

He glanced at Kristin. He had not invited her to sit with his parents since, well…the first day she'd come to the castle and they'd had tea. And a lot had happened since then.

"Are you up for that?" he asked Kristin.

"Well…" she said. "It probably would be a good thing, seeing as it looks like I'll be a guest at the wedding they're hosting."

She was right, of course. And it was just another reason to put Malcolm on edge. He loved his parents, but at this stage of his life, he probably only shared meals with them a handful of times per year. And never with a woman accompanying him. But most important, he didn't want this to be just another source of stress that could send Kristin flying away from him.

AFTER DINNER, KRISTIN went searching for Malcolm. "You've been gone a long time. Are you all right?" she asked.

Malcolm was in the Laird MacDowall's wine cellar, formerly a whisky cellar for the old castle. Malcolm was sitting on a low shelf, holding a bottle of port, just staring into the distance.

When he heard the scuff of her shoes on the stone floor, he straightened. "Sorry. Things were going so well with you and my family that I let my mind wander. I actually got a thought that the answer to our dilemma might be to change the pricing model. That would adjust our profit numbers across the board and we could—"

Kristin laughed and put her fingers to his lips. "As much as I appreciate your working so hard on my account," she teased, "I'm not impressed by the fact that you appear to be a workaholic."

"I'm really not," he protested.

"Then prove it to me." Kristin stepped close to him and ran her hands up his strong forearms, feeling the slight hairs beneath the sleeve of his jacket, and then farther up, to his strong shoulders. She gazed up at him, holding his eyes, feeling so full that she needed to take a deep breath.

Malcolm was a good man. The longer she'd sat with him and his family at dinner, the more she had trusted him, and them. She was probably even falling in love with him a little.

Maybe her feelings were still a bit skittish, but if she

was afraid of being tied down, then in many respects, Malcolm was the perfect guy for her. He lived so far away, after all. He was safe.

She moved in, stepping between his legs, pressing her torso to his. He moved his hand to the small of her back. Lightly first, but then pressing.

She stood on her tiptoes, stretching her feet inside the constricting boots she wore, and extended her spine to press her lips to his in a kiss.

She just seemed so full of pent-up passion. He seemed to be, too.

If their kiss outside the ruins of her family's castle had been chaste, this one was fiery. She couldn't be sure who started it; it seemed to be both at the same time, but they were deliciously slashing and mingling the kiss with their tongues. "I can't keep my hands off you," he gasped.

"Stay with me again tonight," she insisted.

"Your room. It's safer. You're on the quiet corridor."

"Agreed." She went back to kissing him.

He ran his hands up her back, to the base of her scalp, his fingers massaging. She made a small moan. She was in heaven with him, this solid, rock fortress of a man.

He broke the kiss. His hands still cradled the base of her scalp and his forehead pressed to hers. He spoke as if he was out of breath: "Kristy, I may be daft for saying this now, but if you keep this up much longer, I'll have to have you on the floor of this cellar, and I really don't want that, because anybody could wander in here at any time."

She laughed, straight from her diaphragm. "That, and we might never get anything else done, including that report that needs to be approved by your uncle."

"Aye. About that." He wiped his hand with his mouth. "You know why I'm down here, thinking so much about pricing models? It's because I really want to pull this off for you. If I can't—if we can't pull this off together—are you still going to want to be in bed with me before you leave?"

Stunned, she didn't answer. Put like that…

In the darkness, he shook his head at her. "Think about that one, Kristy. Think long and hard."

KRISTIN DID THINK about what Malcolm had said, and the answer was simple. And since he hadn't come to her room as he'd promised, she went to his.

A crack of light shone beneath the door. Earlier, she'd heard the shower running, but now it was silent inside. She had no idea how much longer he would be awake, so if she was serious, then she needed to act now.

She wanted him, physically, at least. She'd felt the need building in her, longer and more intense with each passing hour that they'd spent in the same room together. Looking over his shoulder, so close that she could smell the soap he'd used on his skin. The shampoo she'd given him—her shampoo, in his hair.

Every time his smoldering, intense blue eyes had turned to her, she'd felt herself melting a bit more. It was delicious torment. Sensations that she hadn't let herself feel in years.

Last night, when he'd said, "You are perfect to me, Kristy," that had unlocked something in her soul that had seemed to set her free, to give her permission to actually believe it herself.

That belief freed her. And it had changed everything between them, which was more important than either answer to the question he had posed to her.

There was no doubt about it, Malcolm was a good man. She certainly cared about him—at least, she did in this moment. Beyond that, Kristin wasn't sure just yet how much of herself she could offer him.

But now, tonight, she had made her choice. He could reject what she offered, but she didn't think he would.

Knocking softly, she turned the door handle. It was dark, and though the light was on in the walk-in closet, from the doorway, she couldn't see him. She shut the outside door.

At the noise it made, Malcolm stepped into the room. He wore nothing but a white towel wrapped low around his hips.

She stared at the towel, and then she looked into his eyes. They were steady and burning. It emboldened her.

She crossed the room and, when she got to him, laid her palm flat on his chest. His heart beat slowly beneath her hand. His skin was damp and warm from the shower.

"May I?" she whispered.

She held her breath, waiting for his answer.

MALCOLM STOOD, STUNNED. He had not expected her to come to his room.

"Follow me," he said. "We're going to your end of the corridor. I want us to make as much noise as we please."

She put her hand over her mouth, but he could tell she was smiling. He tossed on a pair of jeans and led the way, barefoot and shirtless.

Once inside her guest room, she turned and locked her door.

Without a word she wrapped her arms around his neck and kissed him. And then, with both hands, undid his jeans button and zipper and slid the pants over his hips until they dropped to the floor.

It was mind-blowing for him. *He* was the natural leader. He'd directed people his entire life. Until he'd met Kristin, this free woman who did as she chose. Who always surprised him. Who utterly fascinated him.

She was the one who slipped a condom on him—new, this time, from a box she must have bought—which made his heart just crash.

This was not the time to think about it, but, in the past, he'd only known women to *want* to get pregnant with him. His last relationship, years ago, had ended when he'd realized what was happening. "You are perceived as being rich, Malcolm," his uncle used to lecture him, even when Malcolm was a teen away in boarding school in America. "You need to be careful, always vigilant, if you don't want to be trapped."

Kristin had no desire to trap him. She didn't want his money or his notoriety.

She just wanted *him*.

MALCOLM WOKE FROM a light doze. The sun hadn't risen yet but would any minute. Faint light was coming through the window.

Kristin was wrapped in his arms, sleeping on his chest. From head to toe, she was stretched out against him, and it felt damn good.

He ran his fingers through her hair, the strands just tickling his nose. Lightly he kissed her, his sleeping beauty, but she was exhausted and didn't wake.

Very soon the rest of the house would be waking. Just four other people besides them for the time being, but before long it would be bedlam, with cousins and aunts and uncles and grandparents all starting to trickle in for the family meeting and then the wedding. That just gave him extra impetus to work as hard as he could to find the angle toward keeping Born in Vermont open and functioning.

If Kristin couldn't move to Scotland and work at Byrne Glennie, then Malcolm could at least hope to schedule frequent business trips to Vermont to check on their investment. That was his personal hope for Born in Vermont. Kristin, he knew, had her community and her people for her motivation.

Malcolm had her.

Oh, Kristy. Everything he'd said to her in these past few days had been the honest truth.

He needed to get a start on the day. They had just a few hours until the castle was invaded—twenty-four hours or so until his uncle arrived for the presentation.

Gingerly, he peeled back the covers on the bed. Extricated himself from beneath Kristin's sleeping form. She sighed and rolled over, her arms wrapping around the pillow he'd slept on. Across the room on a desk he fumbled for a bit of paper and a pen and wrote her another note, similar to yesterday's: *Meet me at nine o'clock by the back door to the garden. We'll get started then.* He thought of signing something more endearing and private, like a lover, but she wasn't his and, given her reluctance to love him, wasn't likely to ever be. But he could wait, giving her time and patience. He signed the note with an *M* and left it beside her on her pillow.

At least he could give her that one gift before she left Scotland. Born in Vermont was something concrete he could focus on and wrap his arms around. He was a numbers guy, after all.

On the way out her door, he pocketed the shampoo vial she'd given him earlier. The floor was cold to his bare feet, the air cool on his bare chest. He pulled on his jeans, zipped them, and then looked both ways before heading down the corridor to his room. Doing the walk of shame, where there had been no shame.

He had almost made it to safety, when his sister stepped out of her door, dressed for her morning walk on the grounds. She took in his disheveled hair, his bare chest, and just raised an eyebrow. He put his finger to his lips.

She smiled her approval.

Inside his room, he took a long, hot shower. He used the shampoo Kristin had given him, just a small amount so he could save it and use it again. Prolonging her presence.

It smelled like her. God, it smelled like her.

He didn't wash the suds out, just stood with his chest under the spray. Everything about her had been explained to him. He saw the reason for her earlier skittishness now. The granny nightgown. The loose, baggy clothing. The woman who longed for adventure, but who was so encased in fear that she never left her hometown.

He would do everything in his power to help her. Because to him, she was worth it.

CHAPTER FIFTEEN

LATER THAT THURSDAY MORNING, the castle became besieged with travelers, stomping up and down the stone staircase, hauling suitcases and lugging hangers holding men's kilts and ladies' dresses. All of Malcolm's cousins had arrived—his whole crazy, extended family that he usually only saw four times annually at the Sage Family meetings.

Rhiannon was nowhere to be found. Locked inside her studio, hiding from all the action, was Malcolm's best guess. His sister just did not appear in crowds. At least among family, they understood her.

Malcolm stretched. He and Kristin were taking a break from working on the Born in Vermont proposal. His mind was just stuck over what to do next in an attempt to make the numbers work. He sat outside, drinking an Irn-Bru, watching Kristin in the garden as she tossed a tennis ball to his mom's golden retriever. Occasionally one of the cousins wandered past them, and Kristin greeted them, happy to meet new people.

It hit Malcolm viscerally. Kristin was such a free spirit. He didn't want to lose her, but how could he ever expect to keep her interested in him if this project didn't work?

He went upstairs, thinking they could try to tackle the project from a different angle. He just wasn't seeing clearly *what* he needed to do to fix the problem. He'd moved his laptop and printer into his bedroom, and he sat down to concentrate anew, leaving the door ajar for when Kristin returned.

But it was Rhiannon who surprised him by entering, rubbing her arms and looking thoughtful.

"Are you okay?" he asked her.

She nodded and went to stand beside the window. "Kristin is very adventurous, isn't she?"

Malcolm put down his pages and went to join Rhiannon. Just seeing Kristin down in the garden with his cousins, laughing with such lightheartedness, tore his heart out. This week had meant more to him than he'd expected it to.

"Actually, for a long time she rarely left her hometown," Malcolm said. "When I met her, she worked two blocks from her job, and she lived in a house her brother owned, directly across the street from her parents."

"Is there something wrong with that?" Rhiannon asked, tongue-in-cheek.

"No." He looked at his sister and grinned.

"So…why did she come to Scotland in the first place?"

Because *he* had blown up her life. But he wasn't going to tell his sister that.

"I think a large part of her wanted to see her family's castle. It turned out that it was only a ruin, crumbled down to the cellar foundation, but we found it anyway."

He crossed his arms. "The point is, Kristin had never left America until this week. But she finally did it. I'm pretty amazed by her, to tell you the truth."

"She came here alone?"

"She had support from her family and friends, but yes."

Rhiannon traced her finger around the windowpane. "And now, she'll go back home soon, won't she? To America—to her family and friends?"

There was his problem. The point Rhiannon made was irrefutable. "Yes. No matter what happens with Uncle John tomorrow, I suppose she will. I offered her a job that would keep her in Scotland, but she's refused it."

"Are you in love with her, Malcolm?" Rhiannon asked him point-blank.

Malcolm couldn't answer his sister. He didn't want to see her hurt any more than necessary when the inevitable happened.

Rhiannon took a jar of the Born in Vermont hand cream from her pocket. "It is a lovely product she makes," Rhiannon mused, hefting the jar in her hands.

"I'm really trying to give her what she wants, Rhi. But it has to fit with our family's interests, too. And so far, that isn't looking likely."

"Are you afraid you'll lose her completely if you don't make your deal work?"

He couldn't voice his fears to Rhiannon. Then again, he shouldn't set expectations too high with her, either.

"To tell you the truth, it's likely that I'll lose her either way. It's just an impossible situation."

Rhiannon appeared to be thinking carefully. "I believe I can help you, Malcolm."

He looked at her. "How do you mean?"

"Never mind. Just let me take care of it."

He shook his head. "Thanks for offering to talk with her, but really, Rhi, Kristin is going to do what Kristin is going to do. We just have to accept that."

Rhiannon smiled mysteriously. She tucked the jar of hand cream into her pocket and, without a word, left.

By late Thursday afternoon, Malcolm had done all that he could.

"Here's how it's going to go down tomorrow," he said to Kristin, pacing inside her guest room. "The family meeting is scheduled for most of the morning. Since my uncle is arriving late, he's asked me to handle that piece of business. What it means for you and me is that our presentation for Born in Vermont will be held as a one-on-one meeting with my uncle and me, shortly after he arrives. I'm expecting that will be just before the wedding reception."

"I'm attending with you," Kristin said. "We've worked on this as a team, and that's how we'll present it, right?"

He didn't have an argument for her, so he just grunted.

"Is there anything more we need to do with the presentation?" Kristin asked.

He rubbed the back of his neck. He had cut down the proposal, focusing on just a few of the products, but still, the whole thing seemed haphazard to him. Something was missing, but he wasn't sure what. He hadn't known how to tell her, because it didn't make complete sense to him either, but he would push it through with his uncle as best he could. The main thing was to remain positive for Kristin. "Nope, we're all set."

"You don't feel hopeful," she said quietly. "Do you?"

"You don't need to worry, Kristin."

"Can I ask you something? If this proposal isn't received well, will that reflect badly on you?"

Of course it would. With his uncle, every slip was noticed.

But Malcolm maintained a bright smile for her. "He's my uncle, remember? Either way, this is good for me. It shows I'm being proactive and adding to the company portfolio."

Kristin nodded slowly. He didn't fool himself that she wasn't perceptive enough to pick up on his white lies, but she chose to say nothing more about it.

"So, is there anything else to be done before tomorrow?" she asked.

He wished there was. He wished he could *see* what was

missing…the magical answer that would make everything work and solve all their problems.

"Kristin?" Rhiannon poked her head inside the door.

"Come on in," Kristin said. "We're just finishing up."

Tentatively Rhiannon joined them. She was dressed as if she'd just come in from the cold. Her nose was red and her hair windblown. She must have walked over from her studio.

"I brought what you and I talked about." Rhiannon held out the jar that Malcolm had seen her with earlier.

Kristin took it. "This is gorgeous! Your design is so much better than I'd imagined." She passed it to Malcolm. "Look at what Rhiannon did for us."

His sister had painted product labels, for the top, side and bottom of the jar. She'd also changed the container. Instead of plastic, the rich, healing cream was packaged inside an attractive glass pot.

His stomach fell. The weight of the pot in his palm, coupled with the new design—made everything come together for him.

"It's to help with your presentation," Rhiannon said. "The aesthetics are important, too, don't you think?"

"It's a brilliant idea." Kristin turned to Malcolm. "Read the labels. The bottom one says, 'Born in Vermont, with love.'"

Yes, he agreed it was eye-catching and beautiful. It also showcased the product as the high-end, luxury item that shockingly, he hadn't seen until now.

And just like that, visually seeing the product as it was—a dainty, high-end specialty purchase—Malcolm understood exactly what had been bothering him about the proposal; the problem that was making everything not work.

Distribution. Sage was a company that sold to low-priced, big-box markets all over Europe and, increasingly, North America. That's what they did, their core business. But even big-box stores were looking for organic, all-green lines these days. Hence, the acquisition of Aura Botanicals.

But Aura had been able to integrate well with Sage because Aura was packaged in inexpensive plastic bottles. Even though the ingredients were organic, they were relatively low-cost organic. In other words, they weren't too highly priced for the big-box-store shoppers.

Born in Vermont, on the other hand, wasn't meant for this market at all. High-end, organic-food grocery stores, new-age healing shops, New England–based gift shops and the internet—that's where this specialty line fit best.

Sage isn't equipped to handle this type of product line.

How could he have been so blind? He'd made a basic, elementary, strategic-marketing mistake. One that someone like him—highly trained and experienced—shouldn't have made. This stuff was like breathing to him.

And yet, Malcolm had jumped right into the details— into creating and filling spreadsheets with numbers— without first evaluating the proposal for what it really was. He'd been blinded by his feelings for Kristin, perhaps, even by her burgeoning friendship with his sister.

"I've been using this hand cream all week," Rhiannon remarked. "I'm always scrubbing my hands with harsh detergents to get the oil paint off, so I'm fussy about what I use. This product is truly remarkable." She laughed, glancing at Malcolm. "I sound like a walking advertisement, don't I?"

"Aye, you do," Malcolm muttered.

"That's how Laura always talked," Kristin said, agreeing with Rhiannon. "You understand her vision completely."

Rhiannon beamed.
Malcolm said nothing.
What the hell was he going to do?

CHAPTER SIXTEEN

OVERNIGHT, MALCOLM'S MOTHER and her crew had transformed the great hall of the castle into a reception area to rival any Highland wedding. The Ceilidh band arrived and set up their staging. The caterers unloaded their truck. The castle changed from a place of quiet serenity to a raucous, busy house party.

That afternoon, Malcolm dressed in his kilt, complete with sporran, coat, waistcoat, flashes and ceremonial dagger. He went downstairs and waited for his uncle on a cold, hard bench, sitting in the dining room by the unlit fireplace while his uncle settled in upstairs, changing into his own family kilt.

As Malcolm had expected, his uncle was late. He'd entered with his bodyguard, had kissed his sister—Malcolm's mother—and could be counted upon to dance one reel, partnering with the bride, of course.

Then he would leave. Such was life with his elusive, demanding uncle.

But before he left, his uncle would likely stop by and visit Rhiannon in her studio. Malcolm was one of the few people who knew that John Sage kept just one piece of artwork in his private office at Sage Family Products, and that artwork was painted by Malcolm's sister.

She was the only person in their family that his uncle seemed to honestly keep a soft spot for. Maybe it was guilt over not being able to rescue her earlier—leaving her with those monsters for eleven days, all those years ago. Malcolm really wasn't sure; they'd never discussed it, and Malcolm wasn't inclined to now. He didn't see where it would help any of them. He only knew that if he let himself get angry with his uncle—if he let himself fall back on old habits and think about the past—then there was a good chance he would make it worse for his sister.

Nothing to do but go forward. Malcolm leaned his head back and closed his eyes.

In the great hall, the Highland band tuned their instruments. At any moment the music and the dancing would start. Malcolm had asked Kristin to wait for him there; that he would join her when he was finished dressing.

He'd needed to think before their meeting. He hadn't completely discussed strategy with her, but in his mind, he'd chosen which direction to take. He'd only had two choices, really.

He could present the recommendation that he would have reached two weeks ago, before Kristin had ever set foot in Edinburgh. This was the safe conclusion; the practical answer.

Or, he could advise that Sage Family Products invest in keeping the Vermont factory open, albeit with a limited crew.

As a business decision for Sage Family Products, it was risky.

It was also the option that Malcolm had finally chosen to push.

He stood and stretched his arms, pacing. Today was a historic day for him. He was choosing his own selfish interests over a practical business interest.

His uncle would realize this immediately. Malcolm could see the resulting train wreck of a discussion coming from half a mile away.

His uncle would say no, of course, because his uncle always chose the prudent path. This decision would stand. Malcolm was pretty sure he would lose Kristin over it, and that would be that. Life would just have to go on, the same way that life had gone on after the police had stormed that warehouse and untied him and rescued his sister all those years ago.

Malcolm braced his palms over his family's stone mantelpiece. Stared into the flames of the now licking fire.

He absolutely did not want to lose Kristin. He loved her with an all-consuming passion, this sunny, free-spirited woman. She was the one complement to his serious rock of a persona, and he had fallen in love completely with her, down to his soul. And he didn't see that there was a way of returning from it. He didn't want to return from it; his constant sense of vigilance and emphasis on safety had put him in a prison of his own making that he didn't want to be in anymore. He saw no way out of it except to blow up that prison and set himself free.

The first step in this process seemed to be blowing up his uncle's solid opinion of Malcolm as a levelheaded man of business.

So be it.

The music had stopped within the great room. A general hush seemed to fall over the assembled wedding guests. Malcolm adjusted his belt and sporran, then gathered up the detailed report he and Kristin had written together, and prepared to face the consequences of his decision.

Inside the great room, Malcolm waited on the fringes, joining with his cousins and relatives in turning his attention to the central staircase. His uncle stood at the top, resplendently outfitted in his mother's Stewart tartan, which most of Malcolm's male cousins wore, as well.

Malcolm wore his father's tartan; his one contrarian move. Until now.

Kristy. Malcolm clenched his jaw. He purposely was avoiding searching her out in the crowd. He stood still, his hand involuntarily gripped into a fist as his uncle made his slow, grand entrance down the stairway. The assembled party clapped and cheered, as they always did for his uncle—the man whose signature graced the monthly checks deposited into his family's trust fund accounts.

Finally, the applause died down, and the fiddles started up again. Malcolm remained where he was, waiting, while his uncle partnered with Cousin Gerry's new wife to head up the reel.

He glanced at his watch. The reel would last approximately four minutes. Then, his uncle would call him in to the sitting room, his impromptu study, and that meeting would likely last approximately four minutes, as well.

The decision would be made quickly: yes or no. Go or no go. Eat or starve, for many members of Kristin's community. Love or lose, for Malcolm and Kristy.

Feeling resigned, he searched for Kristin's face in the crowded great hall. She stood apart, gazing intently at him, also. Life with her was never predictable, except maybe, that the sight of her always made him smile.

He winked, just to send her reassurance. She looked beautiful. She wore the silky rose-colored top and her short black skirt. Her blond hair was up and off her face, giving her an air of sophistication that was new to him. He couldn't wait to dance with her. Hell, he couldn't wait just to touch her again.

Another hush fell over the great hall. Malcolm followed everyone's gazes.

Rhiannon descended the staircase. His sister had on a simple black dress with the MacDowall tartan—the same plaid Malcolm wore—draped around one shoulder. Her head held high.

She walked directly to Kristin, then took her hand and led Kristin to meet John Sage in the middle of the room, before everyone.

Malcolm leaped into action. He strode to Kristin's side.

"Uncle, this is Kristin Hart—I believe you've already met her, albeit briefly," Rhiannon was saying to their uncle. "Kristin has been staying with us this week. She's been a great friend to Malcolm and me." She smiled at Kristin. "Uncle, I hope you will listen carefully to the details of her company, Born in Vermont. This is one of her products." Rhiannon passed the jar of hand cream to John Sage. "I'm very fond of it. It's a therapeutic, aromatherapy hand cream. I've been using it after I paint. As you can see, I like it so much I designed the labels for it."

Uncle John gazed at Rhiannon's handiwork. "As always, my dear, it's exquisite." He moved to return the jar to Rhiannon.

"No, that's a gift for you, Uncle." Rhiannon kissed his cheek and left the jar in his outstretched hand.

Then, with dignity, Rhiannon kissed both Kristin and Malcolm on their cheeks, as well. She headed back up the staircase to her bedroom suite.

Malcolm knew what that had cost Rhiannon, as did most everyone else in that room. He watched his sister with a lump in his throat. She cared about Kristin. She cared about him, too, but there was nothing more he could do for her, other than what he had planned.

The lull in the conversation ended. Talking commenced. The music restarted.

Uncle John turned politely to Kristin. "It's nice to meet you again."

"I'm pleased to meet you as Malcolm's uncle," Kristin replied. "You're important to him, and as such, you're important to me."

His uncle laughed. Malcolm was willing to bet that was the first time anyone had ever called the great John Sage, "Malcolm's uncle."

"So," his uncle asked Kristin, "how long are you in Scotland for?"

"I have a plane ticket home reserved for next week."

"Wonderful," he said. "Well, if I don't see you before then, Kristin, good luck with your endeavors and have a safe journey home." Then, to Malcolm, he murmured, "After I meet with your cousin Gerry, you and I will talk."

KRISTIN WATCHED THE emotion flicker over Malcolm's face. For the past day, her heart had continually gone out to him. She appreciated how difficult it was for him to present this report to his uncle. She had decided to support Malcolm as best she could, to give him the space he needed and to allow for his occasional bouts of brooding. To just let him be himself, as Malcolm let *her* be herself.

But it was the introduction by Rhiannon which she didn't understand the significance of. His uncle already knew who Kristin was. Why had Malcolm seemed so shocked by the encounter?

"What just happened?" she asked him quietly.

"Rhiannon has never come downstairs while the cousins are here," he murmured. "This was the first time."

"She did that for you, didn't she?"

"Actually," he said, turning to her, his gaze softening, "she did it for us."

Kristin swallowed. Honestly, she didn't know what she was feeling about what Malcolm had just said. Were they a permanent couple? Did she want them to be? She wasn't sure about that. All she knew was that she'd hated that

Malcolm had been upset—she wanted him to be happy. She wanted only good things for him.

Without him knowing it, she'd been observing him sit on the bench in the dining room, looking as if he was getting ready to line up for a firing squad. Kristin suspected quite strongly that he planned to take a hit for her. That he hadn't been completely truthful about what he was going to recommend to his uncle, or what the ramifications might be for him. She'd asked, but Malcolm hadn't shown her his final numbers.

Yes, of course, those spreadsheets concerned her. But more than that, she realized she cared enough about him to appreciate that he was starting to matter more to her than getting the green light for Born in Vermont did.

"May I please see the final numbers?" she asked again, indicating the bound report in his hand.

He paused.

"I won't hurt you, Malcolm," she said. "Not ever. Please, show them to me."

His mouth twisted, but he passed the report to her. She flipped to the pages that, by now, she knew so well.

The final numbers he'd inserted were quite optimistic. Likely, with little basis in reality.

She closed the report. "This is what you're giving him?"

"I already gave it to him," Malcolm answered. "I left a copy in his dressing room."

He had? She shook her head. "No matter what he decides, I'll always appreciate what you and Rhiannon, but mostly you, did for me."

"Kristy, honestly, if we stand a chance at all, then it's because my uncle has a soft spot for Rhiannon."

"Yes, I can see that he adores her."

"She has never come out at family gatherings like this," Malcolm said. "Usually, she hides in her room. I really believe that what she did tonight happened because of you. You helped her take that step." His voice lowered, and he smiled sadly at her. "You're a treasure, Kristy. *You're* the castle. Don't ever let anyone tell you otherwise."

Before she could answer, a man in a gray suit, possibly John Sage's bodyguard, stopped before Malcolm. "Excuse me, sir. Mr. Sage is ready to see you in the other room."

"Shall we?" Malcolm said to Kristin.

Her chest feeling squishy inside, she took his offered elbow. "Thank you for including me. I know you would prefer not to."

"There's a lot on the line for you, too. I understand why you want to be present."

"What do you think our chances are?" she asked.

Straightening his shoulders, he winked down at her. "I'd say that luck is on our side. We found a ruined castle in the middle of nowhere, didn't we?"

This man was such a prize. Her vision was getting blurry, and that was too bad, because Malcolm in a kilt was an image that she could stare at all night long.

She squeezed his arm, the wool from his black, silver-buttoned Bonnie Prince Charlie jacket smooth and warm to her touch. "Remind me to corner you later. I've always been curious about what a Scotsman wears under his kilt."

"Ah, lass, all you had to do was ask me."

And while Kristin bit her lip, Malcolm led her proudly across the great room and past the fireplace in the dining room—the plaid carpet matching the tartan kilt that Malcolm wore—to the inner chamber where John Sage was ready for them both.

MALCOLM WAS READY, as well.

He held out a chair for Kristin to sit, across the table

from his uncle, and then Malcolm hauled over another chair from the side wall and placed it beside Kristin's.

His uncle steepled his hands and regarded Kristin's presence with a raised brow.

"Hello, Uncle," Malcolm said. "You and Kristin have already met, twice, I believe, so I'm sure you need no new introductions."

His uncle smiled at him. "Yes, I see you brought a date for the wedding."

Under the table, Malcolm's hand rested on Kristin's. Glancing at her, he nodded as if to a business colleague. She calmly met his gaze and nodded back. She knew how to best play this meeting, even if it meant deferring to him to handle any slights sent her way.

"I won't lie to you, Uncle," Malcolm said smoothly. "Kristin means a great deal to me. But that doesn't mean that our business plan isn't sound."

"Yes, I already read her version earlier in the week, the one without the numbers included." His uncle waved his hand. "Well done, my dear. It was intriguing to me."

"Thank you," Kristin said.

"That's why I was interested in seeing Malcolm's projections." His uncle held up their report. "I read your revised proposal. I can see that a lot of effort has gone into it, on both your parts. This is a well-thought-out plan."

"So, what's your decision?" Malcolm asked.

His uncle tilted his head. "You and I both know that, while I would do anything for you and Rhiannon, this investment doesn't fit with our established business strategy."

Malcolm heard Kristin exhale. Under the table, he clasped her hand and squeezed it. To his uncle, he calmly nodded.

"You're right," Malcolm agreed. "It doesn't." But he

stared at his uncle, placing both palms on the table. "I'm asking you to move forward with it anyway."

His uncle put his finger to his lips. Silently he contemplated Malcolm.

Malcolm maintained the stare.

"There's one thing I can do for you," his uncle said finally. "Take next week off, with my blessing. You never vacation. Spend a vacation with Ms. Hart. Enjoy yourselves." He smiled indulgently again at Kristin.

Malcolm gritted his teeth. "And *then?*"

"I'm sorry." His uncle stood. He didn't look sorry at all. "If you want to carry on with this, Malcolm, you'll need to think about it in a different way. As it is, Born in Vermont isn't right for us. That's all I have to offer you." He turned to leave.

Malcolm scraped back his chair and stepped in front of him. "We're not finished yet."

"Wait!" Kristin interrupted.

Malcolm blinked as she moved between them. "I have a say in this, too." She smiled at Malcolm, as if to smooth everything over. "You're right," she said brightly. "Born in Vermont isn't right for Sage Family Products. I'll simply have to return home next week and see what else I can do." She held out her hand to him. "Please, take care, sir. And thank you for your time."

Malcolm stared at her, dumbfounded. What was she doing? They had gone over this: besides this proposal, there was no other solution that would help her get what she wanted. By stopping Malcolm and agreeing with his uncle, she was working against her own best interests.

His uncle took Kristin's hand in both of his. Malcolm didn't think he'd ever seen that happen before. "Goodbye, my dear," John Sage murmured. "It truly was a pleasure to meet you."

He turned to Malcolm. "Please give Rhiannon my regrets. But of anyone, she understands why I need to keep our financial position strong."

TWENTY MINUTES LATER Rhiannon called Malcolm on his mobile phone. Malcolm picked up, dreading what he would say to her. He was still in bafflement over what Kristin had done.

"Yes," he said, putting the phone to his ear.

"What happened with Uncle John?" Rhiannon asked. "Did you get what you want from him?"

Malcolm's grip tightened on the phone. Beside him Kristin's clear green eyes regarded his.

Malcolm tilted the phone and gestured her closer, so she could participate in the conversation with Rhiannon, too.

In the background, music played, so he spoke loud enough for Rhiannon to hear him. "Uncle is…taking the decision under advisement," Malcolm said into the phone.

"That's good news, isn't it?" Rhiannon asked.

"We need to be prepared for anything." He glanced at Kristin and she calmly met his gaze again.

"What you did for us… I won't ever forget that," Malcolm said to his sister. "That was beautiful of you, Rhiannon."

Rhiannon made a small, pleased laugh. "You're my brother. We do what we can for each other."

She disconnected and the call ended. With Kristin's gaze still locked to his, Malcolm tucked his phone into the sporran hanging on his belt. "Why did you do that in there?" he asked.

"Because we're a team, Malcolm." She leaned against the edge of the now-cold stone fireplace in the empty dining room away from everyone else. From across the castle came a muted shout from the Scottish reels.

With one hand, she pulled him close to her. "What your uncle said to us was right."

"Kristy," he chided, shaking his head because her bare legs rubbing against his bare legs, in his kilt, was distracting to him. "Er, I could have convinced him to—"

She put her finger to his lips, stopping him from continuing in that vein.

"No one has ever championed me like that, Malcolm. You believed in me. You didn't tell me what to do. And you didn't take from me. I've never been equal partners like that."

"Kristy…"

"And even apart from the Born in Vermont business, I will cherish our time together. And I *am* taking that vacation with you next week, by the way. Now shut up and come dance with me, before I'm enticed by some other braw Scotsman."

He laughed. "You're crazy if you think I'll let that happen."

"My God," she mused, "do you know how damn good you look when you smile? And in that fantastic kilt?" She brushed her fingers through the pleats that ended at his knees, and shook her head in wonder.

A man with a passing tray offered them a flute of champagne. Malcolm snagged one and offered it to her first.

"No, I don't want any liquor clouding my perceptions," she said. "I want to remember every detail of this night."

"Kristy…"

"Malcolm, do you want to dance with me or not, you big, dumb Highlander?"

He grinned at her, because they both knew that the last thing he was, was dumb. He knew a great woman when he saw her.

Later, when he and Kristin were inside an alcove, stealing a private moment alone together after twenty straight minutes of cousins and reels, he asked her, "Do you still want to spend next week with me even if I can't give you want you want?"

She gave him a long, deep kiss, her hands lingering on the edges of his kilt. "I'm with you because I want to be with you, Malcolm. Can't that be enough?"

CHAPTER SEVENTEEN

EIGHT DAYS LATER, Kristin stood with Malcolm inside his Edinburgh apartment. Her suitcase was packed, and it was time for her to use her plane ticket and travel home.

True to his word, Malcolm had taken the whole week off from work. He'd been a tourist in his own country, he'd said. They'd spent an amazing week together, the past three days holed up in a private cottage on the wild coast of the intensely secluded, beautiful island of Lewis in the Outer Hebrides.

But now their time was over.

"Will you please drive me to the airport?" she asked Malcolm. "I want to spend every remaining minute with you possible."

A muscle moved in his jaw. She knew he wasn't happy about her leaving. But thankfully, he hadn't said anything to try to get her to stay. She hadn't wanted him to say anything. She needed to do this.

"I'll call a car for you," he said.

She bit back her disappointment. But she watched him pull out his phone, head to the front window of his apartment, overlooking a long stretch of the Firth of Forth in the distance.

While he spoke on the phone in a low voice, he kept his face to the window.

She completely understood. He didn't want to have to actually say goodbye to her.

She pulled her purse over her shoulder and adjusted her woolen beret. Her flashlight was tucked in to her luggage that she would check. Her new phone was buried inside her purse. She carried only her passport and airline ticket in the big front pocket of her coat.

Yes, she was leaving for home. Malcolm finished his call and went over to sit on the couch beside her. His feet were bare. She moved her feet, clad in her traveling boots, beside his.

"So this is it," she said. "Thank you for everything. I'll text to let you know when I get home safely."

He nodded, a lock of hair falling across his face. Tenderly, she pushed it out of the way.

His phone buzzed. He checked the screen. "The car is here."

She stood. He rose, too.

"Goodbye," she said.

"Yes. Goodbye." He smiled for her. One last gift that lit up his face the way she loved it so.

She smiled back at him, grateful.

Telescoping open the handle for her suitcase, she headed for the door. The thing that she was most thankful for was that Malcolm didn't try to push her, tell her what to do or tie her down. He was giving her the freedom that she needed.

She *needed* to go home. She needed to show herself that she had strength inside, that *she* was in charge of her life.

At the threshold, she paused to smile again at Malcolm. He made a small smile, too, and raised one hand to her. Then he stuffed his fists into the front pockets of his jeans, his biceps slightly flexing under a soft, navy blue T-shirt. He looked so sexy to her; he made her ache.

She turned her head and skipped down the stairs to the

street before she changed her mind. Outside the air was damp, a "Scotch mist," as Malcolm called it.

She passed her suitcase to the driver, who loaded it into his car trunk. She looked up to Malcolm's windows. She saw the outline of his face inside, watching her, but she could not see his expression.

One last time, she waved as she stepped into the backseat of the car. Malcolm let her go, and that was the best gift he could have given her.

MALCOLM SAT SLUMPED on his office couch at work. As soon as she'd left, he'd dressed and walked across the city in the mist that had soon turned into a heavy rain. He felt as empty and desolate as the sidewalks in the wake of the storm. He thought he'd been doing the right thing with Kristin, but now he wasn't sure.

He turned the letter he'd saved for her over and over in his hands. She'd forgotten all about it. If she'd asked to read it before she left, he would have given it to her, gladly, with relief and with hope.

He got up and ran the letter through the office shredder.

He was still staring at the chopped-up pieces in the litter bin when his mobile phone rang. He jumped, but it was the ringtone for Rhiannon.

"Cheers," he said to his sister. No matter what happened, he would always keep a positive outlook for her.

"Did you tell her that you love her?" Rhiannon demanded.

He closed his eyes and slumped back on the couch. "No."

"You need to tell her, Malcolm. She deserves to know."

Maybe so. He blew out a breath. Now it was too late, though.

"What happened with Born in Vermont?" Rhiannon asked him. "You never told me."

He tapped his finger against the edge of his phone. At some point, he'd been expecting her question; he just didn't want to hear it today. He'd been dreading telling Rhiannon the truth.

"Sage isn't going to invest in Kristy's company, are we, Malcolm?" she asked.

Malcolm sighed. "No." He waited for Rhiannon's depressed silence.

"But…*somebody* is going to buy it, right?" Rhiannon said.

Malcolm sat up. He felt the force of the revelation. "Somebody might, I guess."

"Are *you* that somebody, Malcolm?"

"No, I don't have…" He scratched his head. He'd been going to say he didn't have that kind of money at his disposal. But, he did have connections. He knew people in Boston who had money, in the business community there. People with deep pockets who were searching for good investment opportunities.

Another fundamental rule of business Malcolm had forgotten: just because a deal was bad or good for one outfit, didn't mean it was bad or good for all.

He stood and walked to the windows. The rain had stopped. On the street, taxis, lorries and double-decker buses rolled by. A massive pattern of commerce, businesses and people interacting with each other.

He ran his hand through his hair. Rhiannon had jogged something in him. Born in Vermont was a good product line, it just wasn't a good product line for *Sage*. But that didn't mean Malcolm couldn't find an investment group to buy a controlling interest in the brand and in the plant. In fact, he was sure he could get his uncle to provide the brand and formulations and use of the factory rent-free for an equity stake in the new company.

Malcolm nearly laughed aloud. Evaluating companies was what he did for a living, but with Kristin, he hadn't been able to be objective. Now, back in his office—and thanks to his sister—he had a solution that would work for everyone.

"Thank you, Rhiannon," he said before ending the call.

But he was already swiveling in his chair, turning on his computer and bringing up his contact list. He'd gone to school in Boston, and he still knew people there. And Boston was not that far from Vermont....

A few hours later, he phoned his sister back. "Rhiannon, do you know you're a genius?"

"Of course I do." She laughed. "Will you come by for dinner on Sunday?"

"Yes. Yes, I will."

CHAPTER EIGHTEEN

THE FIRST TIME that Kristin noticed she missed Malcolm, it came as a shock to her system. She was inside the airport in Edinburgh, purchasing a bottle of water before her flight boarded, and a woman in the shop said something funny to her.

Automatically, Kristin turned to relay it to Malcolm, so they could laugh together. But then, she remembered that Malcolm wasn't there.

Kristin nibbled her lip. Maybe it was because she and Malcolm had spent most of the past week in each other's back pockets, so to speak. A romantic vacation, the first four days spent driving all over Scotland together—east to west and north to south—exploring the mountains and the lochs and the seacoast, and compromising between staying in country B&Bs and full-service, city hotels. It hadn't mattered to Kristin where their bed was, as long as she'd had Malcolm beside her at night.

Kristin smiled dreamily, standing in the middle of that airport gift shop and caressing a magnet in the image of the flag of Scotland.

Yes, she decided, Malcolm was the fantasy man she had always imagined.

Still, Kristin mused, as she made her way through the bustle of the airport terminal, she'd always figured that it was a very good possibility that the newness and the joy she felt in being with Malcolm might wear off. But how was she to know for sure?

One thing she did know, her time with Malcolm had been healing for her. All these years, and she hadn't known what she'd been missing. Now she would never have a need to go back to that worried, skittish woman she had been before she'd stepped on the plane to Scotland.

As she boarded her plane back to America, she felt free and independent. She had gone on a grand adventure.

Once she got home she waited for relief to come, the feeling of having escaped from being tied down.

But three days passed, and it still hadn't arrived.

She missed Malcolm with an ache that she hadn't known possible, and it only grew worse with each day.

ON MONDAY MORNING, Kristin showed up to begin her last few paid weeks at the old Aura Botanicals plant—its sign officially taken down—before the company was closed for good. The first person she saw when she buzzed her way into the building was Andrew.

He stood in the entrance leading to the managerial offices. Lowering his coffee mug, he scowled at her, eyeing her up and down. "What are you doing here?" he asked with a sneer.

Good question. Kristin glanced around the factory. "No one has packed up the equipment yet. It's still here."

"No thanks to you," Andrew snapped.

"Actually, it *is* thanks to me." She put her hands on her hips. "You may not know it, Andrew, but I went over to Scotland, and because I put myself on the line, I was able to get extra time and money for everybody here. Including you." She pointed at him. "Exactly what have *you* done to help?"

Andrew's eyes widened. He opened his mouth, but he didn't say a word.

After he walked away, she just sighed. Standing up for herself gave her a small amount of personal satisfaction, but she couldn't help think that it wouldn't bring Malcolm back to her.

She did miss him. She missed him every aching moment.

She missed him when she woke up. When she ate breakfast. When she walked to work alone—with her flashlight, because some old habits weren't so unwise after all.

But now, no Malcolm meant no one interesting to talk with. No one funny to joke with. No one sexy to share her bed.

If she was a free spirit, as Malcolm so often called her, then to her, he'd been a free spirit flying right along beside her. And she had taken pleasure in having him there with her.

She had changed.

Struck with her insight, Kristin went home to her apartment that night, pulled out her suitcase and packed some clothes.

On Tuesday, she went in to work and told Andrew she was quitting, which only made him laugh hysterically, because wasn't everyone going to be out of work in a few weeks anyway?

Kristin headed to Cookie's Place to break her decision to Stephanie.

"What are you doing?" Stephanie insisted. "This is because of *that man,* isn't it? He lied to you, Kristin. He lied to all of us."

Yes, he had, once. "He won't do it again," she said.

"How can you be so sure?"

"Because I am. I learned everything about him that I

could. Just like I learned everything about you that I could when we were kids."

Stephanie frowned and slid a plate of her excellent New England apple pie across the counter to Kristin. She couldn't say much more than that.

Kristin sat at a stool and picked up a fork to dig in. She was going to miss these daily chats with Stephanie where she was headed.

Stephanie refilled a napkin dispenser and then sat down beside Kristin. "So, what are you doing to do now?"

"Simple, really," Kristin said to Stephanie. "I'm going to take my new passport and fly to Scotland. Then, I'm going to rent a car and head to a place called Byrne Glennie."

"You're crazy."

"Maybe." She paused, her fork halfway to her mouth, remembering the looks on the faces of the people in the plant there, who'd seen her embracing Malcolm. "Maybe not." She licked her fork and smiled to herself.

Her future coworkers would just have to get used to her, wouldn't they? Because she was pretty sure that if she begged Malcolm nicely, she could still get him to give her that job. That was one favor he had solidly in his power.

"What are you going to do at Byrne Glennie?" Stephanie asked, breaking into Kristin's thoughts.

"Accept a job I was offered there, that's what."

"But in Scotland?" her mom said, leaning over to wipe the counter beside Kristin. "That's a terrible idea. Scotland is cold."

"Sometimes," Kristin agreed.

"And wet."

"Yes, often it is."

"And it's not near your family. That's terribly risky. What will you do if something happens to you? Kristin…"

Her mom spread her arms. "Something will come up for work here in Vermont. You'll see."

"I'm sure it will, Mom."

"But how is that safe to just pick up and leave?" her mom insisted.

"Because *I'm* safe," Kristin replied.

And she was. Her adventure had taught her that she could take care of herself. She didn't need to stay in Vermont and hide behind anybody else's views that weren't her own.

Next, she needed to call Malcolm and tell him she was coming.

She also needed to tell him that she loved him.

She went home and picked up her suitcase. On the way out of town, she stopped again at Cookie's Place, since by now school was over and she knew she could find Lily there, too.

To both Stephanie and Lily, she said, "I love you, guys. I'm going to make sure you come and visit me. I will send plane tickets for both of you in the summer, you just wait."

"Um, Kristin," Stephanie said. "When is the last time you stopped by Aura Botanicals?"

"Nine o'clock this morning, and by the way, it's not called Aura Botanicals anymore."

"I think you should get over there, right now, before you go anywhere else," Stephanie said.

"And why is that?" Kristin asked.

Stephanie smiled. "Because somebody is over there showing around a group of new investors." She leaned closer with a wink and whispered, "I'm told he's a very handsome Highlander, with the best Scottish accent you've ever heard. And guess what—his name totally isn't George Smith. Who would have guessed?"

Kristin's heart nearly burst in her chest. "He's here? Malcolm is here!"

And she dropped her suitcase and raced across the street to the plant.

She didn't have her employee badge anymore, so she banged on the window until somebody saw her and let her inside.

Malcolm had gathered the other managers inside Andrew's old conference room. Kristin heard Malcolm's voice before she saw him. Her heart soared.

"With your help," Malcolm was announcing to them, "I'll keep the Aura plant open for the specialty Born in Vermont line. These are the investors who are buying the plant, under my direction." He indicated three men, all wearing suits, standing behind him.

Barely able to keep from squealing aloud, Kristin squeezed into the audience beside Dirk.

"Hey, Kristin," Dirk said. "I thought you quit your job."

"I did." But she hadn't quit Malcolm.

MALCOLM SAW KRISTIN, and his voice actually wavered. Slowly he let out his breath. He'd really had no idea what he would find when he'd returned with a group of investors interested in buying the Born in Vermont brand. He'd hammered out a deal where his uncle would get twenty percent in exchange for the use of the brand name and formulations, and a large reduction in rent on the factory.

He'd just finished telling everyone the news, when he'd noticed her face in the crowd. He'd wrapped up his talk as quickly as he could, then went over to her.

"Malcolm." Her face was ablaze with happiness.

Calmness settled over him. He had absolutely done the right thing.

"May we talk in your office?" he asked her.

She bit her lip as if she had a secret to tell him, too, and grinning, said, "Let's go."

It was all he could do to keep from pulling her to him. But he had to be sure that his solution was right for her, so, stoically, he just nodded. With his breath held, he followed her down the short, familiar corridor, past the old break room, the coffee machines that made the loud noises, and into the tiny corner office tucked in the back, where he was sure he would find a space heater and a table spread with engineering drawings.

The door was wide open. He followed her inside.

But…her space heater was gone. The table was empty. The bookshelves with her personal things cleared off.

"Kristin?" he asked. "Did Andrew let you go? Because I'm telling you, he no longer—"

She pulled him to her. With her foot, clad in a high heel, she nudged the door closed. "I quit, Malcolm," she said, with a twinkle in her eye. "I quit this morning."

"You…" He shook his head, not comprehending. All he could think about was how beautiful she looked. With his thumb he caressed her cheek, nudged her hair from her face. He drew her closer to him, wanting so badly to kiss her that he could taste the longing.

"Malcolm, I was traveling to *you*," Kristin said.

"But I—I…" He shook his head, remembering. This had to be her choice. He could not dictate to her what to do. "You're welcome to whatever job you would like…in Scotland or Vermont, or both or neither."

What was he doing? "No…scratch all that. Kristy, the most important thing I came here to tell you is that I love you. I want a relationship with you. Long-term. A commitment where I promise to never tell you what to do, or to…what word did you use? *Trample* you."

Laughing, Kristin nibbled on his ear. "It's okay if you

want to make suggestions once in a while, Malcolm." She kissed him, teasing at first, and then tender, with a sigh. Her eyes grew moist, and she wiped the corner with the heel of her hand.

"Kristy?" he murmured tenderly.

"I'm thrilled with what you've done for Born in Vermont, and for my hometown. But I know what I want, Malcolm." She paused. "Take me back to Scotland with you, please," she whispered.

"Honestly? That's really what you want?"

She nodded, blinking harder now. "I love you, Malcolm." Her face seemed to crumple with happiness.

"Say that again, love."

"I *love* you."

He threw back his head and laughed with joy. Of all the sweetest hours. This one topped them all.

* * * * *

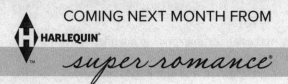

A Promise for the Baby
By Jennifer Lohmann

"I'm sorry to drop in on you like this," Vivian said, gesturing to the luggage near the door. "I didn't feel I had any choice."

"Were the terms of our divorce not sufficient?" Karl's elbows rested on the arms of the chair and he'd laced his fingers together in a bridge over his charcoal-grey suit. Vivian was certain Karl must have soon-to-be ex-wives drop in on him all the time, since he managed to remain so self-possessed about the whole thing.

But his absolute composure was the reason she'd answered "sure" on that fateful night in Las Vegas when he'd gestured to the doors of the wedding chapel, and asked, "Shall we?" with that half-smile on his face. She had wanted to be a part of his stability then, so she supposed it was unfair of her to be irritated by it now. And if she also longed for the passion they'd shared…well, that had gotten her into this mess in the first place.

"Yes. I mean, no, they were fine. I mean, I don't want a divorce—at least not right now."

If she'd shocked him, he didn't let it show. His only reaction was to lean back in the chair and lift his left foot to rest on his knee. Vivian was glad he hadn't sat on the couch next to her. She felt crowded enough by his presence without having to make room for his knees, elbows *and* infinite placidity—which took up far more space than any single lack of reaction should.

"I'm pregnant and I want to keep the baby."

How will Karl react to this news?
And will they stay married?
Find out in A PROMISE FOR THE BABY
by Jennifer Lohmann,
available January 2014
from Harlequin® Superromance®.

HSREXP1214

REQUEST YOUR FREE BOOKS!
2 FREE NOVELS PLUS 2 FREE GIFTS!

◆HARLEQUIN®

super romance®

More Story...More Romance

This cowboy deserves a second chance...

A Ranch for His Family
by Hope Navarre

Bull riding means everything to Neal Bryant. In his quest for the championships, he's let everything else go—including Robyn Morgan, the woman he loves. Then he has a bull-riding accident that could turn his rodeo dreams to Kansas dust. It's fitting—or maybe it's fate—that she's the nurse at his bedside.

While recuperating on his family's ranch, Neal learns how much he's missed. Robyn is widowed *and* has a son Neal can't seem to resist...especially when he learns *he's* the father. It's a dream he never allowed himself to have. And now he needs to show Robyn he's worth a second chance.

AVAILABLE JANUARY 2014 WHEREVER BOOKS AND EBOOKS ARE SOLD.

HARLEQUIN®

super romance®

More Story...More Romance

www.Harlequin.com

HSR71898